Rescued ex Inferna
a Knights 15 13 story
by Carl Michael Curtis
A Prequel

Cape and Swordstick Press

Gladstone, MO 64118

www.capeandswordstickpress.com

The characters and events in this book are fictitious. Any similarity to real persons, living or dead, is coincidental and not intended by the authors.

This is a work of fiction intended to be in communion with the Holy Catholic Church. It does not bear an imprimatur or a nihil obstat, but the authors have taken pains to ensure it does not conflict with anything the Church dogmatically teaches. If the authors have missed a detail that does conflict, the mistake belongs to the authors; The Holy Catholic Church does not teach error when it comes to faith and morals.

Cover art by Patrick Sayles

Cover and back cover layout and lettering by Paula Hays @ Floraliescreative.com

Copy editing by Catherine Lueckenette

Rescued ex Inferna
a Knights 15 13 story
by Carl Michael Curtis

CARL MICHAEL CURTIS

Other works by Carl Michael Curtis
  <u>The Knights 1513 series</u>
  Stigmata Invicta
  Vindicare Hope

RESCUED EX INFERNA

For Matt James, the friend who read an early draft of *Stigmata Invicta* and said, "I'd like to know more about Brother Cleopas." Here you go, Matt. Hope it was worth that single sentence since you probably never thought would equal a novel.

Rescue those who are being taken away
to death;

hold back those who are stumbling to
the slaughter.

Proverbs 24:11

Site of operations:

Asteroid 3021 KD, also known as "Stake" in orbit of Zaffre Asperity, fifth planet in the Torizza System

On-site resources:

Spec Ops Unit #7-1a, Brigid, F. Commander

Saint Eligius, Xiphos-class fast attack ship, Lieutenant Commander Walter, P. pilot

3rd Commandry of the Knights of Those Washed in the Water and Blood from His Side ("Knights 15 13")

Mission details:

Stealth extraction of asset from decommissioned asteroid facilities by any **just** means necessary in accordance with Knights 15 13 Rule of the Order

Mission designation:

SANCTIONED by the Federal Interstellar Governmental Network/FedNET

SANCTIONED/UNSANCTIONED by local solar system governmental authorities is not applicable/none exist

SANCTIONED/UNSANCTIONED by corporate owner of asteroid locale/none exist

SANCTIONED by Knights 15 13 Supreme Commandry in accordance with Christ the King's commandment to LOVE THY NEIGHBOR AS THYSELF and TO RESCUE THE LOWLY AND THE POOR; TO DELIVER THEM FROM THE HAND OF THE WICKED

Combat permissions:

Granted in full

Patron Saint(s) assigned to ops to request intercession from:

Saint Michael the Archangel (*Angel*, eternal)

Saint Philip of Agira (*Homo Sapien*, birth and death dates disputed)

Saint Numor the Hure (*Quasi-homo Euloterrax*, 2998-3112)

Part One:
A Simple Extraction

Mission Briefing

"I wonder what Saint Louis would have done with a bunch of these," Brother Santa Cruz asks as he sets his rail gun down on the workbench.

Freshly returned to their home world of Nicaea Neo from a combat mission, Santa Cruz goes through the post-firing rigamarole of maintaining his firearm. Their mission was a quick one on a moon orbiting another sun in another solar system. The transport back uneventful, boring even. He could have done this then but wanted his own shop. His own tools. They go where God sends them, do what He asks of them. But it's nice to be home.

The combat-length barrel is still attached. Shooting with that short of a barrel always adds stress to the recoil dampener. He plugs a small cable into the dampener that runs to a tablet and sets it to auto-troubleshoot. Checking fatigue.

Santa Cruz places discharge contacts to the rifle's high-concentrate capacitor and waits. Hears the telltale sizzle as it shorts out the stored charge. His hand open, palm facing it just a few inches off the surface. Done it for years. His old instructor told his fledging sniper class they'd learn the glow of the weapon that way. Learn her temperature, predict her moods. To this day Santa Cruz finds it ironic that a class of warrior-monks learns their firearms as the opposite sex.

Oh, the heat. A capacitor the size of a 64 fluid ounce bottle carries some juice. Now discharged, he disconnects it and puts it in an explosion-proof box. Latches the lid. Just in case it decides to fail and explode. Begins disassembling the coils.

Those Washed in the Water and Blood from His Side, the Knights 15 13. When Santa Cruz swore his final vows to the religious order in service of Jesus Christ, the one true God, he did so with this rail gun slung along his chest.

The workbench is in a shop which is in a militarized facility next to a Catholic Basilica. The Blessed Virgin immortalized in iconography on the very front. Bells toll on the hour. Holy Mass said twice a day by a rotating corps of priests. The whole thing, vibrant, full of life. Architecture reaching towards the heavens, drawing the eye to the abode of the All-loving Creator.

"Saint Louis? Saint King Louis the ninth?" Brother Cleopas walks over, leans against the wall near Santa Cruz as the man works on his rifle. Cleopas shrugs. "I imagine he probably would have had a better time at the Battle of Fariskur, that's for sure."

"He was captured there, correct?"

"Yessir. Seventh Crusade of Earth." Cleopas leans over and shuffles through Santa Cruz's precision tools. Small things, like surgical implements. He picks one up, examines its end. "This one is better than mine. I'm jealous."

"Jealousy is a sin." Santa Cruz says dryly. Smirks.

"So is stealing," Cleopas says as he stares absurdly hard at Santa Cruz while sliding the precision tool in his pocket. Wags his eyebrows, gives an obnoxious glance down to his pocket. Buttons it up. "Those always come in handy."

Santa Cruz huffs and ignores the action, uses a thumbnail to scrape at the end of a coil. No pitting, no arcing wounds. He sets it down; grunts and leans back in the stool he's perched on. Asks, "Ever been?"

"What? To Earth? No. Have you?"

"Nope. Our confessor during shoot school was from there. He told a lot of stories." He smiles, taps a finger on the bench. "Said it wasn't the same after they moved the Supreme Commandry off-world."

"It'd be weird. I hear only the Vatican is left now." Cleopas pats his chest with his forefinger absent-mindedly. "You know, I think the commander has been there."

"Our own personal Saint Louis."

Cleopas huffs a laugh. "Sure."

The shop is small. Concrete flooring. A single light overhead that is almost too powerful. The walls covered in religious art and pegboard overflowing with hanging tools. Tools next to scenes from the Gospels. For men who do little more than both pray and train for war, it is as natural as anything they've ever known.

The door opens and a man whose shoulder width blocks out the light from outside steps in. Brother Gonzaga. He looks twice at the two men inside, then tries a smile. The way it crumbles off his face makes it look like he tried and didn't like it.

"How are you guys?" he asks and moves over to a second bench. Sets his TechHaft down on it.

Cleopas gives another shrug. "Not bad."

"Next mission, Gonzaga, and I'm hiding behind you," Santa Cruz says.

"Why's that?"

"You're a better door than window."

"Sure," Gonzaga says and then lifts his TechHaft and slides on a pair of darkened glasses. "Eyeballs," he warns and ignites it.

The TechHaft, like a beefed-up hilt from a sword, expands two very bright laser constructions, one from each end. It becomes a bow, and Gonzaga pinches the string and draws it back. The TechHaft generates an arrow from where he pinched. The shaft extends forward, a tiny triangle for an arrowhead. He flexes it back and forth a few times, just feeling the resistance.

"I adjusted the draw weight earlier," Gonzaga says as he brings the arrow up to his eye.

"Those explosive?" Cleopas asks.

"No," Gonzaga says. "The little, tiny arrowhead? I have it set for training."

"Cool. You can shoot it over there," and he motions to the far wall. Sure enough, there's a metal target affixed to the wall, scorched all along it.

"Lots of burn marks on that thing that aren't center mass," Gonzaga says. He lets the arrow fly and it hits the bull's eye. Remains for a moment before fizzling out into nothing. He collapses the bow, says, "Feels better."

"Isn't there settings on it that allow you to virtually shim the angles?"

"Yes. I tweaked those also. Lots better now."

Santa Cruz points at the target. "You're so new the academy training is still helping you out. Get a few missions under your belt. You'll be just as terrible as the rest of us."

Gonzaga smirks. "Says the guy who, yesterday, shot a stabling fin off a missile coming right at us."

Cleopas nods. "*That* was a bull's eye."

Santa Cruz shrugs. "The Lord guided my hand."

"He guided you to shooting off the correct fin that caused it to veer off to the south where an enemy transport was coming right at us."

"Like I said, the—"

"—the Lord guided your hand," Gonzaga laughs. "I know, I know. But just so you know, I've got a couple missions under my belt now. And I'm still hitting bull's eyes."

"The Lord can guide your hand also," Cleopas says as the door to the shop opens again. Commander Brigid walks in, eyes crawling along the room. Papers in one hand. That serious look on his face his men recognize as business for them.

"Brother Cleopas, you know anything about asteroid mining?" Brigid asks.

"Yes, sir. I grew up on—"

"On asteroid 3021 KD? They call it Stake? Outside the orbit of Asperity?"

"Zaffre Asperity, yes sir." He stands up straighter. "But I guess we just called it Asperity. Zaffre is a weird word."

Brigid looks at the men. Wags his eyebrows. "You're why we got this gig, then."

"What gig, sir?" Cleopas asks, taking a step towards the door. Santa Cruz and Gonzaga both watch Cleopas as he moves. The man's body tenses. Brigid is talking about home.

"Remember how the higher command promised us a week's downtime after yesterday's combat op? Yeah... Conference room. Five minutes. I'm getting the others."

†

Brothers Pio and Nonnatus join Brothers Santa Cruz, Gonzaga and Cleopas in the conference room. Cleopas rolls his Rosary beads in his hand, forefinger and thumb gripping one and tilts his head down. Lips move in prayer.

Pio sits down, fidgets. Watches the door, chair pushed out from the table, legs bouncing. Commander Brigid strides in, slapping some papers against his thigh, says, "Don't waste time."

Pio jumps to his feet. Clears his throat, prays, "In the name of the Father, and of the Son and of the Holy Spirit, amen," and all the warrior-monks rise, make the Sign of the Cross over themselves.

"Gory be to the Father, and to the Son and to the Holy Spirit, as it was in the beginning, is now and ever shall be, world without end, amen." They cross themselves again. They all sit. Brigid pauses and prays as he approaches the podium at the front of the small room.

He finishes and fiddles with a remote control as he readies himself. Shuffles the papers. Inserts a cartridge into an interface board. Before him and between the two rows of tables where the Knights sit, a large waist-high machine whirs out of power-saving mode. On its surface a two-meter-wide transparent circle. From underneath it a light swells to life and above its surface a laser light 3D volumetric display lights up in a rotating hologram.

"Oh, I wanted our time off. . ." Bridgid says. He huffs, rolls his head on his neck.

The room is clean and bright. Expansive picture window on one wall, opening to a breath-taking vista. A shoreline cutting like a curved blade; a rocky edge dotted with evergreens and monumental boulders. A waterfall almost one and half kilometers wide thunders over a stony lip a hundred and fifty meters above the water. The shore itself outlining a plunge pool so vast it laps at the earthen edge like a tide. From the falls, a white cloud of thick spray extends out, loosening into mist before diffusing into the rest of the grand world. The sun high in the afternoon sky, refracting in the cloud all the colors of creation. Kilometers into the atmosphere, it glimmers off the constructed ring in orbit. A moon's worth of metal and carbon fibers, glass and polymers. A tribute to God's power as it encircles the planet. Glorious.

A fleet of ships convoying from the planet's surface to the ring dotted like birds against the clouds. Some are warships, but others have a wide square base and bell towers rising off it like masts on old sailing boats. Giant airborne Gothic cathedrals, complete with a tower sporting a rose window done in the flamboyant gothic style. Crucifix in form, each containing Christ in the Eucharist atop nuclear drives that propel it to the heavens and adoring priests who want nothing more than to offer the Mass. Stand in their places where God needs them to aid in the salvation of souls.

Glorious, indeed.

"Thank you, Pio," Brigid says. "All right, brothers. I know we just got off a mission, but our Lord needs us."

The Knights nod their assent and Brigid feels a good measure of relief; these are good men, and they are his. Some teams would balk at back-to-back operations. Not these men. "This is an Intel Special; our boys have been sleepless, rushing around in the last few days. The mission details are cobbled together, so you know what that means." He grimaces, holds up a hand and brushes away nothing but air. "Anyway. Word came in three days ago that Archbishop Theodore Hrutt from the archdiocese of Polycarp on Xewl—" he loses his words and points at the left wall and by extension, outside into the great beyond, "—in some galaxy whose name I can't pronounce. Anyway, a terrorist faction has kidnapped him. From the—" he references his papers, offhandedly says, "—sorry, brothers. I just got these. He's been kidnapped by a militant sect of the UnZerre FulZzhea WarHeight. Ever hear of them?"

He looks up, sees three of the men nod. "ZZH for short. I'm going to use the initials. Like I said, they snatched him up three days ago. Killed a few people doing it. It's considered a hostage situation."

Brigid turns and aims his remote at the monitor behind him. A picture comes up, and he clicks to an info graphic. "ZZH. Heretical offshoot of the Catholic Church. They immigrated to the city of Xewl several hundred years ago and set up shop with a bunch of other folks on a colonizing mission. Tame the planet, all that stuff. They use Xewl as their capital. Their Rome, so to speak.

"The religion itself— a group of progressive clerics and laymen broke off from the Catholic church as a response to Pope Michael-Julius's encyclical *In Amore et Alignment*. Hard disagreements on the Church's moral teachings. They supported all sorts of disordered sexual and biological conditions, denied God's plan in biology.

"Using biotech—hormonal, surgical, vat-grown multi-purpose organs, whatever else, the ZZH altered themselves into what's known as a sequential hermaphrodite. SQ. For generations now, they've done this. More or less, they can hormonally trigger a gender change. I hear it's not super quick nor super accurate; their sex organs

17

don't function as intended, and they're for the most part, sterile. They try, though. I guess when they can achieve pregnancy they're considered especially blessed. Works towards their social rankings.

"They reproduce in artificial wombs after collecting sperm and eggs. They have ice banks full of literally millions of preborn children, just waiting. Many of those they'll alter in utero to be SQ as well."

Santa Cruz flips a page on his handout, flips it back. "But these ZZH folks are Catholic?"

"Heretical," Brigid says. "They've moved so far away from Christ's teachings now. . . they're sedevacantist, they've 'retranslated' portions of the Bible to fit their more extreme beliefs. And, like any good schismatic group, they claim to be the only church that possesses the fullness of Christ's truth."

Pio nods along as the commander speaks. Examines his handout. Runs a searching finger down the information. "Altogether sketchy intel. These are my favorite."

"It is sketchy."

"Lots of room to play."

Brigid smirks. Gonzaga watches them, trying to read the room. He picks at his own handout, asks, "Intel states somewhere between twenty to forty armed ZZH members?"

Brigid nods. "Yes. We call these types of briefs Intel Specials. There's a lot of moving parts, and they're moving quickly. Blurry. Only bits of info, maybe they've been validated, maybe not. We're behind on the entire thing but we still have to react properly and win. Get used to these. We get a lot of them."

Pio leans back in his chair so he can catch Gonzaga's attention. Pio smiles broadly, says, "Lots of room to play."

"Just don't get bogged down arguing with them about the faith," Nonnatus says. "I've met a few ZZH folks over the years. They're. . . zealous, to say the least."

Brigid pats the side of the podium, drawing all eyes back to him. "Okay. Half a millennium of erroneous doctrinal beliefs aside, we're here to retrieve an archbishop from a terrorist group. And word came in an hour ago where they're holding him."

Brigid looks at Cleopas. Cleopas's eyes light up in recognition; the final piece falls into place in his mind. "Stake."

"Yes, brother," Brigid says. He holds out an arm as if he's at a loss for anything else. "This is a rescue mission. It was assigned to us because we're blessed by our Lord Jesus Christ, we're good at what He asks us to do, and we've got the only Knight who grew up on Stake." He flaps a handful of papers at Cleopas.

"Well," Cleopas begins, "I lived there about fifteen years total as a kid, and that was almost fifteen years ago besides. I'm not sure—"

"Santa Cruz," Brigid says, the tone of his voice flatly serious.

"Yes, Commander?" The sniper perks up.

"How many years have *you* spent on Stake?"

"Sir, I don't even know what a Stake is."

Brigid looks around. "Pio?"

"None, sir." Pio leans back in his chair again and finds Cleopas, that smile still beaming.

"Gonzaga?"

"Same, Commander. None."

Cleopas nods and concedes the point. "I understand, sir. I'm just saying—"

"You're the best we got, brother," Brigid says. He presses a few keys on the podium controls and the volumetric display switches from the 3D placeholder graphic that has been silently revolving around its vertical axis. A blue-lined schematic of an asteroid takes its place. Along one side of it is a series of rectangular shapes.

"The asteroid Stake." Brigid announces as if he's in front of a convention full of investors. He turns to Cleopas, "Would you agree?"

19

Cleopas studies the laser graphic for a moment and nods. "Yes sir. That was home when I was a kid."

"Okay," Brigid checks his timepiece and looks out the Knights. "Our sources of information about the environment are limited. Cleopas here hasn't been there in— what? You said—"

"Just about fifteen years, sir. Not too long before I became a novice in the Order."

"Copy. Your parents are still alive, correct?"

"Yessir. They retired to a place called Harmony, out in the Zeti Reticuli galaxy."

"Anybody else you can think of, by chance?"

Cleopas rushes through his memories. "Not really. My younger siblings— my folks were limited to two children during the stay just for practical reasons. Even then, Cayna, my younger sister, she was only something like eight when we left. And friends... they're all lost to the cosmos somewhere. I never kept in touch, really."

"Family photos that happen to be here?"

Cleopas makes a frustrated sound. "Outside chance. Maybe I have a few. I'd have to dig. Most of that stuff didn't really make the trip with me."

"Well, maybe we can pray to Saint Anthony that you find a few." He looks back to his timepiece and behind his eyes some new calculation occurs. "We'll need to launch here shortly. Okay then, quick and dirty. Facts and figures here."

He aims the remote at the volumetric display and clicks. The display itself of the asteroid is blue. A single floating text block next to it highlights red.

Brigid squints and begins to read. "3021 KD is the official asteroid designation. Stake is what, Cleopas? Your all's name for it?"

"Yes. The mining company my parents worked for, they... well, there's a ton of companies that do this. They make claims on asteroids and I forget what astrological authority approves them, but they do. So, when it's just being observed in the sky, they get letters and numbers according to some official scheme. 3021 KD became Stake once we technically owned it."

"Copy." The next block of text highlights red. Brigid reads, "C-type asteroid, C for carbonaceous. They have water, primitive metals and carbon compounds in them. Hauled from their discovered location to orbit around Zaffre Asperity. Thar's a gas giant, correct?"

"Yes, sir. We just called it Asperity."

"Roughly two and half kilometers by one and a half. . . so we've got some room to land, hide and sneak around. The Op Order says there's danger of cave-ins and unstable terrain. . . from the mining, I assume."

Cleopas nods. "Yes sir. They followed veins of anything valuable and mined it out. They could adjust the GravCore on pinpoint locations—"

"Grav what?" Nonnatus asks.

"GravCore. It's a brand name. It's a gravitational anomaly engine. It's weird alien tech that I can't explain. But basically, it's a device that exudes a gravitational pull. They had it set pretty standard, 1G, I think."

Pio nods along. "I've heard of them. They're adjustable, you say? The whole field or can you—"

"It's pinpoint," Cleopas says. "I remember that much. My dad was excited about that. See, they'd hit a lode of something—ice, let's say—and start to chunk it out, collect it all. As soon as they'd find a wall of asteroid rock they'd just go in another direction. Well, they could pinpoint adjust the GravCore to not exert 1G in that spot. Kept them from having to buttress the mine nearly as much. No gravity pulling down the ceiling."

"It prevented cave-ins?" Brigid asks.

"Prevent? No. Not really. But it would, you know, keep things from falling really fast. Killing folks. Saved a ton on costs with having to frame in the holes they made."

"All right. Keep a watch on your footing," Brigid says. "The plan is to land about here—" a small red ring with a solid dot in the center appears on a partition of open terrain. "We'll exfil from the same location. We're still discerning the best method of entry, and where to even enter at. Intel Special."

"Sir, I can probably call my father for his advice. He was a mining foreman. It was his job to know that stuff."

"Great idea. Just let me get clearance from the brass before you send out details of this. Top secret and all."

"Yes, sir."

Brigid motions to Pio. "You just might need to make a very quiet but very effective boom."

"Because we're sneaky, Commander?"

"Yes. Very sneaky."

The commander turns back to the volumetric display and they continue the briefing. He, checking his timepiece every few moments only to see how much of their cushion is flecking off like bits of rust. And yet too soon with too many variables leaving their loose ends flapping in the wind the Knights prepare to sail on, time is up. The 3D image of the asteroid collapses as one laser light after another after a thousand others clicks off.

"All right," Brigid says. "Any questions?"

"When do we roll out?" Santa Cruz asks.

"Father Savvison is on is way for us to receive the sacraments. I want guns loaded and us suited up in ten. Move out."

Close Enough to I Love You

The Intersolar line takes an agonizing moment to connect from telecom waypoint to waypoint. With each staticky click then open, fuzzy pause, Brother Cleopas grows anxious. He looks at his mission-timer countdown—fed through his armor's wrist piece like a watch—knowing they'll have to launch very shortly.

Finally, the telltale beeping of the actual call speaks up like a song in his ears. Three rings in, Cleopas hears that old gruff voice that never modulates in tone. He is immediately a little kid again. "Yeah, hello there?"

"Hey Dad," Cleopas says, cheerful. "How are you?"

"Good, good. Your mom was just talking about you. She said you were awarded something. How come you didn't tell me?"

"Oh, Dad. Yes, I— I was awarded for bravery— the Order awarded me, anyway. . . a few months ago. The Order doesn't like us to brag about accomplishments. It helps us towards true meekness and being humble. All things through Christ."

"Yeah, yeah. Meanwhile my boy is being so brave he's being awarded by it and I don't hear about it."

"Sorry, Dad. I'm not sure how Mom heard of it either."

"I think they sent a message or something to the house and she read it. I'll read it too, since my own boy—my own *hero* boy—is on the phone right now and isn't telling me more about it."

Cleopas huffs. His father, a blue-collar miner his whole life, is a straightforward man without much use for anything outside of the tools he needs to do his work. Cleopas knows his father's ethos can be summed up in the idea that when there's something to say, you say it. Otherwise, quiet is bliss. And as his father, he expects to receive a report from his son say when he's accomplished something. That's worth breaking the silence.

"Sorry, Dad."

"Well, go on, then. Bravery."

Cleopas smiles sadly, wanting to brag to his father. "So, Dad. I'm sorry I have to rush, but I'm up against a clock here."

"Okay, then. Fine." He can hear his father's scowl. His brow must be furrowing. "You okay?"

"I'm going on a mission," Cleopas pauses just because it's a unique thing to say. "To Stake."

"Stake? *Our* Stake?" His father mumbles to himself, "Of course *our* Stake. What other Stake could there be? Anyway. What does a hollowed-out asteroid have to do with a religious order?"

"Everything I'm telling you is top secret, Dad. You have no idea how many security filters this call went through just to connect us."

"Yeah, yeah. Who am I gonna tell?"

"I know, Dad. But still. Listen, some terrorists kidnapped one of our archbishops. Took him there. Me and my team are going in to rescue him."

His dad actually lets out a bit of a laugh. "Well, of course *you* are. How many kids from that rock became Knights? You're the only man for the job."

"Exactly. So, my question for you is, where do you think they'd hide him?"

His dad goes quiet. Clears his throat. "Well, quite honestly you should have called a guy named Xiong Ping. Head of security. He knew that place— well, now that I think of it, he's probably dead, actually. I think I heard he passed back— oh. Doesn't matter."

Cleopas looks at his mission timer. "Sorry, Dad. We've got to move this along."

"Calling me and then rushing me. Tell your order I don't like that."

"I will, Dad." And that redirects the conversation enough.

"Okay. Let me think." His father grumbles, shoving ideas through his mind, examining them. Throwing most away. Then,

"Listen, when we decomm-ed the place we took all the modular structures with us. That means the living quarters, medical, most of the facilities. Anything we didn't build on-site or need to anchor directly. So, all you've got left is the hangar, the office structures, the actual processing facility, the morale strip and security. And those go pretty much in a straight line. You'll need to start in the hangar, then you can move right through."

"That's great info."

"Security to me sounds like the best place terrorists would take a hostage, for a few reasons. Number one, unless you're drilling through the surface to it, you can only reach it basically in the order I just laid out. So, start in the hangar and go through. Security is one way in, one way out. If it was a castle, that'd be the most defensible spot."

"I'll let my guys know."

"I guess you could just sneak in through the hangar—"

"I don't think so."

"Why not?"

"I imagine they'll be watching it. They'd expect that if they're expecting a rescue at all."

His dad starts to speak and then stops. Groans. "How many bad guys are there?"

"Don't know. Maybe forty."

"Tight squeeze for what we left." His dad looks off in the distance, the gears behind his eyes turning. "Well, I think you'd have to start looking there, anyways. Plus, it's the only way in unless you want to blast— wait. There it is. You can go in on the far side, down the shaft where we did core drillings. Remember, you kids would always go there and drop rocks down the shaft?"

"Yes, Dad." Memories of him and his buddies—the Vear brothers, Tim, whose mother was the head liaison between the union and the company, and a kid everybody called Flip who was only there for a year before his father died in a bar fight in the morale strip—doing exactly what his father is saying. Sneaking off to the surface of the asteroid and making their way in those cumbersome exosuits they'd borrow from old equipment lockers. Making their way to the shaft. Heaving rocks down. Laughing. The musical notes of the mirth still in Cleopas's child's mind. The best they could hear is if the rocks struck the sides as they plummeted. Having a great time.

"That shaft runs right near one of the primary mines. Get through the wall there. You'll be inside."

"Got it, Dad. That's fantastic. Thank you."

"Listen to me, boy." His father says with that authoritative tone all children hear in their father's voice from time to time. "The GravCore, it'll work until the end of time. But the rest of that place is in disrepair. Everything. Electrical, water, mechanical, even the structure. We left it idling so maintenance crews could come by annually and upkeep it, but it's been what? Twenty years?"

"Around there."

"So, trust nothing. Unless these terrorists brought their own stuff, you can't trust nothing. Not the atmosphere, not power. Don't drink the water. Don't flush a toilet. Got me?"

"Yes, Dad. I'll tell the team."

"Now, son. Those grid defense cannons; they *do* still work. Got to."

"I think our pilot is aware. He'll get us in cleanly."

"He better. My hero boy is goin' on a rescue mission."

Cleopas feels proud of that. His father was never the type to talk about his feelings. Even when he'd been drinking, he'd sit there quietly contemplating whatever was going on in that opaque mind of his. "High praise, Dad. I love you."

"Yeah, yeah. Your mother and I love you too. Wait'll she hears what you're doin' now."

"Top secret, Dad."

"What do mean? I can't even tell her? She's your mother. She was there, too."

"Sorry, Dad. When it's over. When it's over I'll try and take some time and come see you guys. I'll tell you everything."

"What if I put her on the phone and you ask her the same question? Maybe then? She'll tell you things. She was a process tech. She knows things."

The countdown timer is so low, if it were an hourglass the last grains would be shuffling their way out. "I'm sorry, Dad. My time is up."

"Come back to us, boy. I don't see you enough as it is."

"I will, Dad." He stays quiet for a second and watches his timer count end. "Oh, hey, Dad? Want me to bring you back a souvenir from Stake? For old time's sake."

"Nah, son. Everything I wanted from that place, I took with me when we left. Your mom and you kids. Hear me?"

"Yes, Dad." Close enough to *I love you* for Cleopas.

Negotiations and Zealotry

"Your Excellency, our compression-beam signal has been received and approved. They're waiting on the other end for us to get going." The Knights 15 13 tech says as he finishes the settings on the camera-enabled monitor.

The bishop nods and takes one last sip from a glass. Ice cubes inside it clink and bob as he sets it down, the condensation on the outside of it enough to where he wipes his hand on his knee. He feels his forehead; cool and dry. The glass is doing all the sweating. At least for now. He adjusts in the chair he is in. The tech notices.

"Comfortable? I can get you another—"

"No, no thank you." The bishop waves his hand. "I fidget if things get tense. It's worse when I'm on my feet. My academy trainer, Father Deeves, he used to ding me for it all the time."

"I see."

"Twenty-two years of this and I've never gotten better about the fidgeting."

"Okay, okay. . ." the tech says to himself as he types a few numbers into a touchscreen. Squints as he reads the information. "The dark address these guys attached to that. . . that hostage video they sent us, it's buried all right. Buried deep. Our compression-beam is bouncing off something like four hundred receiver/emitter satellites across five systems. No doubt the signal is being washed and examined by all sorts of monitoring equipment. AI, the whole bit. Trying to make sure we don't trace them."

"We are, though, correct?"

The tech turns to the bishop, half a smile unturned on his lips. "Of course." Even if the dark address they've just connected to is next door, the lengths to which they've gone to mask it are extraordinary.

The bishop says, "Good. Praise our Lord. I want the archbishop returned."

"Yes, Your Excellency. We're all set when you say the word. As soon as he appears on this monitor, it'll be go-time." He points to the blank screen as if that one finger will assign where this conjuring occurs.

"Thank you. Give me just one more moment, please," the bishop bows his head, and his lips move silently. A prayer of supplication, then he says out loud, "But You, Lord, are a shield around me, my glory, the One who lifts my head high. I call out to the Lord, and He answers me from His Holy mountain. I lie down and sleep; I wake again because the Lord sustains me. I will not fear though tens of thousands assail me on every side." The bishop concludes with a silent bit and crosses himself. Looks up. Nods to the tech.

"We're live."

The monitor flips on, and there is a man, lean and muscular, dressed in all black with a Roman collar about his neck. Strangely plump in some areas as compared to others. His shoulders and hips seem to be equal in width, but that may be a visual trick of the few segmented pieces of armor he has on. It's short-sleeved, and his forearms are matted in wiry black hairs. His hands look small and smooth—at odds with how built he is. His chin and jaw are weak; he possesses a patchy beard mostly along his neck. His eyes are effeminate but look determined. Sharp.

"With whom am I speaking?" He demands. His voice over the inter-solar comms crackles slightly. Behind him is a hanging black drape covering everything. Behind it is a source of light, dimly glowing through the fabric. But nothing more.

"My name is Bishop Treasach Tauthail of the Archdiocese of All Saints in Glory. Thank you for accepting my invitation to speak."

"It was I who sent you this address. The invitation is mine."

"Indeed." For his part, Bishop Tauthail decided to have the negotiation in the church proper of the local parish, Our Blessed Savior. He wants to have Christ all around him in the Eucharist and in the icons. It is a calculated risk, what with having this talk with an avowed heretic. "I was hoping we could begin in prayer."

"A prayer," the man says with a note of rumination. Rolling the word around like a bit of clay in his hands. Maybe trying to take what the bishop said and mold it into his own definition of it. "You know, I've always had such a hesitation in my mind about that."

"Prayer?"

"No, no. God hears me. Knows me quite well. My hesitation is simply whether or not we're even praying to the same god."

"The ZZH and Catholics?" Bishop Tauthail considers it. "Yahweh, God of the Israelites. Jesus Christ, the Godman. The Holy Spirit, paraclete. The Holy Trinity. There is only one true God of the universe and we both worship him. I don't see—"

"Yes, yes, I'm well versed in your Catechism." The man says as if he feels like he's being spoken to by a child that is convinced knows more than he. "The ZZH corrected the errors in the Catholic Catechism long ago. Hundreds of years now. That's not what I mean."

"Please help me understand, then."

"It is simple. Your God hates us, and my God loves everyone."

"My God—our God—loves everyone. But He does not love what we do, sometimes. We are all fallen and in need of Him."

"Let me put it another way," the man says as he leans in. "Your God makes us and then hates us for being what He made. My God makes us and loves us. Simple. Does that help you?"

"May we pray?"

"Not together," the man says. "But we should open in prayer, yes. We will each take a silent moment to pray to our gods."

The bishop nods. "So long as it is done. I wish blessings on you and this conversation."

"I, as well."

Each man bows his head and speaks with God. Bishop Tauthail finishes and looks up. The man on the screen is staring at him, smiles. Says, "That's quite a name you have. All Knights 15 13 take a Catholic saint's name upon ordination or final vows, am I correct?"

"Thank you, and yes, we do. I took the surname Tauthail on my ordination. It's Old Earth Irish, and belonged to a saint whose name, in common tongue, is Lawrence O'Toole."

The man wags a knowing finger at the bishop. "Ah, yes. Yes. All glory to God that Saint O'Toole graced Ireland with his love. He was known for his negotiations, correct? I seem to recall as such. He was successful against invading nations, barbarians, all the classic high-stakes events."

"He was. I was in the transitional deaconate when I was assigned to become a negotiations consultant for the diocese. I felt it was appropriate to don myself with the cloak of such a magnificent saint known for it."

"Maybe to receive some of his gifts. And also hence, why I'm speaking to you." He says the word *you* with an accusation. Like he's tearing the veil off some hidden weapon the bishop was planning on using later. The bishop can tell the other man—if that is truly what he is at the moment—already has a vivid idea of how this will all play out. Suspect.

"That's a big reason, yes." The bishop clears his throat and returns a smile. Asks a question to which he already knows the answer. "May I know your name, please?"

"And there it is," the man sits back, smug. "The negotiator's psychology. I can't tell if you're not very good at it or if I am just particularly good at sniffing it out."

"How do you mean, the negotiator's psychology?"

He counts off on his fingers. "The very even, measured tone of voice so far. No ripples in the water, so to speak. Asking me to define the words I say, hoping that I'll think you're trying to understand me.

The way you posture your face to communicate openness. Trying to humanize yourself to me, a man you think is an aggressor. You're not the enemy but rather somebody just like me who happens to have a different viewpoint on a critical item. You, trying to build goodwill by sharing your name and a personal anecdote about it, then asking me to reciprocate. I assume if I refuse to tell you who I am, you'll try and maneuver that into a reason why the Knights 15 13 will kill my people."

Bishop Tauthail suppresses a sigh. He has had a dialogue with the ZZH before, and this the standard fare. Useless. They make these types of things useless with their obstinacy. "Fine. We can drop the pretenses. But you go first."

"There are no pretenses with me, understand that."

"None? I am very aware that a common play out of the ZZH's book is that you'll be aggressive towards another religion—as you have been towards us—and then very publicly accuse that religion of preparing to murder your innocents. A publicity stunt for the Court of Public Opinion. Pick a fight, and then scream that you're the victim."

"You are so aware of our methods, I see. So aware."

The bishop says, "It's a transparent one-two punch that carries no weight. You know good and well the Knights 15 13 are not going to drag your innocent members out into the streets and execute them. We don't do that. We've never done that. So, knock it off."

"I can never be fully sure your religion will not kill us for our beliefs. It *has* been done in the past—"

"The Catholic Church has never issued any form of murder decree against your belief system. It simply—"

"You have pronounced us as a heresy! That alone is insult tantamount to a proclamation of death. The more zealous of your church hear about heresy and think they need to root us out. Kill us to keep us from spreading our beliefs. We are treated as cancer! And you are the healthy scalpel!"

"They will try and evangelize, yes. Murder is never an option."

"Stuttgart? The Shooting Star Massacre? The Slaughter of Pinpoint? Need I go on?"

"You can't go on, first of all. And second, none of these were sanctioned by the Church. There's no historical proof Catholics even took part in them. This isn't getting us anywhere—"

"Come and read my histories and then tell me such nonsense."

"ZZH histories written very favorably by the ZZH for the ZZH. The ZZH will blame the Catholics today for those incidents because today we have a disagreement. In the past, the ZZH has blamed Islam for Stuttgart. Then they blamed fascists for it. They blamed other Protestant denominations for Pinpoint and then they blamed a secular militia. They blamed a passing Tak'thaNar cruiser for the Shooting Star incident—"

"Ah! See? You diminish our agonies and blood loss to mere vague happenings! And as an aside, when you say *other Protestant denominations* it implies we are one of those. We are not protesters of your faith. We are the correct form of it, as Christ Himself intended. And Shooting Star... It was no *incident*. I had family on the Shooting Star transport. Five thousand passengers plus crew. And almost thirty thousand fetuses in cryostasis. No one survived. They were all reduced to radioactive vapors and detritus. How can your religion speak about God's love and then—"

"I apologize for saying *incident*. It was a grievous wound to the ZZH people. I am simply pointing out that the Catholic Church did not request, sanction nor participate in those attacks. We denounce them as gravely evil. I recall very clearly, we offered Masses throughout the galaxy for the souls of those affected, which includes you."

"One of the Catholic Church's many publicity stunts."

"We did them in earnest, out of love for our brothers and sisters in Christ."

"Brothers and sisters. Call us what you really think we are. Gender-neutral siblings at best. Deviant is more accurate, though. Damned to hell. You say so yourself."

"The Catholic Church does not damn anyone to hell."

"Archbishop Hrutt was very fond of saying how we will all suffer in fire for eternity with God turning his back on us."

"You take him out of context. Just as you so fervently believe that your interpretation of God is correct, so do we. And God has revealed that sin must be avoided to the very best of our ability, with His help. We must be holy. Your belief system. . . it normalizes sin and has enshrined it in your very way of life. Your definition of life, even. The archbishop simply preaches against it."

"He commits violence against it."

"His words constitute nothing but truth. There is no violence."

"And that, Bishop Tauthail, shows exactly why you have no understanding of our faith, and therefore, of God's truth."

Not to be deterred by this man's absolute zealousness of his ideas, the bishop continues, "He was chosen of the archdiocese of Polycarp in Xewl to bring the light of truth to those who might be suffering in their particular sins."

The man smiles like a predator when he realizes his prey has a set of claws he was previously unaware of. "You say it so nicely. As if I can't see through your filthy but sweet sugar coating. Hrutt was specially chosen because he preaches so well against *us*. Our beliefs. He is a capable weapon against our armor. Our religion. *Particular sins*? You mean our very way of life?"

"Yes."

"This is why I hate you all so much. So haughty. You dare to say we're—"

"When the founding fathers of the ZZH on Earth could no longer force the Catholic Church to tolerate their manifest sin, they simply blew off God's truth and made their own. Then they called *that* God's truth. Your predecessors went so far as to retranslate the Bible to fit your belief system. We are not wrong here." The bishop sips from his glass and is not rebutted. He says, "We must love, but we must love correctly."

"Tell that to your archbishop, then."

"I will, just as soon as you give me back to me. May I have him back?"

"More negotiator psychology. You ask me for permission. *May I.* Always the phrase, *may I*. Changing course. You don't want to talk about our persecution. Our graveyards, full of children. You ask me *may* we do something instead of *can* we do something. Instead of telling me what we will do. You want it to be my choice, with my permission. Then you'll get what you want but I will feel as though I am running the show."

Bishop Tauthail does not fight his sigh this time. He holds his hands out, a starving man begging for a morsel. "Your name, father..."

"Father Amit Hiram Loognar."

"Thank you."

"And you must know that Archbishop Hrett will not survive. And tomorrow, the Knights 1513 will not either."

Infil

"These feel a lot more. . . restrictive than they did in training," Brother Gonzaga says as the lid to his Individualized Drop Pod closes and seals over him.

Inside the deployment bay of the *Saint Eligius,* a *Xiphos*-class fast attack ship, there is only enough room to bump armor plates against one another as they mount into their pods. The bay's deployment hatch is open, and the maw of space lies just beyond. Beneath the ship and dominating the view outside the hatch is a sweepingly gorgeous view of the gas giant Zaffre Asperity. Hundreds of kilometers away is a small speck. Stake.

"On station now," Lieutenant Commander Walter of the *Saint Eligius* says over the comms. "Finals preps should be done in the next sixty seconds and the window will open for launch. Please acknowledge."

On the opposing wall is a countdown clock. The number sixty appears on it like a phantasm materializing. When it hits zero, everybody that wants a trip to Stake needs to be inside their IDP.

"Acknowledged," Commander Brigid says, standing outside of Gonzaga's sleek, pill-shaped IDP and looking at him through the viewing port. "Were you in your full frontal assault kit in training?" he asks. He gives command acknowledgment to the readout displayed on Gonzaga's IDP that is sealed, functional and ready to launch. All team leads must inspect their men and verify everything is in the green or the IDP's auto-protocol won't allow it to leave the bay.

"No. They let us do it in our PT gear."

"Shirt and shorts?"

"Yes, sir."

"They really should have done better, I think. The armor is enough, but they should have asked for your gun too." Brigid slaps the viewport where Gonzaga's helmeted face peers out. "You'll be fine. And if you're not, your armor will keep you alive." He walks to Brother Pio's IDP and Brother Santa Cruz shuffles up to Gonzaga on the way to his own pod.

Santa Cruz leans over. "These are set for auto landing. If it crashes, try to grab the surface before you float away. Got a grappling hook or something?"

"No."

"Darn. Okay. If you float away, turn on your personal transponder. The ship can find you that way. You got one of those?"

"A personal what? No." Gonzaga's inexperienced eyes half-cover under his furrowing brow.

"Darn. Okay, well, the commander is right. Your armor will keep you alive. For a few days as you float off into the void of space. Then. . . . just keep praying. I hear it's cold by the end." He pats the lid and the mannerism slaps away any real concern because it's obvious to him there's no point in having it anymore. No personal transponder. No grappling hook. "Yeah. Just pray."

"Are you serious?" Gonzaga asks.

Santa Cruz stares at him blank-faced through the viewport for a second, then goes over to his own IPD. Gets inside.

Lieutenant Commander Walter's voice comes over the comms. "Window will be opening in T-minus twenty seconds. We'll have seventeen seconds after it opens to complete the launch."

"One thing we'll need to keep watch for is the debris field," Brother Cleopas said during the briefing. "In its heyday, numerous companies used Asperity's orbit for mining. My folks' company used a modified version of underground mining, whereas several others blast-mined the asteroids and picked through the pieces. Those pieces are still out there, all around Stake."

The *Saint Eligius*. The dot that is Stake still hundreds of kilometers off. And between them, a jagged debris field of mangled asteroid chunks. Blast-mined over the course of decades and left to float. Crunch together, knock apart like billiards. All gently stirred and held in a very loose cloud by the gas giant's gravity.

"We can use it for cover," Brigid said.

"Or we can ram right into one," Cleopas said.

Santa Cruz looked up, asked, "Do they ever strike Stake? Is that a concern for the op?"

Brigid and Cleopas both shrugged. Pio laughed. "Pray to Saint Barbara. She's the patroness of miners."

"How do you know?"

Pio said, "She's also the patron saint of explosive workers, and as the resident CQ4 guy, I ask her to intercede often enough."

The ship is rounding Asperity to its starboard side. The planet is gorgeous this close. Even from outside the atmosphere by hundreds of kilometers the whirling storms inside the gas giant streaked in brilliant rivers of colors so absolutely vivid they defy basic description. Currant red and macaroon yellow with the odd but thick vein of cobalt blue darkening under alien pressures into castleton green at its edges. Blotches of orchid purple swirl like hurricanes against the resplendent backdrop, and somewhere in all of that is a continent-sized storm that thrashes with such immense pressure it's squeezing the hydrogen and carbon in the high atmosphere into diamond-like pellets that are raining down below.

Using the color pinwheel of a gas giant as a shield, the *Saint Eligius* maneuvers around with its profile obstructed to Stake. The *Xiphos*-class carry three crewmen: its pilot, Lieutenant Commander Walter, Lieutenant Pascal Baylon the co-pilot and Chief Warrant Officer 3 Andre Bassette, their systems engineer. They make their final adjustments and strap in for the run.

In the deployment bay, Brigid keeps one eye on the countdown clock and sees how much time he has. He walks up to Santa Cruz's pod smiling, says, "Stop messing with the new guy."

"He's stressed. It'll relieve it for him. I'm doing him a favor."

"Cite me one example where Christ did that to His Apostles?"

Santa Cruz slides down into the pod; more of a missile barely wider than his armored shoulders than anything else. He grunts. "It might not have been written in the Gospels, but even John the Evangelist wrote that Jesus said and did many more things than were recorded and—"

Brigid laughs softly. "Knock it off." He acknowledges the readout and goes back to Gonzaga's. "Hey."

"Commander, I don't have a grappling hook or a transponder—"

"None of us do. Santa Cruz was teasing you."

Gonzaga stares out. "So, what if I float—"

"You won't. The asteroid has artificial gravity. We'll be fine." Brigid starts to turn away, turns back, says, "It was in the briefing. Just— pray and do not worry. We're forbidden to worry by Christ Himself."

Gonzaga grunts, mad at himself. Then he considers everything for a moment and exhales large and long in relief. "I remember, I remember. A grappling hook would be fun to have either way."

"Sure. If you need one, use your TechHaft. You can make grappling hook arrows. I thought you knew that?"

Gonzaga is speechless. Brigid turns away. Sees the status board where all his Knights are confirmed in the IDPs and ready to fire. He taps his helmet mic. "Might as well ask our Lady to bless us, eh, brothers?" He enters his own pod and the lid seals. He clicks over to a separate channel, "Walter, I'm in."

In only Brigid's speakers, he hears the pilot's voice say, "Brigid, I've acknowledged the ready status of your pod."

"Copy. Thank you."

Brigid clicks over to the main comms channel, hears Pio's voice praying, "—of grace, the Lord is with thee. Blessed art thou amongst women, and blessed in the fruit of thy womb, Jesus, holy Mary, mother of God, pray—"

The countdown timer beeps, interrupting like a stab into flesh inside their helmet speakers. The clock on the wall turns from green to red, flashes. Three seconds.

"—for us now, and in the hour of our deaths."

"Amen." All the Knights say, and it is undergirded by a quiet strength.

"Lord, lead our hearts in our actions with our misguided brothers," Pio says. Two seconds.

"And bless the work of our hands," one second.

"And carry our souls to Heaven if you grace us to sacrifice ourselves this day, amen." no seconds.

Then Commander Brigid's pod fires off at twice the speed of sound, razor-edging the curvature of the awesome gas giant beside them. Hurling towards the hollowed-out rock containing the archbishop. Behind him, silently in the void of space, are five more missiles with men of God inside them.

†

The *Saint Eligius* dives and swoops away in a huge curve. Positioning to monitor the Knights as they race towards their landing. Threading the needle of the debris field, each of the IDPs vanishes. The ship's propulsion flares brilliantly as its maneuvering thrusters burst in half-second jets of compressed gas, nudging it this way and that as its trajectory keeps it on the line of sight edge of Asperity's silhouette.

The bridge is as tightly packed for the crew as the bay was for the Knights. The *Xiphos*-class ships were designed more as knives to secretly stab into an area and then withdraw than anything for combat. It has a small compliment of light-armament turrets and a single cache of needlelike missiles, but the real defenses are in the ships' anti-detection design, obscuring profile and electronic-reflective skin materials. It also possesses a battery of clutter-generation devices that overload enemy sensors, RADAR and the like with electronic noise.

The *Saint Eligius* station-keeps in its position, a slow pour of clutter leaking from it; not heavy enough to look like active avoidance but just enough to appear as an error on enemy tracking. It keeps a small observation window open for themselves in the clutter to monitor the Knights.

Lieutenant Commander Walter presses two buttons in sequence on his touchscreen and begins adjusting a virtual dial to tune a piece of equipment. "Hey, Pascal, do you have the telemetry on them yet?"

Lieutenant Baylon flips one switch and nods. "Yes, sir. They look good. Reached full acceleration, already on the decel. Still on course. Should have contact in—" he presses a button, "—three minutes."

"Copy that. Andre?"

Chief Warrant Officer 3 Bassette, scrutinizes the flow of numbers along a monitor, taps the screen once, twice. "Pods held up to the acceleration. All levels acceptable. Same with the rescue pod they're towing. All statuses are green in the foam projectiles as well. Those are prepped to launch in ten seconds."

"Copy that. We're sitting where we want to be, then." Lieutenant Commander Walter says. "Let's watch the foam deploy and then we'll do a quick round of prayers. Three minutes will be a lifetime to request divine aid."

"Yes, sir."

†

The six Individualized Drop Pods plus the seventh Brother Nonnatus is towing for the archbishop's hopeful escape are all little more than aimless missiles rocketing towards Stake. All have the same anti-detection design and skin materials that the *Xiphos*-class have. A mere three meters long and almost two meters wide with a single thruster in the rear. Each Knight is laying on his back, surreptitiously hurling feet first towards their unsuspecting target.

In the nose of the dagger-shaped IDP are two things: the decel engine and the landing foam packet. The decel engine glowing brightly, fighting the acceleration the pod received when the *Saint Eligius* launched it. The foam packet little more than a box with a long range proximity sensor at the front.

When their final ten seconds expires, the packet spring fires from the pod and races ahead. The whole thing is mechanically engineered to reach the landing surface first and detonate, creating a five meter wide wad of foam that the pod can strike into. As long as the decel engine does its job and takes the acceleration force off, the foam should be able to absorb the rest of the impact.

The IDPs need to launch one more time using their own thruster. A crash landing tends to interfere with that.

†

"Foam packets are go for launch in five seconds," CWO3 Bassette says as he examines a readout. A flashing light on his monitor catches his attention. His head darts to it and he squints, frantically taps on a button. "Sir, two of the grid cannons on Stake have started tracking—"

"Knights?" Lieutenant Commander Walter asks. He looks to Bassette and then out their front window screen as if he could see them clearly.

". . . I'm not— I can't tell. . . muzzle trajectory is close on one. Real close."

On the surface of the asteroid a small but long-barreled installation turns on a circular ball bearing track. The barrel tilts up and adjusts to coordinates fed to it from some automated monitoring station on the asteroid. Its muzzle flashes. A chuck of debris half a kilometer away from Commander Brigid explodes.

A second grid cannon looks up to the eternal night sky of space and aims far away from the Knights. Fires. Another debris chunk flashes in the silent darkness and the cannon resets to its home position.

Bassette slaps his face. "Not our guys. Just. . . just doing their job against the debris field."

"Don't do that to me again," Walter says. He looks back to the Knights' monitoring screen, says, "Go time."

†

The Knights are not connected by comms inside the IDPs, for fear of their traffic being discovered by the enemy. Commander Brigid, shaken deeply by the debris explosion off his side, can see through his viewport as Stake swells hugely. He breathes with slight relief as he feels the *thump* of his foam packet launch, making distance between him and his pod. He barely sees as the packet hits the rocky surface; a small disturbance of dust kicked out in a halo.

A lightning-fast chemical reaction in the foam as it boils out, stiffening as it goes. A circular tide, a ripple on the pond of stone before him. The nose of the pod hits. The whole thing shudders like a fault line and he can see a ripple travel through the foam around him and he hammers deep into it. The pod folds over—he can feel it in his guts as all of a sudden, the single g of gravity on this hollow rock takes him.

He jostles like a giant has slapped him. Thinks he blacks out for just a moment. Snaps his eyes open and heaves in a breath. Sees his pod settle out and through the viewport he is looking at the twinkling blackness of space. He hits his open button, and the pod obeys. Lid up, he grabs the edges and pulls himself out, sees three other globs of foam near to his.

Another packet strikes just off his own mound, bursts open. A blast of self-perpetuating foam roils about, climbing high and wide and fast. Brigid looks up and can see his Knight's pod strike into it. An impressive impact. The whole thing jiggles and he sees the material stretch and peel in long gelatinous pulls, but never falter.

A sixth strikes far enough away from the others, and it too softens the crash landing. All the Knights emerge within thirty seconds and Brigid gives the rally hand signal. Points to a boulder nearby. They dismount and meet up, far enough away from the landing foam that if that patch of unnatural growth and color catches the enemy's eye, they won't be there to suffer immediately.

Brigid taps the left side of his helmet twice. They all dial in their comms to line-of-sight-only with each other. Much harder to intercept during stealth ops. "Anything broken?" He asks.

Everyone shakes their heads. Brigid points to the small, shed-like structure ten meters from their landing zone and they move out.

†

"Sally port," Brother Cleopas says to himself as they reach the structure's nearest wall. Three meters in height and maybe twice that in length and width, the metal is old and pockmarked with age. Micro-collisions. Abraded by particulates and graffiti-ed by children like Cleopas. Just four sheets of cheap stamped metal tacked together at the seams with a roof on top, the sally port is little more than a space-age lean-to. That's all it's ever been, and all it was ever meant to be.

Cleopas takes the lead and moves around to the left while his childhood memory reminds him where the hatch is. He scans the corners before proceeding. If the ZZH were smart, they'd identify this abandoned shack for what it is: Stake's original front door. Unmonitored. Unguarded. Dusted over with spaceborne cobwebs now. Cast into memory's oblivion, except the Knights 1513 have a man who, as a mischievous little boy, used to violate every safety standard on this rock and come out for exterior walks with his friends. Rascals. Playful rascals.

Hide and seek between grid cannons. Try to catch hand-sized bits of errant debris floating by.

Come into the prospector's sally port and see where they took the original core sampling to determine if asteroid 3021 KD was worth capturing, towing to orbit and commit decades of resources to it.

"Oh, Mom. If only you could see your little boy now."

He reaches for the hasp keeping the hatch closed. The hasp is newer than the hatch itself, but still worn down by mounding years. Scan reads clean. No booby traps. His full frontal assault kit greatly augments his strength, and he turns the hasp and snaps whatever metal mechanism inside is holding it locked. Opens it up, and in his mind's eye his armored hand gets replaced with a memory of his youthful one all those years prior, still in the exterior suit he and his friends would lift from old lockers. He'd asked for one for is birthday every year, but his parents knew better.

"Them suits are to go out into space," his dad would say. "And no kid belongs out there. There's a reason I've never spent the money. Stop asking for one."

Cleopas couldn't for the life of him remember Flip's real name now, but he remembers the boy sneaking in there with him and their friends. The brothers. Then there was Kent and Diggs. Kent's squeaky voice saying, "Yeah, well my dad said those guys carved out a long, long hole in here and my dad was part of the team that examined all the rock and stuff they took out. Said it was super deep and they knew right away they could make huge caverns in this thing. There's a huge cavern right next to the hole. My dad said so."

"My dad said so too, Kent," Cleopas says to the recollection of the little boy now and swings the door open.

RESCUED EX INFERNA

Stake used to be a clump of rock identified simply as 3021 KD, hurling through space for untold eons of God's creation. And then one day a prospecting drone did a basic scan of it and marked it for further investigation. A spherical satellite with a dull hardened exterior and numerous clusters of antennae reaching off it like feverishly placed growths. A few comms dishes and a multipositional scanning array.

The two of them, meeting out in the universe as if they were against-all-odds lovers. The drone wanted to know every secret of the hulking rock as they ripped past one another at thousands of kilometers per hour. The drone made note of it in its software. Sent a communication light years away to some massive dish collecting loads of communications from all over. Assigned it out.

Years later a prospecting duo managed to locate it in a different part of the solar system. Matched course and speed, came alongside. Pulled a sally port kit off their storage rack and hastily assembled it, drove it into the asteroid's surface. Brought their coring machinery inside. Drilled their way through to a vein of metal or ore or carbon or frozen water that any mining company would kill for.

Sold it but left the sally port where it was like a signature. Just three meters in height and maybe twice that in length and width, the metal is old and pockmarked with age.

†

The team pushes inside. Clearing the corners—nothing but crusted-over ground anchors driven deep enough into the surface to embed the thing. No fancy tech. No low tech, either. Not even a light. Just bare walls sprinkled with ice. Brother Cleopas silently claps his hands, points, "There it is."

The team looks at the center of the port and they all see the gaping hole leading deep into the asteroid.

"Praise our God for prospectors, eh?"

"Praise our God for everything," Brother Pio says as he leans over the rim of the hole. It leads down into abysmal darkness, machine straight and smooth. His hands on the rim, blackened and honed to an edge from the friction of the drilling.

"Careful, Pio," Cleopas says. "Those edges were sharp enough back in the day we could slice through the rubber soles of our boots with it. A kid named Greb or Griff or something, we came out here and sat on the ledge of the hole as a dare. The rim of it cut through his exterior suit and he nearly died of decompression."

"Your company didn't seal this hole after that?"

"Nah." Cleopas says. "They put that lockable hasp on the hatch. Before it had no lock."

"The one you just broke?"

"Yes."

"Okay, excuse me," Brother Nonnatus comes over and works his way to the lip. Stares down into the coring shaft. A pinpoint of deep black at the bottom that gradually lightens to a shadowy gray at the top near him. He deploys the three small drones he has stacked in position on his back.

They buzz to life, their hover engines igniting on either side. They drop down inside the tunnel and the twin illuminations dwindle as they descend.

Nonnatus pulls up their scanning array in his Visuals and slings the feeds over to the other Knights. In their helmets, they watch as the drones reach a position in the tunnels where the blueprints show a significant mining cavern. The drones inspect the wall of the tunnel for a moment and find the cavern on the other side. Test for rock depth between the two. Find the thinnest point. They drop a marker on it and ascend.

"Bingo," Pio says and withdraws a handheld device almost a meter long. On the bottom of it is a handle and he presses a few buttons while the drones buzz back up and pass him at the tunnel's lip.

The device's far end unfolds and fires up into a glowing mechanism that begins to lift upwards, pulling his arm with it. "Give me just a moment," Pio says and steps off the hole's lip. His weight counteracts the lift of the device, and the effect causes him to slowly descend into the shaft.

As he goes, the team can see the compartments on his armor that contained all their explosives. They also see where Brother Santa Cruz had once painted *don't shoot me!*" across his back. Pio, the team's demolitions tech, agreed with the sentiment and left it there.

He makes himself as narrow as he can in his wearable tank of a suit. The device glows brighter as he puts his full weight onto it. He thumbs a dial on the handle that adjusts his descent.

Down to the marker. He reaches out with both legs and digs into the sidewalls of the coring tunnel. Withdraws a brick of CQ4 with one hand and tweaks its settings. Consonance quattour or CQ4, a "tunable" demolitions device that uses sonics to create an explosion disproportionate to the size of the weapon.

Getting what he wants from it, he sets it on the marked spot and prays, "Lord, let this make the boom I want and not the boom the ZZH would want. All glory to You, oh Lord. I love You, amen."

He kicks off the tunnel's side and ascends. Reaches the top twirling his index finger in a small circle. The other Knights acknowledge. Brother Gonzaga grabs Pio from over the tunnel's mouth and pulls him onto solid ground as a flash erupts below them. A small tremor communicates up through the rock and directly behind it a gust of dust and pebbles. And atmosphere.

Pio rushes back over to the lip, removes a small handheld rack of four devices. Jumps back into the tunnel's mouth. Descends faster than he did before.

He scissors his legs out again, scraping down the tunnel sides and comes to a stop about where he was. The hole punched into the cavern. Stake's maintained atmosphere now freely rushing into the void the Knights are in.

Pio unhooks one of the square devices. He sets one directly outside the small blast hole. The other three he hurriedly paces around the hole at the four corners of it. He activates one device and from its barrels it shoots a translucent but shimmering beam. Those beams meet the next device's corners, and they do the same with their two barrels. The four devices in the corners light up with a square covering over the hole, and a temporary patch forms. The vacuum of space no longer pulls at the atmosphere inside, and hopefully it didn't cause so much a disturbance or drop in levels that the enemy noticed.

Pio scans it for leaks. Satisfied the patch is holding, he reascends. Meets the others and nods. "Got a front door now."

"For His glory," Commander Brigid says as he touches a crucifix etched into his armor.

"For the life of Archbishop Hrutt," Pio says.

†

"Why Archbishop Hrutt?" Pio asked.

Brigid said, "He's an outspoken preacher against the ZZH's abominations and heresies. He's very accomplished; he's a medical doctor. He's got advanced degrees in philosophy and bioethics as well. He was custom-made by God to evangelize against the wrongs of their beliefs. He's orthodox while still being pastoral. Apparently, he has a decent track record of converting their folk, too."

"If that's the case, how do we know he's not already dead?"

"Because," Brigid said as he clicked over to another video feed. "They sent us a live feed link, presumably so we know both the archbishop is alive, and we can watch him be executed when we inevitably fail."

And there was Archbishop Hrutt. Stripped of his vestments, strapped down inside some kind of tight chamber. Obviously beaten. His eyes closed, lips moving in prayer.

"What is that he's inside? A medpod?" Nonnatus asks.

"Could be. Maybe they hurt him a little too much getting him off-world," Santa Cruz says.

"His breathing is labored... broken ribs." Gonzaga said. "It sucks trying to take a deep breath when you've gotten one of those."

"And we can trust the link is actually a live feed?" Pio asked.

†

Gun out, Santa Cruz takes the hovering device from Pio. Drops into the blast hole. A moment later the device comes freely floating back up, Santa Cruz left behind. Gonzaga grabs it, sets off down the tunnel. It comes back up emptyhanded again, and Nonnatus grabs it. Brigid and Pio look at one another, nod. One by one they drop inside.

Shadows, Broken Rock and Rust

The breach leads into a dark womb, claustrophobic and nerve-racking even for men trained to go into adverse places. Encased in armor more a combat machine than a simple protective suit, the feeling is still there.

Brother Santa Cruz is first inside. Abandoned mine. A seeping gloom surrounds him, deeper shadows than even what was on the surface with actual space as their backdrop. His suit reflexively switches through visual modes to remain as stealth as possible. It settles on a light filter/amplification mode, and he looks around for movement. Traps. Pitfalls. The first thing everywhere is wet stone. Rusted and broken pieces of metal. Dinge.

The roof is low and uneven. In some spots Santa Cruz has to duck. There are brown- and orange-scaled tracks along the floor; metal worked over into rust by age and moisture. Along the roof in places there are torn metal nets holding back crumbling sections. Bands of metal anchored into the roof for structural stability.

Brother Gonzaga is behind him. One by one the Knights emerge and take up defensive positions. They've emerged into a hollowed-out corner. Beyond where it grows even darker, they get the sense there is a much larger cavern.

Brother Nonnatus comes through and sends his drones up for a bird's eye view of the space. One ascends at a wrong angle and strikes an outcropping of stone less than three meters off the surface.

"Home," Brother Cleopas announces as he turns in a circle. Touring the cold rock, the remnants of industrial processes. He smiles.

He enters a low-hung section of a larger cavern. Brutalized stone all around. Chunks and rocks and pebbles strewn everywhere. Careless mess. He steps forward and gently toes a larger chunk out of the way. It lifts and drifts before gently settling back down.

"Less gravity here," Santa Cruz says. At his feet are pools of water. Stagnant, lying in mineral-encrusted troughs and breaks. The parts they step through leave water droplets suspended in the air, playing about like billiards knocked on a break. The interplay is lovely, even the way the breaking ripples in a pond stab upwards and split, descend. Like slow motion. Droplets scattered in handfuls as they step through. Merging into larger droplets. Sinking back down. Some floating off on their own as the weak gravity takes double and triple the amount of time to reclaim them under its power.

"The GravCore," Cleopas says. "It's tunable. Pinpoint tunable. They would adjust it anywhere they're mining. One great way to avoid cave-ins is to lessen the gravity in a particular area. Rock isn't as heavy if it's literally made less heavy."

"Fan out, advance five meters and wait," Commander Brigid says. The Knights move as best they can in the cramped mine. Everywhere the edges of stone, gouged by cutting and drilling tools, the dips and crests of an uneven floor. The way the roof seems to be leaning down into its long-lost family of rock in the floor, taking another eon to rejoin it, but rejoin it will.

Scrapes of remains from the industry that entered in here, took what it wanted, forced its will on the ore lode and left when it grew tired. Orphaned electrical junction boxes with all their conduit cut. A single stand with a wide baseplate and a small controller box at waist height, attached to nothing. Some errant bolts, mostly broken or sheared off. Left like shell casings on the battlefield. Soaked through food containers, ancient and grease stained. Lengths of chain, hung in pairs. Some short, some draped down to the floor and curled like snakes, some links stressed so badly they sheared.

Decaying ladders here and there. One leading up to nowhere. Another leads up to a square platform of expanded metal that is two meters by two meters and has nothing else attached to it. One ladder buckled just off the floor, rent over as if it was struck by something larger. Hungrier.

Brother Pio finds a length of cabling strung along one wall. The loops of it sink down, and at their lowest points moisture collects and drips. Almost the dead center of each loop's nadir is a crust of minerals. Fish belly white but dirty all the same.

"Commander, I'm not getting anything adverse down here." Nonnatus says. "Drones are reporting back that there's one sensor in the roof. I'm scanning it now, but I can tell you just from looking at it, it's dead. Left behind by the miners."

"Verify."

"Yes, sir." Nonnatus switches to another thumbnail in his Visuals and remote pilots the drone to the sensor array. Runs through a list of options on the drone and uses an electromagnetic spectrum scan to see if there's any traces of electricity. "Nothing that I can detect, sir."

Cleopas clears his throat. "They're required by regulation that when they seal a decommissioned mine, they leave behind a sensor array to monitor it. But it's a formality. The abandoned mine is sealed off; you'll need tools or explosives to get back in and there's nothing of value in here. The sensors are cheap, and they die in a couple of years."

"Why monitor it, then?"

"Technically, they've maintained the atmosphere inside here. The sensor might watch for drastic leaks of it, indicating a cave-in. Stuff like that."

Nonnatus says, "Verified, commander. The sensor is dead."

"But it looks like it's from the decomm? Not the ZZH?"

"Yessir."

"Praise our Lord. Good catch, brother. Now, look for the next thing. An entrance. Ask Saint Anthony if you need to."

"We ask him to intercede a lot, I've noticed." Cleopas says.

"In our line of work, we need him, ever present." Brigid studies the info sent from the drones for a moment; a square box growing a few antennae off of it, with rusty bolts in each of its corners drilled into the rock above. A single cable runs to it. All of it dirty, dank. Everything is this way. Brigid looks about. "That's it? Nothing else?"

"No, commander. Just rock, rust and grime."

Brigid flicks on his helmet light and one hundred thousand lumens in a tight cone blasts forth. He huffs and says, "All right. There's a door or something leading out of here, right?"

†

An archway large enough to accommodate elephants appears in the flashlight-pierced gloom. It is sealed over by a plate metal slab. Like a quilt, it's composed of several smaller sheets of metal connected. It's rusty and crisscrossed with raw welding seams. Whoever put the slab together did so out of scrap and didn't feel the need to do any finishing work. Around the plate, embedded in the wall are anchor bolts drilled through the stone, presumably into the metal on the other side. The mine cavern itself sealed off.

"Door," Commander Brigid says. Points his gun at the slab.

"Not on the prints, either," Brother Nonnatus says as he takes up a position beside the commander.

"Not even on the set from when they idled this place," Brother Cleopas adds, "But it makes sense. Legally they'd shave to plug up this mine when they're done. Probably didn't even occur to them to notate it."

"What else didn't occur to them to notate, then?"

Cleopas grimaces. "Pray that it's not much."

"Pray anyways, and in all things." Brigid says as he comes up to it.

Nonnatus and Cleopas scan the metal, examining the edges, the welds themselves. Cleopas runs his finger down the rusted surface and comes away, rubs his finger and thumb together. Watches the rust turn to powder under his pads. Falls to the floor of his childhood home.

Cleopas turns to the commander. "This has to be decomm work. They must have thrown these things together and slapped them up on their way out. It might not be too solid, especially after a few decades." He points to the floor, where twin rail tracks disappear under the slab.

"The other side?" Brigid asks.

"The tunnel we want. To the main hangar." Cleopas pulls up the schematic on his Visuals and sends a marker for it to his brothers.

"That tunnel is long," Brother Santa Cruz says. "Fatal funnel if they know we're here."

Brigid says, "Peeper hole."

"Roger, sir," Brother Gonzaga says. He pulls out a kit and removes a small cylinder from it. Attaches a drill chuck to it. It has a magnetic lock facing the same direction as the chuck. He inserts a drill bit, then holds it up to Cleopas who has a camera snake ready. Cleopas compares the snake to the bit and nods.

"Should be a good size," he says.

"Yup," Gonzaga says and puts the drill up high on the metal plate. The magnet holds it in place. Fires it up. The drill was designed for covert operations. Its motor is whisper quiet. The bit is louder, but with such a thin atmosphere inside the mine the noise isn't terrible. The old metal squeaks as it goes. A few times the bit bites in and the metal shrieks. The Knights brace every time it does. Gonzaga presses a button on the side and a nozzle sprays cutting fluid onto the bit.

Gonzaga looks at a display on the cylinder as it auto-plunges the bit. A steady rainfall of gleaming chips come down from the bore hole, and the bits curl and float off in the lessened gravity.

Every rotation of the bit, an opportunity to be discovered. All at once the squealing changes pitch and the cylinder stops laboring. It spins freely. "We're through," Gonzaga says. He looks at the display on the side of the drill, says, "Fifty mils."

He removes the drill as Cleopas steps up and eases the snake through the hole. In his hand is a screen, and he interfaces with it via fine connections on his gloved thumb. Broadcasts that to his brothers' Visuals.

"Everybody online with this?" He asks, and they all respond affirmatively. He maneuvers the snake, on the end of which is a pinhole infrared laser and camera.

"No obvious booby traps," Nonnatus says.

"No welcoming party either," Brigid says.

"For all we know the miners put up another steel plate at the other end and no one has been in this tunnel for decades," Pio says.

"Could be," Cleopas says. "At worst they're waiting for us further down."

"In the fatal funnel." Santa Cruz says.

"Be ready with covering fire," Brigid says. "We've got to breach it. Best option?"

"Cut through it," Santa Cruz says. "Or I can use the breaching foam."

"Foam is loud," Nonnatus says. "I think we should cut it."

"Good enough for the girls I date," Brigid says. "Pio, TechHaft." The commander taps a fingertip on the slab as if he's knocking on a door.

"My pleasure," Brother Pio says. He ignites his TechHaft and a brilliant short, thick sword forms out of the laser weapon. "By the way, Commander, when was your last date?"

"Thirty-two years ago, when I took my wife to coffee, and she would want you to cut through that instead of asking me questions." Brigid crosses himself, thinking of his old life.

Pio lets out a quiet laugh and stabs his sword into the metal. The laser heat instantly turns the edges around the blade red hot, then a piercing orange-yellow as it begins to slag and melt. Pio efficiently draws the blade down until he has a two meter high vertical line. Then a matching one on the other side. He runs it horizontally at the top to connect the two and as soon as he does Gonzaga magnetizes the drill back onto the slab and uses it as a handle to pull the makeshift door inside the cavern.

Santa Cruz rushes through, gun up. Gonzaga next, peeling off to the left. Cleopas to the right, Nonnatus, Pio and Brigid pouring through the opening.

No assault waiting for them. No blockade against them. Brigid snorts. "Move, move."

They silently stalk, one foot rolling in front of the other, heel-toe, ambling at a pace that gets their hearts quickening. Heavier breathing. Checking pools of shadow. Each crevice that, through tricks of light or uneven feature of rock, looks like it might conceal a gun or security camera.

The tunnel itself is tall and wide enough to accommodate the old equipment the miners brought in and out: transport carts, laser cutters, the works. Sloping walls up to an arched ceiling, ribbed all throughout with supports. More wet, slimy weeping trails down the stone. More rust eating away at the supports. More metallic netting holding back cave-ins, chewed up in spots, dribbling pebbles like saliva.

More shadow than anything. The Knights do what they can to avoid puddles, streaks of faux-slow-motion water spills as one of them treads through the puddle. Sideways cascades of droplets and splashes taking their time in the one-third gravity. Using their headlamps to spotlight every collection of darkness in front of them. So many. Any one of those could be concealing enemy tech. All down the tunnel are coring holes where the miners must have continuously taken samples, searching for that next vein of riches.

"Nonnatus, get the drones down further. I want a picture."

"Yes sir," Nonnatus actives the drones and maneuvers them with eye flickers as a rear-facing camera inside his helmet watches. The compact stack of circular drones zips up and maintains a half-meter distance from the roof of the tunnel.

Using infrared, they scan. "Nothing but rock so far, sir," he reports, then, "Wait—"

The entire team halts and sidesteps to whatever side of the tunnel they're closest to. Gonzaga and Santa Cruz take a knee, post up with weapons hot.

"What are we looking at?" Brigid asks.

Nonnatus huffs, says "Cave-in." Tense, quiet. "A huge cave-in."

"ZZH?" Pio asks.

"Toss me the view." Brigid says. In a flicker of his Knight's eyes, a window pops up inside Brigid's Visuals. Lit by the infrared beam the drones are showering the area with, the tunnel is mouse-still. In that moment all the Knights cease breathing, their hindbrains begin running through a checklist of training. Easing the tension in muscles, relaxing. Focus on front sights and long-range monitoring. Identify the enemy. Remove their threat.

And give praise to God.

Brigid looks at each of his men at the ready, says, "I don't think it's ZZH. Looks like the miners' overhead netting catastrophically failed."

"Plan B?" Santa Cruz asks.

"Move up to it," Brigid says. "Let's see how thorough it is."

The Knights acknowledge and move forward. They come up on the spill of rubble and it becomes obvious there is no way forward short of using powered equipment and an entire excavation crew.

Cleopas studies the cave-in, wipes a hand over a settled stone. Looking at his glove, sees a thick ribbon of dust on his fingertips. In his headlamp the dust is flaked with an extremely fine bluish glint, and if he moves his fingers just right those nearly infinitesimal particles roll. Shimmer. Takes him back to his youth, skirting this very tunnel. The passage from this particular mine to the main hangar. How he used to play, how they'd get in trouble for being too near the automated ore carts moving back and forth on the ruined tracks beneath his feet.

"We solved that problem. . ." he says to himself.

"Say again?" Brigid asks.

Cleopas fills with the Holy Spirit as it grabs a handful of long-forgotten memories and shoves them right back into the forefront of his mind. He takes his dust-coated fingers and touches a Rosary bead he's painted on his armor. Smiles so warmly that even though his brothers cannot see it, they can feel it radiate.

"EcoPassage 2." He says and turns around. Orientates himself.

"Fill us in." Pio says.

"The Blessed Virgin is never far," Cleopas is half in a daze as he moves over to the opposing wall and comes up on a run of old, dented conduit fixed to the ground. He begins to follow it forward into the shadows. There the cave-in is thinner, and he moves a few large pieces and can step around it.

"The drones examined back there," Nonnatus says. "There's maybe five more meters and we're closed off completely."

"I only need four. Take a look."

The Knights follow around the disgorge of rock. Cleopas is standing next to an old panel that stands two meters high and about the same in width. Conduit and heavy cabling run into it, rope out of it like a nexus. Behind it, in the tunnel wall, the rock is squarely sheared away in a dugout.

Cleopas shines his flashlight onto the roof of the dugout and there is still the scraping marks and black marker he used as a child to draw. Brigid kneels and takes a look.

"Madonna and Child," he says with a note of puzzlement. Drawn on the surface of the dugout is a woman holding a baby, both with halos.

"I drew that a long time ago. The Blessed Virgin is never far," Cleopas says. Several lengths of conduit run into the dugout and pass through an old, ruined grate before disappearing off into some other portion of the world here. Cleopas grabs the grate and yanks. It snaps free and reveals a dark entrance beyond.

He sets the grate aside and removes a glowstick from a compartment on his armor. Snaps it and it comes to life with a soft green light. He throws it at the dark entrance and whatever is on the other side amplifies the soft glow stick's illumination. The space beyond diffuses into a vibrant panoply of blues.

"EcoPassage 2." Cleopas announces. "We used this as a way to sidestep all the industrial traffic. It'll take us right into an adjoining mechanical room of the main hangar."

Brigid asks, "Was it on the schematics?"

"No. But God put three of them here. This asteroid, I guess the region of space it came from, a small planetoid billions of years ago or whatever, it had a particular kind of fauna and flora on it, and a few species of it survived in deep space cryostasis. It's all inside."

Cleopas looks down the dugout's length into the glow stick-lit area. A sea of jeweled blues. Sees the familiar structures he was used to playing around with as a child, sneaking about as some kind of prophetic statement about how he as an adult would one day do. "For Christ's glory."

He enters and disappears on the other side.

Brigid motions to Santa Cruz to keep on Cleopas's tail. He says, "Stay tight. Gonzaga, maintain our six and make sure to get that MedSled through." and he enters.

Arteries of Jade and Emerald

Brother Gonzaga exits the dugout's shaft and enters what might as well be a dream.

His new brothers are circled around one another, their headlamps shining beams this way and that as they turn their heads, cutting like lightning through crystalline structures that refract it in all the cool colors of the rainbow.

Like being inside a geode, washed over by dark admiral blue with ribbons of kelly green, several glimmering shades and hues thereof. A thick wall of stone all around them—as low and craggy as the mine itself but bejeweled in shotgun blasts of hefty mineral crystals. Thick, squat stalagmites and spiraling, almost curlicue stalactites adorn the space. Like frozen trees and handing vines from some far off, long dead alien world. These structures, stalks made of cut glass that wind in coils and heave up to the ceiling and back down to spill in ice formations onto the uneven floor.

The shaft is narrow, and along one side of it service cables and piping run in a compact formation as if they are one species and know they are only being tolerated here so they keep their formations unobtrusive.

"EcoPassage 2," Brother Cleopas announces, and one can see in his eyes the boyhood memories of the time he spent there. Dodging around these foreign branches, trying to climb them, swing on them, sliding down them, tracing their alien curves with his fingertips. Putting his flashlight right up to their flat, smooth surfaces and playing the light through their astounding prisms.

Commander Brigid looks to Cleopas. He motions with his hand and says, "Lead the way."

"Yes, sir." He has to hunch in order to make it under the nethermost overhead features. The Knights follow him, and all notice how Cleopas's boyhood muscle memory comes right back as he smoothly angles around some jutting crystals and weaves about others. His hand reaching out and touching one here and there as if in familiarity. Old friends reuniting.

"This is the flora I was talking about," he says, patting one with remembrance. Fondness, even. "A type of silicone-based fungus I think is what the on-board scientists said. Just, little, tiny glass seeds that were lying dormant in the stone surface. Heat and atmosphere reached them after eons and they sprouted."

As his brothers examine the structures with tempered admiration for God's hidden beauty, Cleopas says, "The fauna. There were these. . . clutches of eggs all over the crystal when our miners first arrived. They were embedded in the— everything. All around. Just, everywhere. They burrowed holes in the crystal and laid clutches."

"What did? What did they hatch?"

"These half-meter long centipede things. Really thick bodies. Mandibles like scimitars. But the big deal about them is they swarm and exude this caustic fluid. Damaged all kinds of metal. Our guys spent months eradicating them."

Here and there the Knights notice pockmarks in the surfaces. Brother Nonnatus peers inside one. "Here. Narrow hole, burrowed in just deep enough. Then a little rounded space."

Cleopas nods. "Anything inside?"

"No. Empty."

"They're all over. Like I said, they were eradicated."

"Did they jeopardize the mining operation?"

"They stuck really close to the EcoPassages. I guess they don't survive long on cold rock. There's something I didn't understand about their physiology and these crystalline structures. Dependent on it I guess. They were very specialized. Anyway, they would sneak out long enough to damage things really badly, yeah. They were exterminated."

"You sure about that?" Gonzaga asks. "I'm wearing metal."

Cleopas laughs. "Yeah, I'm sure. They'd be all over us by now if they were still around. Trust me." He aims his light at where decades-old initials are carved into them. M.R. + R. F. and dozens more, many inside carved hearts. Like high school sweethearts marking up trees, Cleopas smiles. "See this? Memories."

He pauses long enough to draw back to those days in his mind. Walks over to one and examines a feature. Doesn't see what he wants, so he goes over to another one. Then a third. A fourth and he claps his hands silently. Shows off another two pairs of initials faded from time, nestled comfortably in a heart. "Me and Kasi D'Vear. Her folks were in logistics. She was from a little island chain on Xerra IV." He rocks back and forth on his heels for a moment, thumbs hooked along his weapons belt. "She was blonde."

Cleopas wags his eyebrows, not that any of his brothers could see it. But the tone was in his voice. The Knights blow raspberries and wave him off. Brigid pats him on the shoulder and says, "Stories for later."

"Sure," Cleopas says. "Anyway, I think she joined the Sisters of Saint Telavor-in-Mercy. They're Dominican. So, you know. Very holy."

A sadness fills his eyes. He clears his throat and turns and points at the service cabling bundles. "Our facilities guys did a good job of keeping their footprint in here down to a minimum. This cave is a natural tube in the asteroid. Stake's arteries, we'd call them. That's why the floor and walls are so uneven. But we as kids would come in here and play all day. Just look at God's beauty here. Hidden away from intelligent life for literally tens of thousands of years."

He starts going again, looking back to his initials one more time. The Knights can hear him say a Hail Mary under his breath, finishes it with, "For Kasi." Brigid has some idea of why he does it but leaves it alone.

They zigzag through another twenty meters or so of glistening treasure on earth and in the short sky. Cleopas absently says, "There's no mining value in this stuff outside of chintz jewelry and decorations. Technically it's living, so it has to be treated like a house plant. And it's invasive. That's why they left it alone."

He comes up to a hard ninety-degree turn in the conduit along the floor, says, "But it'll always be Kasi and I's place."

Cleopas follows the conduit run and halts. Kneels, taps at another grate in the wall. Through it, the conduit disappears. "Mechanical room into the main hangar."

Brother Santa Cruz comes up to it, tense. "Showtime."

We're Not Alone

The railgun's large bore muzzle appears from a service corridor followed by its combat-length barrel and finally the body of the gun itself. Brother Santa Cruz's finger indexed along the trigger guard. He and the gun push forward through the thin atmosphere, leaving EcoPassage 2 behind. Sight hovering near his eye, he moves into a cramped side space three meters wide and four meters long.

The wall to his right continues onward out into what he assumes is the main hangar. It terminates a hundred and fifty meters directly ahead where the hangar bay entrance divides them from outer space itself just beyond. The wall on his other side takes a drastic curve to the left. They're emerging into a corner of the hangar.

"One g," Santa Cruz says just above a whisper as his body registers the difference in gravity immediately. The GravCore must be tuned higher here.

"All copy," Commander Brigid says as he emerges into the alcove with Santa Cruz. Santa Cruz stops at the corner made by the left wall's turn, goes bolt still. He looks all around, then turns to the commander. Gives a look and then nods at the wall's edge near his head. A fresh rend in the metal glimmers in the pale light leaking like a spill into their claustrophobic alcove. Bullet ricochet. Brigid nods.

"Light," Santa Cruz says as he looks above. Brigid follows his gaze, hearing his own breathing become heavier as he sees it. The light fixture on the ceiling before them has been shot out. A trail of bullet holes, pockmarks that ripped through the overhead, one or two shattering the light as it passed by.

The fragmented remains of the fixture twinkle on the floor in the dim, watery illumination spilled over from far off to their left. Santa Cruz steps off to the side, points down at the floor just past the corner.

"Blood," he says. A fling of crimson comes from somewhere beyond the wall. Jagged fingers of a spray pattern reach into where they can see.

"Brother Cleopas, on point with the peep camera. The rest of you hold fast."

Cleopas emerges and points ahead. "Primary hangar. Business offices in the far corner., all the way down this wall." He pats the wall to their left.

"Take a look," Brigid says as he moves for the Knight. Cleopas takes a half step and stops. Realizes what they're showing him. Resumes going forward.

"What'd they shoot at?" Santa Cruz asks. "Not supposed to be anyone here but the ZZH."

Cleopas aims the long-necked camera around the corner. Whistles.

"What do you see?" Brigid asks.

Cleopas sends the view to the other Knights Visuals, says, "Trouble."

Brigid snarls just a moment as he watches the video feed, says, "Brother Nonnatus, get the drones up here."

†

"Get to the landing gear and take up posts," Commander Brigid says as the Knights flow out from the alcove in single file. They have to step over the blood spray as they hustle out into the main hangar.

Before them the expansive space unfolds. Bathed in flickering, damaged flashes of struggling light from the shootout overhead shattered most every ceiling light fixture. Shards of light popping like fireworks from the damaged fixtures. Weak and mostly futile.

They exit from the top left of the hangar. The bottom wall from corner to corner is an open airlock. Rimming the wide-open cataract into space is a glowing field that retains the heat and vacuum of the hangar against the frigid void outside. All along the top wall is open storage; an absolute kill zone should the Knights run there.

The abandoned asteroid hangar is full of new ships. And full of new bullet holes.

The Knights reach the closest ship, situated on six massive landing gear feet. Scurrying inside its shadow, they fan out, covering all angles as the drones overhead zip from one spot to another, scanning for the ZZH and potential traps.

Gonzaga, trailing the archbishop's Fast Recovery MedSled behind him, maneuvers it under cover and sets its auto-controls to hover in place.

All the Knights are getting back from the drones' video feeds are scatters of blood. Spent shell casings.

"These aren't ZZH ships," Brother Santa Cruz says. "Whatever happened here was a slaughter."

The ship dominates this side of the hangar. Effectively a large, flat square casting an equally substantial and boxy shadow. The edges of it are captured in the flickering going on above between the roof of the ship and the hangar's ceiling. The marred lighting system pecking out what few bits of radiance they can.

On the other side of the ship is the crew gangplank. Still extended down, a ramp from the vessel's belly to the hangar floor. Trickles of light cast through bullet wounds in the gangplank. At its base is more blood. A smear mark runs off towards the far end of the hangar where someone must have been drug away. Jumped.

The Knights stay at the ready, hunkering behind the gear.

Brigid taps on one of the landing gears; his finger comes away with hydraulic oil on it from a leaking cylinder above. A gouge in it is a perfect circle the size of an entrance wound.

†

"Tech did a flyby on it an hour ago," Commander Brigid said, clicking the remote. "They found some observatory satellite passing by Stake within a few hundred thousand kilometers and it had an eye sharp enough to see it. They commandeered it."

He calls up a few photographs of the asteroid.

"I'm assuming we only got one side of it?" Brother Pio asked.

"Yes. The satellite wasn't going to make a loop of that magnitude and not be unnoticed by the ZZH. And it would eat up more time than we have."

"Okay, so whatever is waiting for us on the other side. . . we'll get to find the fun way."

Brigid smiles. "Whatever we find, God will be with us."

"Yeah, but I wish the satellite found it first," Brother Nonnatus says. "God can still be with us then, too."

"Wishes are for little girls. I'm pretty sure a pope said that." Brother Santa Cruz said and tossed a small wad of paper at Nonnatus.

"The other side is where the sally port is located," Brother Cleopas said. "That'll come in handy."

"Good," Brigid said. "Do you remember that structure?" He pointed to a hexagonal feature on the asteroid. It is white with a red outline running down its geometric features. At the four corners, the Knights all recognize vacuum-capable VTL thrusters.

"No, it's sitting. . . uh," Cleopas strained back into his memory. "This right here—" he touched a spot on the permanent boxes that faces the exterior, "—was the main airlock. They'd never attach mobile stuff right up to the working and living spaces. If it accidentally detached, they'd lose atmo, temp, instant rad exposure, you know the drill."

"Makes sense," Brigid said. "Intel states this is a late model Huskvar STV interplanetary barracks unit. Self-propelled campground is what the Huskvar sales material says. No hull numbers, no transponder that we can ping. We think the ZZH acquired and modified it to run dark.

That's what they're staying in and using the facilities on Stake as needed."

"Defenses? Tracking?" Nonnatus asked.

"Minimum package to take flight is what we can gather from its profile. Who knows what the ZZH did to it, though."

"We going to hit that, then?" Brother Gonzaga asked.

"Last, and only if necessary." Brigid said. "We can't just missile strike it and roll in afterwards. Just in case that's where they're keeping the archbishop. I'm not answering for that, in this life or the next."

"Why not keep him there?"

Brigid shrugged. "If they were keeping him inside the Huskvar, they wouldn't need Stake. I have to assume he's inside the asteroid. The Huskvar is mostly likely just transportation and barracks."

†

Now, in the shadow of the cruiser and Commander Brigid's finger tapping on the landing gear, he decides he might be a little girl too and wishes they had better intel. "ZZH reinforcements?"

The cruiser has so much patchwork, layered metal over its skin it looks like sedimentary rock grew wings. Some company logo painted on the side; chipped and faded from years of travel. The same logo is printed in three different languages; Brother Cleopas recognizes two.

"ZZH? No," Cleopas says, caution in his voice, looking up at the underbelly of the behemoth above them. "This a maintenance transport. That company logo—I can't pronounce it, but I recognize it—they're the tech company that travels from asteroid to asteroid performing annual checks, preventative maintenance stuff. Cleaning. They're here."

"Why?"

Brother Gonzaga leans back from where he's watching the hangar. "Looks to me like this is all brand-new excavating equipment. Opening the mine back up?"

"No way. . ." Cleopas says as a thought dawns on him. "You know, they probably are, now that you mention it."

"Really?"

"Yes, sir. Looking at these particular vehicles right here—" he points to another ship, basically a flatbed with the equipment Gonzaga spoke of mag-locked down to it. "—specialized stuff, right there. I read somewhere a year ago maybe— yeah, somebody has been taking contracts to gather and process mining wastewater. They've got some system now that makes it cost effective. That looks about right for what the equipment is."

"So, everything we stomped through in the mine shafts is going to be reclaimed?" Brigid asks.

"Yes, sir. These ships must be part of the new fleet, come to open it back up alongside the maintenance crew that cleans and maintains Stake anyway."

"Then they're hostages too," Brigid says.

"Doubt it, sir," Brother Nonnatus says. "I agree with Brother Santa Cruz. Looks like a slaughter."

Brigid groans and makes a fist. "Copy. Cleopas, How many, you think?"

"Ten? Tech techs with maintenance, anyway. They usually bring a deep cleaning crew also. Specially trained janitors. Maybe somewhere near ten of them as well. I couldn't tell you the flight crews, equipment operators, all that."

"There should have been a report about this before we got here."

"Well, maintenance anyways, these guys rush to get their work done. Staying ahead of schedule means a bonus and more time off before have to start their annual rotation again. And since Stake is decomm-ed, there's nothing to interrupt if they show up unannounced and get their work done. Plus, they're working ahead of a new mining crew now. Pressure to get here and get it done."

"Lord, guide us. All right. Nonnatus, what's it look like?"

"Got us a clear path, I think."

"Mark it out on the Visuals. Santa Cruz, you're up."

†

Their footsteps are quiet in the hangar, and the stillness is deafening. Commander Brigid's full frontal assault suit's sensor array is constantly scanning. He lines into his Knights' arrays as well; sees them scanning. Alone. They're alone in the space. At least, they're the only living things in the space. Stepping over the blood enforces that notion.

Brother Gonzaga says, "We need to avoid this kind of treatment if we can," He points to the side of the crew transport ship as he moves past it.

The other Knights move around to him. There alongside the ship is a blast hole, scorched and twisted metal. The ship's gaping wound big enough for three men side by side. Inside is savaged as well. Its guts pockmarked by gunfire, trash and clutter along the deck. Outside is no different; blast debris strewn about the hangar floor. Shell casings like spilled jewels twinkle in their flashlights.

"Gonzaga, you and Brother Pio sweep it. One minute." Brigid says. "The rest of you, fall in tight. Hold what you've got."

Gonzaga again parks the MedSled and he and Pio move inside, worming their way around the jagged edges of the blast hole. Brigid pulls up their feeds in his Visuals. As he's watching them hastily flow through the space, his mind drifts to the other vehicles.

"Brother Nonnatus," he says, "Can you break off one drone to inspect the equipment?"

"On it." Nonnatus says. Along the hangar ceiling a single small disc drops away from two other dark spots just like it and soundlessly cants in a swooping arc towards the nearest excavator-like vehicle.

Brigid has the Knights' feeds pulled up in his helmet. Watches Gonzaga's sweep across the cockpit of the ship. Next to the control panel, the type of cup holder that is more like a sealable can than an open round compartment. Can't suddenly go into zero G and let that liquid float up and out. Pio's watches him move through the crew berthing compartment. Bunkbeds bolted to the floor stacked three high with just enough space to probably sit up straight. No more. A solid curtain drawn across each space to keep the sheets and pillows from floating away just like the cockpit coffee.

"Nothing," Brigid says to himself. The video feeds turn and head back the way they came. Pio and Gonzaga appear at the blast hole and jump down.

"Commander," Pio says. "You saw?"

"Yes. Best I could through your feeds, anyway."

Pio nods. "No bodies, no evidence of violence. Looks like they landed not any the wiser and got attacked as they were exiting on the gangplank and—" he motions to the blast hole, "—there, which I'm pretty sure was an equipment unloading door before it got hit with whatever munition did that damage."

"All right," Brigid says as he looks out into the hangar. "Where are the bodies?"

"That way," Brother Cleopas points to a nearby wall. "You can see the blood."

Brigid looks that way, crosses himself. He sees the drone ascend from one vehicle and head over to another. "Let's get this show on the road, Nonnatus. We're sitting ducks."

A Bad Last Stand

There was a significant splatter of red leading up to the sealed hatch in the far wall. The Knights drive that way unmolested. They reach it and fan out; the corner is open to the entire bay. The hatch leads into the business offices and along the wall leading to the bay door are two reenforced windows looking out from the offices. No movement behind the windows. Past those are wall-mounted racks for storage that reach deck to overhead. The Knights take note that there are only three pallets on the racks, and all are new.

Brother Santa Cruz posts up with his gun trained on the hatch as Brother Pio opens it. The hatch slides back into the wall and there are no monsters on the other ready to pounce.

Just a gaping dark maw; a tunnel like a throat to swallow them further into Stake's decommissioned belly. The tunnel itself is ravaged. Wounded beyond life in some kind of vicious struggle.

"Last stand," Brother Cleopas says as the Knights move into it.

"Yeah, but all the way down?" Brother Nonnatus says. His drones move forward, scanning as they go.

"Why didn't they get back on their ships and try to fly out?" Pio asks.

"Jumped from behind?" Santa Cruz says. "Herded this way, maybe?"

"If somebody blew a hole like that in the side of my ship, I might not trust them to get away." Brigid says.

There are trails of smeared blood that run into the shadow-soaked tunnel. "Somebody got drug through here," Brother Gonzaga says, sidestepping the worst of it.

"Hopefully to medical," Cleopas says. No one adds anything.

The tunnel's recessed lighting is damaged. Apparently set to motion sensors, the lighting reacts poorly as the Knights push through. Soft where they are not, flickering and harsh where they are.

Like misfiring lightning bolts, the lighting tries to grow in intensity as the men pass but only succeeds in struggling embarrassingly.

The tunnel is hewn from the asteroid in what was a fantastically angular rectangle. Running from the hangar to wherever it leads, ninety-degree angles in all four corners. Now chunks are missing from all the surfaces, spent shell casings like party glitter here and there. Small clusters of them marking where the shooters paused, fired and moved, paused, fired and moved.

"This tells us a lot about the ZZH here," Brigid says. "Disciplined, armed. Merciless."

Santa Cruz says, "All the shell casings are small arms fire. Shouldn't do much against our armor. Unless they fire whatever they hit that ship with at us, I think we can walk into a wall of their fire."

"Let's hope that's all they have," Brigid says.

Blood in puddles. Flung sprays across the wall. Up onto the ceiling. Brigid comes up to one such mess and extends a blade from his armor's forearm. Scrapes it through the crimson. In the spasmodic flashes of lighting, it takes on a nightmare quality. From black to deep life-giving red and back to black.

"Fresh enough," he says and flicks the knife at the wall to clean it. "Just now getting tacky." He looks down at the tunnel. "Let's move."

They step around bits of mothballed office equipment used for cover. Waist-high copy machines, draped in plastic to keep dust off. Now blasted into ruins. More pockmarks on the walls. A line of blackened bullet holes tracing a sweep across one wall and crawling up the ceiling like a sutured scar.

"First door coming up on the left," Cleopas says. He has the schematics overlaid on his Visuals. "Should lead to a facilities machinery room, no way out from there."

"Nonnatus?" Brigid asks.

"Yessir. Drones reported it. Two more after this one."

"Clear it."

"Looks like we're too late," Cleopas says as they get up on it. The door's control panel has been shot. The door itself is a sliding one. No hinges. It slips into the wall and is jammed a quarter of the way into it. Bullet dents adorn the exposed threequarters.

Gonzaga sets the MedSled along the wall. Nonnatus comes over and takes the control for it off of his armor where it's attached to his lower back. Like a beacon, an invisible leash for the pod to follow. Snaps it to his own. "I've got rear guard anyway," he says. Gonzaga nods his appreciation.

Santa Cruz and Gonzaga get on either side of the door. Pio and Nonnatus grab the door's edge and pull it further into the wall. The hatch grinds into the recess. Its internal gearing groans and the damaged metal screeches. Santa Cruz shoves in. Gonzaga holds the space at the open hatch.

Inside the room there's service equipment for plumbing and an electrical panel with the requisite thick tubes of conduit branching out of it. Fresh and wastewater piping painted black with red gate valve handwheels dominate one wall. A single touch screen monitor that has been smashed dead center.

And two bodies dressed in flight jump suits crumpled in the back corner, huddled in their final moments. One looks to be of *Homo Sapien* origin, though born and raised outside of Earth. Like so many billions now. He wears a breathing apparatus to supplement the lean air. The other is of Mariol decent, which is obvious by the fact he's not wearing an environmental suit helmet. The substantial bulges behind his jaw hinges that allow his body to extract and better process gases from unsubstantial atmospheres. His needle-like hair and significantly larger eyes add to the evidence.

"We got two dead males. One Terran diaspora and one Mariol. Same logo as the maintenance ship. I imagine chased in here and executed." Santa Cruz says. "Otherwise, clear."

"Mark it for a work of mercy. We'll return to collect them for burial when this is all over and done with."

Santa Cruz drops a marker in his Visuals to note where they are. Assuming Stake is cleared and later deemed safe to move about, a crew of monks will treat the dead with respect and dignity in accordance with Jesus Christ's command to bury the dead.

They step back out into the sea of languid darkness, move on. The tinny clink of empty shell casings rattling about with their footsteps announces their travel. The damaged lighting still tries to do its job. Overhead motion sensors turn the light on full blast—or as best as they can—directly above them while fading out the one behind them. Fading in the one before them. The effect is some kind of diabolical revelation. Flickering, stuttering. Snatches of extreme violence in the light, only to be hidden underneath the blankets of shadow in the blink of an erratic eye.

"Second door up on the left," Cleopas says. "Another mechanical room. Larger this time. Contains atmospheric controls and GravCore monitoring."

"Same drill, Santa Cruz, Gonzaga."

Pio gets to the door first, magnetizes his gun across his chest in an arms ready position. With both hands free, he turns, says, "This one will be bad too."

"Damaged?"

"Blood," he motions to the red floor, then to a crimson handprint on the control panel. "Ready?"

Santa Cruz and Gonzaga get up on it, poised for a dynamic entry. Santa Cruz looks to Gonzaga and nods. Gonzaga looks to Pio, says, "Ready."

Pio stabs at the bloody button and the hatch slides back into the wall. A corpse falls out into the hallway. Santa Cruz catches it with a handful of jumper suit—maintenance logo bright and cheery across the breast—while keeping his rail gun trained on the room. "Almost fired," he says windlessly as he pulls the body off to the side.

Cleopas takes a large step forward and grabs the body, lifting it from Santa Cruz's burden. Pulls it off to the side. The Knights make entry. Cleopas looks down at the deceased he has—another human man, so bald he has no eyebrows but does have a thick tattoo across his skull and some kind of cybernetic implant over his left temple—and finds a streak of bullet wounds in his back.

Inside, Santa Cruz goes to the right, Gonzaga to the left. Sure enough, there is a large control center with the brand name of the GravCore Stake uses emblazoned along the top. It has two wounds from a fire axe in its metal cabinet, but the system has power and hums under load.

Near enough are the atmospheric controls. They too are damaged, with the fire axe still sticking out of it. Fresh blood there. Gonzaga stops as he reaches the console. Boots sticking out from behind it, one leg cocked off at an impossible angle.

"Here," he says. Moves in an arc around the console to full view and Santa Cruz keeps one eye on him. There on the floor is another twisted victim of the ZZH. Obviously past help but never beyond their prayers. "Both were Terran diaspora males. Looks like these two came in and tried to cripple the asteroid rather than let the terrorists use it."

Santa Cruz says, "Commander, we're clear. We got another body. Looks like they came in here to disable the asteroid."

"Offline now?"

"No, they didn't get that far before they got laid down."

"Copy, mark it. Let's move."

"Roger," Santa Cruz says. Stops mid-stride and looks at the GravCore system. A freshly drilled hole is in the side, with three red wires trailing out to a box set on a ledge behind the cabinet. The box has a blinking light on it and two thick, short antennae much like insect wings coming off it.

"Standby," Santa Cruz says. "Nonnatus, take a look at this."

Now Nonnatus parks the MedSled, comes inside, moves up to Gonzaga and Santa Cruz. Sees the box, tilts his head in question. "Scans show its online. Some kind of input/output transmission and receiving."

He reaches and unlocks the GravCore cabinet door. Gently pulls it open. The red wires go into the cabinet and are landed on terminals inside. Nonnatus points to a small box with a screen on it. "Detachable controls. It just snaps in and out of place right here in this cradle, but I'm sure it's OEM equipment. Linked by wireless comms. This I/O system that's hardwired in, it looks to me like something the ZZH did."

"Why?" Brigid's voice comes over their headsets.

"Remote control of the GravCore, I assume. Overrides the asteroid's facilities systems if they want."

Gonzaga clears his throat. "So, if they get wind of us, they can just fire off this GravCore thing and what? Cleopas, how much did you say this thing can exert?"

Cleopas thinks back, shakes his head and says, "It's tunable. They've got the occupied parts at 1 g. If I remember correctly, they can ramp it up pretty high. But less than 10 g, I think."

"More than 5 g?" Brigid asks.

"Sure."

Everyone shares a collective groan. "We'll be crushed," Brigid says. "Can we disable this?"

Nonnatus keeps his hands at his sides but sticks his head nearer the device, studies it. AI inside his suit generates possible wiring configurations—there's only the three to contend with—and he checks basic electrical current with leads built into his armor, designed for field work on the drones.

"It's pretty basic, dumb. But that's worse, I think." He says. "Taps supply power off the cabinet right here with one wire, runs it to this outside I/O box. The signal comes back on the next wire and the box essentially just serves as another stop on the path that tells the GravCore to maintain what it has."

He squats down and looks at something, then stands back up. "Problem is that third wire. I think it sends the kill signal. If we remove power from the I/O box, the kill signal will send, or maybe it's a constant signal that is stopping the GravCore from crushing us, I don't know. But either way, if we remove either the power or the kill signal wire, the GravCore will crush us."

"So, that's a no?" Gonzaga asks.

"Correct." Nonnatus says. "Our best bet is to get to the actual GravCore unit."

"Okay. Nonnatus, you've gotten us this far. Can you undo that at the unit?"

"I'm just the drones guy," Nonnatus says. "I get basic technology, but I can't run the drones and do this."

Brigid looks at Pio. Pio shrugs, says, "EOD, sir. But I pray for the best out of everybody. We'll need that for this thing, I think. I'll get to it. Then Nonnatus can patch in, and we can put our heads together."

"Pray to Saint Attar Otto. I hear he was a modern-day genius with this stuff."

Brigid says, "Let's go. We're running late."

Nonnatus closes the cabinet, takes a look at the dead maintenance guy and says, "In Your Divine way, Lord, thank you letting this man swung his axe and miss those wires. It'd be a short mission if he'd hit paydirt."

"Amen," Gonzaga says as he walks past.

†

"Third door coming up on the right," Brother Cleopas says as they make it that far. "This one leads to the offices."

"We all make entry on this one," Commander Brigid says as they line up on the door leading in. "Schematics look to me like they're boxcar style. A total of four compartments plus a larger open space labeled as the main lobby. Two meter spacing, cover alternate sides, peel off as we clear under desks and whatever man-sized spaces we encounter, then fall back in on the end. We've done this before. Nothing unusual now."

The Knights acknowledge. Brother Santa Cruz has his rail gun up, reaches to the door controls, poised and ready.

"Make entry," Brigid commands and Santa Cruz hits the open button. The door slides into the wall and they flow inside.

Santa Cruz leads, aiming forward and covering the left. Brother Gonzaga next, covering their right. Brother Pio third, covering left followed by Brother Nonnatus, covering right. Cleopas and Brigid pull up the rear.

The first office they enter looks like it was little more than storage even when Stake was alive and well. A stack of crumpled boxes fills one corner, disheveled with browning papers leaking out. A desk set up on its end with its writing surface pushed flush along the wall. The bottom half of a cheap office chair stuffed in between the protruding legs.

They move into the next space, which unfolds out around them. "Lobby," Santa Cruz says and peels off, his left shoulder to the wall. The reception desk occupies the room like a wrecked sailing vessel in a narrow trench. Massive and out of place for the gray walls around it. Santa Cruz steps behind the desk with aggressive speed; if there is a surprise waiting for them, he has it countered.

"Clear," he says as he walks the length of it.

The Knights keep driving forward, Gonzaga leading. Other than the reception desk, there are three wire-framed chairs with plastic tops and backs. Not even worth stealing when the crew vacated. Everything else in the room is small, dust-covered detritus.

Santa Cruz falls in behind the commander, covering left again as Brigid covers right. They move into the next office and Gonzaga steps off to the side where two desks are. He charges behind them as well, smooth and steady, ready with firepower.

"Clear," Gonzaga says as he pauses for the line of his new brothers to pass by. When Santa Cruz passes by, he joins back in, covering right.

The third office is empty save one end table that is little more than four long legs and a plastic top affixed to them. Pio leads, seeing the familiar glint of light on metal along the floor as this office transitions to the final one.

"Shell casings on the floor here," Pio says, holding up his off hand to indicate their position to all members. He gets a few steps further and stops dead in his tracks. Says, "Our lord Jesus Christ, son of the ever-living God, send your blessing down upon these souls."

"What do you mean?" Gonzaga asks. The others seem to know. They enter the room, file out to both sides with the door between them.

There, along the far wall, are the bodies of every other traveler on the maintenance ship, hands bound and executed. Mostly Mariol females, with a few males and Terran diaspora males.

Brigid makes the sign of the cross over himself, and the Knights follow suit. Cleopas goes down to a knee beside the first body and examines it. Find a mortal wound and moves to the second. Then to the third.

"Brother, they all received head wounds," Nonnatus says. "A move straight out of the universal evil handbook. Lined up, shot, abandoned. You're not going—" Nonnatus spins around towards the door. Gun swings up. "Drones. We've got movement outside."

The Knights move with intensity. Silence. All backs turn to the execution, facing the door. Outside, someone clangs around in the far office. Shouts. Moves closer, oblivious to the walking war machine wearing Christ's cross as a badge in this room.

Brigid sends a message scrolling across their Visuals. *No sound, even if it goes down.*

Outside, footsteps come closer as someone begins shuffling through what little the asteroid crew left behind. The spilling sound of a sheaf of papers pops suddenly in the room next to them. A man's voice curses and then kicks through the mess.

"Behn, any luck?" comes a second voice.

The man in the nearest room says, "I mean, there's a bunch of old papers. We could burn those. I think I saw some boxes too. Not a lot of kindling, though."

The second man joins the first, Behn, in the room outside the Knights. "We're on a rock. Metal and plastic. Nothing that likes to burn."

Behn snaps his fingers, says, "You know what? We should check the maintenance ship. I bet they have—"

Cleopas is distracted. Some quiet sound. He looks down, sees the corpse of a Mariol woman with blood running down her head. He squats lower to her, moves her acicular hair where he wound is. A few of the male corpses were destroyed by the entrance wound, but hers is obscured. Moving her hair, there is damage but only a bad graze. Very bad, but a graze.

The woman's prodigious eye flings open like the shutters over a window sprung wide. She takes a shocking, rasping inhale and begins to tremble violently. Cleopas puts a hand on her shoulder as the other Knights take a cautious notice.

"You hear that?" Behn asks.

"From where we waxed those heretics," Their footsteps come towards the door. "You left the door open, too."

"I'm glad I did. What if whoever's making those sounds got back to the ship? The radio still works, I think."

Cleopas gently presses his hand, trying to communicate reassurance. Her eye rolls up to the Knight; an armored soldier completely encased in a battle suit that aesthetically mimics plate armor with the technological advancements of spacefaring science. A helmet of white and red with a black visor. Sleek, efficient. Weapons everywhere.

And his hand on her.

All she remembers in her fractured memory is assault. Rocket attack as soon as they landed and cut the engines. A gunfight. Karm and Teller, Mizrofi and Pin, Joff and the new girl she brought with her, all getting gunned down, drug away like sacks of trash. Others running. The screaming. Shoved around. Herded like cattle. Blood and deafening explosions as one after another of her friends falls. Gored and ruined.

The white armored soldier whispers something like, "You're safe with us. Quiet." And shushes her. His hand on her.

Another voice from outside the room says something like, "One must still be alive in here."

She takes another agonizing breath and screams.

Cleopas tries to quiet her, and he sees Gonzaga reaching for his weapons.

Negotiation and Evil

"Any fool can trust God while he is in Eden," Loognar says as he rubs his face. He fixates pointedly on Bishop Tauthail and asks in a dry, quiet voice, as if the question and its answer will either be a source of eternal light or a nail into the palm for eternal crucifixion, "but do you trust God during evil?"

"Yes," the bishop responds out loud and thinks to himself, *as I do in this moment.* "I think for some, that is when it is harder to trust God. But, for those of us who know Him, it is easier."

Even still, the bishop is only half paying attention; Loognar has stated plainly Archbishop Hrutt is either dead or will be, and boldly taunted an end to the entire Order. While the second claim is nonsense Tauthail worries about the first.

"I am sure you must trust in something, bishop," Loognar says. "For you trust Him even as you believe in your religion, which is from the Evil One."

Bishop Tauthail can only laugh. "Listen, Father Loognar, I don't want to spar with you. I don't want to debate with you—"

"Because you cannot."

"—what I want is to negotiate with you for the archbishop's release. You must want to do the same thing, I presume, since in your original transmission you supplied us with this comms address. Am I wrong?"

Loognar considers him for a moment, then leans back. Settles in. "You are correct. You still haven't asked what I want. For a negotiator—"

"Wrong foot, my good sir. We got off on the wrong foot for sure." The bishop breathes deeply. So thrown off track was he from the very beginning the bishop now must clear his mind. Reorient it. He thinks, *this has gone from me requesting we pray together to this man—hair trigger extraordinaire that he is—to controlling the conversation with his accusations, his ridiculous assumptions. Reactionary. You're better than this.* The bishop smiles, says, "Let us try again, please."

Loognar smirks. The bishop thinks he is going to make some noise about that last statement being *negotiator's talk* or something, asking him for permission to restart, but instead, Loognar nods his head. Waves a dismissive hand. "Fine. So be it."

"Excellent. What are your conditions for the archbishop's release?"

Loognar claps his hands like a child receiving a gift it has been pining for. "Simple. One, Hrutt is to leave the planet—not the city, the *planet*—immediately. Hrutt is the recognized embodiment of Catholic intolerance to our faith, and I want him gone. It will be public, as well. All are to see his tail between his legs. There will be no quiet fading into the night. He arrived very publicly to preach your so-called truth; he will leave very publicly as a failure." His smile vacates and the bishop thinks he sees hints of fangs.

"Two, the entire Catholic presence in Xewl and the surrounding country will be phased out over the course of year. Not a soul who believes in your filth will be left behind."

The bishop stifles a scoff at that.

"And three, we the UnZerre FulZzhea WarHeight are to be recognized by the Vatican as legitimate. Not some heresy. Not some cult of perverts who believe our genders are malleable. Legitimate."

"I see." The bishop tries to drink in the enormity of what Loognar asks. It's a flood. "I can understand wanting the archbishop gone because he has an immediate effect on your people. I can even see why you want it to be a public—"

"Spectacle, bishop. A public spectacle."

"—yes, but I'm— I... well, how the head of a church on another planet views you—"

"Your pope and magisterium mean nothing to me in the sense of authority or correctness." Loognar stiffens. "The revelation of our truth did begin on Earth, and that is where it first fell under assault by your church." He swipes the air in front of him, as if to indicate everything, all at once. "And all others followed suit. But to expound on that in general: I don't care what your incorrect leaders think of us. I don't care what the Mormons or their so-called prophet and Quorum of the Twelve think either, but here's where it matters: both of you claim to be the one true church that Christ founded. The God of the universe became our species and gave His salvific plan, and each of you falsely claim to have its fullness. Both of you hold beliefs that are simply incompatible with one another. Both of you sent missionaries to Xewl to preach against *us,* the true church. It wasn't enough to persecute us on our home of Earth, you have brought your satanic lies to our new backyard as well. The Mormons. . . they have failed already. And now you will be made to fail also."

The bishop looks quizzically at Loognar. Yes, the bishop has heard through official reports of the local Xewl authorities that a few months ago a prominent member of the Latter-Day Saints in the city had disappeared. Is Loognar giving a flash of his cards here?

Deciding against more careful wording simply because if nothing else, Loognar might interpret it as negotiator-speak, the bishop asks, "Did you also kidnap a member of the LDS church?"

Loognar rubs a thumb and forefinger along the top row of his teeth. Tauthail has been briefed that is a cultural custom of Xewlians as if to say, *let me choose my next words properly.* Not *carefully. Properly.*

He settles on something in his mind and says, "They were given the same offer as you. To their credit, they denied the truth of our beliefs and stuck to their own. I would do the same if I were placed in a similar situation. The man we took possession of. . . I'm convinced he would've rather them meet our demands."

Loognar lights a cigar of some kind and lets the flame die off on the end. Smoke envelops his face, and he exhales a thick cloud through his nostrils. "By the end he was more than willing to admit we have the correct beliefs. If only Joseph Smith could have heard his claims." Loognar comes to some amusing thought and says with a flourish, "And maybe God did permit Smith to hear them through the deafening crackle of his private hellfire. I don't know. But, God does seem to favor me, so I might be permitted some revelation. One day."

The admission hangs in the air like the declaration of a terminal illness. And joy. The bishop clears his throat. "Can you point me to scripture where Jesus condones such things?"

Loognar stares, unwavering. "We were told to sell our cloaks and buy a sword in order to follow Jesus. We have learned over the last several years we need more swords. And since simply brandishing them doesn't seem to work, it's time to test their edges."

Tuathail chews on the information for a moment. Asks, "Are you implying you will torture Archbishop Hrutt until he dies or until we meet your demands?"

"There is no implication. We *will* do it."

"Have you hurt him yet?"

"Certainly you have seen the live feed I sent you."

"I have."

"Well then, you know. I have instructed my personnel to cancel the feed. You will receive it again if you do not meet my demands."

"So we can watch—"

"Watch it, yes."

"I condemn these threats as anti-Christian in the fullest."

Loognar remains blank faced. Smokes his cigar. The bishop keeps his gaze, but he knows Loognar will not respond.

"I can certainly arrange to have the archbishop taken off-world," the bishop says. "But I'll need time and concrete assurances from you that the archbishop is alive and well as I speak to the Vatican."

Loognar points his cigar at the camera facing him, jabbing the bishop with its hot tip from however many millions of miles away he really is. "The negotiator is coming out in you."

"As you knew it would. As you know it has to. You're to provide me with proof of life for the archbishop all throughout. That will go a long way towards your end."

"I will not negotiate. Maybe that bothers a man such as yourself, but alas. The truth does not shrink back in the face of its detractors. And neither shall we. These things are firm."

Bishop Tauthail adjusts in his chair. Looks down at the ground. Wonders if the Knights have even landed yet. The last update he received is woefully old. Glances back up at Loognar, who is chewing on his cigar and the expression he wears is a bizarre mixture of an aggressive male and a bitter female. Maybe a product of the sequential hermaphroditism. The bishop prays for Loognar. "Can you help me as I help you, at all?"

"I can. I knew you would ask."

"And?"

Loognar adopts a barbarous air, reaches down with one arm and lifts an object. The bishop stares in disbelief as the severed head of a man appears, Loognar's fingers clasping a curly mop of red hair. Rising from below the camera feed like some surfacing leviathan. "Lehi Orson, the Mormon fool abandoned to die by his people."

The bishop knows the outcome here, now. He stares directly into the camera to make sure that Loognar does not see him avert his eyes. But rather, to meet this challenge of hideousness through the strength of Christ emboldening his heart. In a steady, commanding voice he says, "Proof of life of Archbishop Hrutt. Anyone can provide proof of cruelty."

Loognar makes a show of callously opening his fist with his arm still fully outstretched. The head plummets. A hard, wet thud from below. Sounds of it rolling, settling out. He meets the bishop's gaze. "Not enough?"

"Not in the least. Proof of evil is not a substitute for proof of life. And certainly not if you want what you're asking for, which I must assume you do." The bishop considers not asking, but the information might be useful later. "Are the LDS members leaving Xewl?"

Loognar smiles triumphantly. "Seven ships over the last five weeks. I haven't done a head count—no pun intended—because they understand the gravity of truth. I fear they understand it better than you. Sometimes a team that has some good wins behind it gets on the field with a team that is essentially playing a different game. The Mormons have done that, and they are now leaving the game. You need to recognize this for what it is."

"I'll send word to the Vatican," the bishop says. "And let them know that you're sending proof of life. I'll recontact you in two hours' time. I expect it by then."

"You do, now?"

"I do, Loognar. If you really want what you ask, and you have seemed clear-minded up until now, so I think you *do* want what you've asked, you'll give me something to work with. We're not the LDS. The Vatican knows it has glorious martyrs in its past and in its future. I can assure you they'll consider Archbishop Hrutt one of those unless you give them a reason otherwise."

"Not what I wanted to hear, bishop."

The bishop shrugs and tries to communicate some measure of the firmness that Loognar has been exuding. "You started this. Blame who you want for provocation, but you set this path into motion. You. You orchestrated killing people and took our man. If you just wanted to murder Catholic clergy, you wouldn't be negotiating with the Vatican of the Catholic Church. To alter your course now and harm the archbishop will only solidify you as a terrorist and nothing more. Ever. Not to mention the damage done to the reputation of the ZZH. So, see your own play through and send me proof of life. There is still time and goodwill between us for a satisfying and nonviolent—on both sides—resolution."

Loognar sits starkly, the rage shimmering like heat snakes on his skin. Capitalizing on that silence, the bishop leans forward and presses the disconnect button for their feed.

The tech looks up, shocked. He turns to the status screen, clenches his jaw ever so slightly. "Connection terminated, your Excellency."

"Good," the bishop says as he stands up. Rolls his head on his neck. "I've grown tired of arguing with a man who feels comfortable carrying on a conversation with a severed head at his feet. That's a new level of psychotic, even for me." The bishop looks up to the ceiling and closes his eyes. "Forgive me, Lord."

The tech stands also, cracks his knuckles. He checks the feed, as if a connection request would be coming right back from Loognar. The screen stays blank, and after a moment the tech eases just enough to ask, "Your Excellency, if I may, do you think these people have harmed the archbishop? After. . . what happened to the LDS man?"

Bishop Tauthail shakes his head. "The answer is most likely no, but as long as Loognar keeps mum the threat is harsher because it is vague. A solid no means he is short on boldness and a solid yes means the Knights have a reason not to play ball."

"Praise our Lord."

"For all things." The bishop turns to the altar and to the Eucharist displayed in the monstrance on it. He adores it for a single moment, basking in the intangible love it emits like rays of a sun's light. He closes his eyes and returns to an innocent place where he is not arguing with killers about what is a false dogma, and who possesses the truth of Jesus.

He continues, "But it lets me know all I need to know about who we're really dealing with. It took us too long to get even this far. A man that zealous, that unhinged, he doesn't need a negotiator. He needs an exorcist." The bishop turns to the tech, "And he needs to be stopped."

He faces the altar again. Over his shoulder he asks, "Join me in prayer, would you?"

"Of course, bishop." The tech says and comes over.

"I'll need a few minutes with Our Lord before we request a link with the Vatican."

The tech nods and offers a forced smile. Both men kneel at the communion rail and the bishop crosses himself. The tech follows, and they pray.

Quiet Actions and Hard Choices

I've got the shot; Brother Gonzaga sends the message across their Visuals as he ignites his TechHaft. Draws an energy arrow back in the bow. Crackling with luminescent energy, the laser haft brightens the room.

The other Knights take up covering fire positions. They're all off to the sides of the half-open door; the ZZH outside will need to either tactically enter in order to engage or simply walk straight through before they see the opposing forces. Brother Pio steps to the wall with the door in it, readies a small device in his hand.

Their talking gets louder as they approach. And just like that, one pushes the door open and steps inside.

Gonzaga takes a huge sidestep, arrow already lined up. The first soldier sees the brilliance of the TechHaft, eyes widen in shock. Pio thumbs a button on the device in his hand. A distracting burst of flare goes off.

Disoriented, the soldier shouts and doesn't know whether to shield his eyes, grab his weapon or retreat.

A half second later, Gonzaga looses the arrow. It strikes the first soldier in the neck, passes cleanly through. The second ZZH soldier coughs a strangled noise as the arrow strikes him as well. He falls flat on his back, the sizzling bolt of energy lodged firmly in him. It lasts a moment longer and then dissipates. A single flourish and then into thin air.

Brother Santa Cruz grabs the first soldier and drags him off to the side in a single heave. Path through the door clear, he moves. Pushes through the door and takes a position, looking for the next threat. All stay quiet

A breathless minute later and he cautiously says, "Clear."

The two soldiers are wearing the standard light body armor their ZZH sect has been pictured in; Intel was right about that. Full chest wrap and abdomen protection as well as shin guards below knee pads. A bland gray color that works well enough in industrial environments. They all have a respirator covering their noses and mouths. Their heads shaved except for a ponytail situated at the center of their skulls. A ZZH fashion that is intended to display their warriorhood in both male and female forms.

Commander Brigid motions to clean up the mess. His Knights take the two soldiers and respectfully move them. Hide their bodies. Take their weapons and disarm them. While they're not a considerable threat to the full frontal assault suits the Knights wear, they might be a threat to any other survivors. Always best to leave your enemies unarmed.

"Check the rest of the maintenance crew. Verify she's the only one who still needs help," Brigid says. "And get ready to move. Two down, dozens more are still out there."

The commander remains still for a moment, the big picture scrolling through his mind. He tilts is head down as he considers their options. After a moment, "Pio," Brigid says.

"Sir?"

"Remember where we saw the ZZH's wiring for the GravCore?"

"Yes."

"Go disable it. I figure you'll have to follow those cables to the actual unit. Do whatever you can to buy us time. Message me when you're back out. We'll rendezvous."

"Yes, sir." And he leaves.

Brother Cleopas moves along the line of executed, says, "She's it, sir."

"Copy." Brigid turns in a circle once, twice. Pondering. Finally, he says, "Cleopas, get her to the surface."

"Yes sir," Cleopas looks decidedly confused. "But I'm. . . I'm the resource here."

"I know. Believe me, I know. I don't want our experienced soldier away from the mission, but the mission has changed. You're the medic. And she needs a medic."

"We've got the schematics—"

"Which we've already seen are woefully out of date."

"—and we've got the knowledge you've already passed along. Until she's on board a rescue we'll treat this like any other Intel Special, any other rescue. You yourself said there's not much left here. It's nothing we can't comb through nearly blind."

"Understood."

"I'll open up comms and get the *Saint Eligius* to come and evac her, stat."

"Yes sir," and without anything further, Cleopas goes to Brother Nonnatus. Sets his comms to between them two only and holds out his hand, says, "The beacon, my good sir."

Nonnatus detaches it from his armor, hands it over. "I thought about volunteering myself for this, but you heard the commander. He's already had that argument in his own head before he ever said anything."

"You're right," Cleopas says, attaching the beacon to himself. "It'd do no good. He's his own worst second guesser. This is for the best of the entire mission."

"Hopefully the MedSled will be enough."

Cleopas looks over at the woman, unconscious again. "I think so. I could use your help one more time, though."

They team lift the Mariol woman into the device and secure her.

"Here goes nothing," Brigid sends a message to the *Saint Eligius* and receives an acknowledgment. "Let's hope that went unmonitored."

Gonzaga shrugs. "We'll know soon enough. You think Cleopas could use a second guy? In case they heard you?"

Brigid considers it for a moment, looks back and forth. "I hate to say it, but probably. However, he's got to go solo. With him taking the MedSled, we're going to need all the hands we have to carry the archbishop out if he's hurt."

Nonnatus perks up. "From that live feed, it looks like he's already in a full-scale medpod. Those are also mobile."

"Pray for the best, prepare for the worst," Brigid responds. To Cleopas, he motions to the door. "Get to the surface and send them your coordinates."

"There's the grid cannon problem."

"Deal with the cannon, then. They'll be counting on it."

"I will. I'll get her safely off."

"I know. We'll pray for you, please pray for us." ·

"Of course, sir." Cleopas hefts his rifle and cracks his neck. Turns and leaves, the MedSled obediently following behind.

"Be careful, Cleopas," Brigid says. "There's bound to be more of these soldiers about."

He stops and turns. "Yes, sir. I know a place where I can sneak her out."

"I bet you do," Brigid says. "You're the resource here."

And Cleopas leaves as well.

Brigid turns to Nonnatus, Gonzaga and Santa Cruz, "You three, come with me. We've got a few more stops to make."

Part Two:
All the Complications

Promise Me You'll Stay Out

"The company brass ordered EcoPassage 3 closed off, son," Cleopas's father said to him when Cleopas was a young boy, adventure fresh in his mind. "They did it years ago. That's why there's a big lock and all the signs reading keep out.*"*

Man and child were standing in the maintenance artery where the boy had been caught by security. He was trying to get through an access hatch into the crystalline vein hidden in the surface crust of Stake. A dare by friends. But now busted, little Cleopas was worried he'd be hauled off. Maybe arrested and sent to an all-boys school. Lose his family. Or his parents given the ultimatum that it was either him, a little troublemaker, or their employment. What then? He was trouble, and trouble didn't pay the bills. Or firmly in the clutches of the ruthless security he'd vanish. Disappear. Maybe put into an airlock and punched out into space. Sold into servitude while his parents were never told anything.

Posters everywhere read things like A Lack of Discipline Equals a Lack of Survival. *And here little Cleopas was, trying to enter a restricted area. A* forbidden *area. Stake ran a tight ship; it had to. But instead of some quiet execution, they just waited there, security officers and a young kid worried his death was around the corner.*

His father arrived and received custody of the troublemaker. His father, called off shift from the work site, still dirty and in uniform. He groaned and signed for his son on an official document. Company record. A few more of those and the family would lose their employment on the asteroid.

Security said a few things to his father and walked off. One of them mumbled something about boys being boys but this couldn't happen again. His father nodded and agreed with everything. Thanked them for their help in saving his son. His father stood there, amused but upset. "The company brass ordered EcoPassage 3 closed off, son. They did it

101

years ago. That's why there's a big lock and all the signs reading keep
out."

*Young Cleopas furrowed his brow. The elation at having his life
spared, the fear of costing his father work, the confusion as to why the
world wasn't as a boy wanted it to be, his father thanking the security
guys for saving him. Saved from what? "Closed off? Why? The other two
aren't. They're fun."*

*Taking him by the arm, his father firmly stated, "The other two are
safe. Promise me you'll stay out of this one. This one in particular."*

"But why? What's the difference?"

*His father huffed. "This one. . . the roof is really thin. On the other
side of its ceiling is outer space. I know that much. One wrong move and
you'll. . . you'll break through and cause a vacuum and son. . . you'll get
sucked out into space. That will kill you." His father knelt beside him
and stroked his hair. "Now, I want you to promise."*

*A young Cleopas thought about crossing his fingers behind his back
and making the promise, just as he'd seen in cartoons and heard his
friends claim to do. But he didn't and made his promise to his father out
of love and respect. And from then on out, the other EcoPassages were
his limit. He'd promised.*

†

"Well, Dad, I meant to keep it," Cleopas says as he stands before that
same hatch again.

In that same maintenance artery again. In front of that same
closed off hatch again. The MedSled behind him, the Mariol woman
inside dying. His full frontal assault kit's armor enhances his
strength, and the big lock doesn't stand a chance. He snaps it off, sets
it aside. Slides the hatch into its recess in the wall and investigates
EcoPassage 3.

"You and me both, miss, are seeing this for the first time." He says as he turns to the MedSled. He looks at its dimensions, scowls a bit. "It's tight in there."

Cleopas uses his Visuals to measure the size of the MedSled, and then turns to the crystalline tunnel. His Visuals overlay the best route to take through the sea of stalagmites and stalactites. The uneven floor of the cavern. The dips and surges of the walls and ceiling. These abundant features are sharper, more bladed and needlelike than he remembers from either other EcoPassage.

"Could be because we're one layer of strata away from the surface of the asteroid," Cleopas wanders aloud. He turns to the MedSled, "That's why we're going this way. A little bit down and the roof will be thin enough I can just punch a hole straight through into space. We'll climb out that way. Skip any problems with the ZZH. I'm sure you're not upset to hear that."

The Mariol woman is sedated, and Cleopas knows she can't hear him. Respond to him. Offer a suggestion. He steps inside and the MedSLed follows. He pulls the hatch shut. It squeaks a tinny, shrieking note and cuts off like closing a book.

†

Outside the maintenance artery, two ZZH patrolmen come around the corner, guns up.

"You and me both heard that metal snapping sound just a second ago," one says as he shrugs his tight armor up a little higher. In one arm he has a medical port that has an IV leading down to a pump on his waist. His beard is noticeably thin and his nose soft. His skin becoming translucent with a gelatin quality to its coloring. Some of his words were deep and rich while others nearly hand a sing-song quality to them, as if they were the same sentence spoken by a man and a woman and then clipped apart and reassembled from both.

Even as the two walk, some of the black wiry hairs on his forearm fall out as he brushes his arm along the tunnel's corner.

"Yeah, I heard it," the other says. "But that metal squeaking is what got me."

"Somebody from that maintenance ship hiding in there?"

"Probably."

"I'll call it in. Then we need to get 'em. I'm worried they'll get a distress signal out."

"Let 'em. When we're done with this walk-through, we're done altogether."

"Loognar's called it twice already. This one will be no different." They come up on EcoPassage 3's hatch, and one points to the torn off lock setting on a lip in the wall nearby. The other nods.

The one with the medical port says, "It'll be different this time. There's dead bodies this time."

†

The GravCore is tuned differently here. Brother Cleopas noticed as soon as he stepped foot inside and he found no more than a half g.

Headlamp refracting through all the cool colors of the EcoPassage, Cleopas moves quickly as he can in a quasi-swimming motion. Admiring the watery ghosts of all the crystalline shades and hues spilled and animated along the surfaces. Lapis and cornflower blues, verdun and castillian greens, even plum and orchid purples. And those come to life and dart away, leaving aquamarine and even a flourish of rosewood pink. And then on to others, and back to the same.

He gets ten meters in and the MedSled scrapes along a stalagmite. A fine powder of shavings drifts about before slowly settling to the floor like chalk dust. Cleopas turns and sees it. The MedSled has a shiny new rasp mark down the side. He adjusts the path in his Visuals and tries to get the MedSled to hover higher but it will not. Across the screen it cites power output as the reason.

"We've got to keep your contact down to a minimum. These flora growths are gorgeous but as you can see, they're not hip to move easily for anybody."

Cleopas tries to balance caution and urgency as he weaves in and out of the tighter entanglements. These features are jagged like melted teeth inside a dragon's mouth. He continuously scans for a spot in the roof where there is high likelihood of making a big enough hole to the surface.

Directly ahead he sees a stalagmite damaged from years prior. A chunk laying on the floor. A decapitated trunk standing sentinel nearby. That fine powder everywhere. It sparkles like jewels in his light. He aims to avoid it but the surrounding features are like statues of guards with their spears tilted down, blocking passage.

The temperature inside the EcoSystem is dropping as he combs his way deeper. "We're getting closer to a good exit point," he says. "Just a matter of a few moments and then—"

Cleopas slips violently in the powder mess. Even in the half G, his heavy suit pulls him. He Collapses on his side on a stalagmite, rolls forward. Behind him a crash and the MedSled alarms. Noise clatters behind him; a tide surging. Up on his feet, he spins. Sees the MedSled dumbly trying to follow his beacon and when he took his nosedive, it canted. Yawed. Crashed.

Four stalagmites and two stalactites suffered in its haphazard wake. Shards abound, scattering in slow motion through the EcoSystem's air. Fresh crush marks. More damage to the MedSled. Powders still floating about and down. Glistening fairy dust in his helmet light. Cleopas gets up and grabs the MedSled, straightens it out. Sees a bizarre mark on the nearest stalagmite. Leans in to examine it.

A tube, bored from inward the exterior. He looks to the adjoining wound on the MedSled. Pieces of the crystalline flora are scattered along it. A few larger chunks. He brushes them away and the biggest piece falls but disgorges an oddity onto the roof of the medical device. A tightly packed cluster of black pearlescent globs.

"Eggs," he mutters as he sees something tick to life under the leathery skin of it. He stifles a gasp and swipes the entire clutch away. It spins aimless in the air, hits a nearby feature. Bursts into individual pieces. They pirouette away in a scatter. All wiggling. He stomps the ones that have settled as he can, but numerous eggs rolled out of sight. "These things have— hibernating— the crew never bothered to clear this passage. Just shut it off. We've got to roll out, miss."

Even as he speaks a wad of those eggs slow motion fall from the damaged stalactite. Cleopas turns in every direction, feeling himself hyperventilating. "Lord, bless us. Please."

He darts forward and the MedSled crashes again. All Cleopas can see are cracks in the crystalline fauna, each now holding the threat of those caustic centipedes. His Visuals sends up a warning about his sudden heart rate, hormone levels. "I can't believe how fast— Saint Michael, protect us. Saint George, protect us. Saint Hik—"

"Protect you from us?" One of the ZZH soldiers asks as they flood the EcoPassage with light from shoulder-mounted lamps. They lightly float inside, one hand on their guns and the other grabbing features to slow down or dart in various directions. "The saints are clearly on our side. You're the sinner here."

Cleopas stops. The MedSled between him and them. His Visuals beep at him. A new scan shows an area thirteen meters away where he can break through to the actual surface.

He clears his throat, swallows. Trying to even his voice out, he says, "Listen fellas, we've got—"

The ZZH soldier with the medical port fires a single round and it strikes Cleopas. Ricochets off and snaps into a spike of emerald flora nearby. "Shut your filthy mouth. In the eyes of God, and so reflected in our culture, it's a punishable offense to use gendered terms. And since you're on our turf—"

"Friend, you have no idea what claim I can make to this asteroid," Cleopas says. In the corner of his eye, he sees squiggling, coordinated movement in the shadows. "But right now, we have bigger problems. And we're on the same team. *Believe me.*"

Black Cubes

Commander Brigid hears it before he sees it, and he sends the message *back up back up* across his Knights Visuals as he himself shoves backward. The Knights react and instinctively collapse into hiding spots as best as they can in their armor.

"Get down," he whispers in a harsh push, dropping to the deck of a crowded passageway. He tucks in behind a discarded cardboard box. Sides old and moisture-ruined, the empty box lays on its side with its open end aiming at Brigid. Flaps like limp wings dangling on a bird's corpse, they point at Brigid's shoulders. Its opening like a mouth, ready for his head. He looks over it and sees what he heard.

A hovering train of sleek, featureless black cubes, all connected into a worm-like configuration as it patrols down the passageway they were about to turn down. The cubes, though all connected by some unseen mechanism, one after another, no cube ever actually stands straight or still. But rather, they constantly slide along each other's surfaces as if each individual cube is its own organism and through touch is examining its world. Deriving pleasure, even. The sensation of activity like a drug. The train of them slides through the air effortlessly.

The passageway, an old boxy footpath and nothing more, seems to hold its breath as this glossy thing moves through. No feature on its absolutely onyx surface. Flawless. Nigrescent like its surface eats light. Aloof but somehow absolutely predatory.

A message scrolls along Brigid's Visuals, *what is that?*

Death, he sends back. *Be silent. Pray.*

Brigid watches as the thing reaches a hatch. A single spindly arm unfolds from under its belly. On its end effector what looks like a needlesque pointer finger. A pair of protrusions coupled like a scissor. A red eye on a small silver bulge. It runs the eye over the hatch controls in efficient, sharp flicks. Then the needle finger presses a button; the hatch opens with a hiss and as it does the train of cubes rearranges in a sudden thunderclap of motion. The arm collapses and disappears.

The cubes fold themselves open, revealing even more cubes, and the entire thing takes on a T formation; from the crossbars stubby Gatling-like weapons emerge. Their multi-barrels begin spinning into a blur. With aggressive flits back and forth the guns cover the new passageway. All the while the thing flashes brilliant blue lights, filling the hallway with near-blinding patterns. By the time the hatch has fully retreated along its track inside the wall, the cube had transformed, armed itself and checked for targets.

The guns stop their blindingly fast rotation. Vanish back into the midnight surface of the cubes that bore them. The cube rearranges again in a sinewy, fluid motion. The cubes break up geometrically into smaller cubes and shuffle, sliding across one another and then merging into larger cube configurations like a puzzle being solved. Perfectly square on all sides. Unsnapping and then re-snapping back into place in some other location. From T back to train. Fluid as mercury flowing downhill.

And it proceeds into the new passageway as if it had never stopped. The hatch shuts. Brigid exhales in relief, says, "Praise our Lord and Savior, Jesus Christ. I didn't know the ZZH had a 20de9. No wonder they are so lightly armed." He stands back up and wipes an errant crumb of trash from his forearm. "I hoped no had a 20de9 anymore."

"Sir?" Brother Nonnatus says. "I've heard of the 20de9. You have experience?"

Brigid looks off for a second, then to the closed hatch. With ghosts in his eyes, he says, "Yes."

"Okay," Brother Gonzaga says with a note of expectation. "Are we in trouble?"

Brigid stands and checks his weapon, says, "Let's get out of here." As he starts to move he says, "And close every hatch behind you."

†

The Knights move down the corridor, Brother Santa Cruz pulling point. He says, "Commander, if that thing was patrolling, we should pull up the schematics and see where it can get to from the hatch it went in."

"Good idea," Brigid says. "Brother Nonnatus?"

"On it." They are approaching a T intersection. Placards on the wall with arrows pointing in both directions have directions of what is found down each path. Nonnatus's drones move ahead and scout out the passageway to the right, then come back quickly and work on the one to the left.

"Sir," Brother Gonzaga says, "Not to be pushy, but what are we dealing with, with that d2 thing?"

"20de9," Brigid corrects. "The 20de9 is a combat drone outlawed by the FedNet, along with I-SAW. It is—"

"Sir, would you clarify I-SAW?"

Brigid reaches over and pats Gonzaga on the shoulder. "I-SAW, the Intersolar Commission on Acceptable War Practices. Bureaucrats. Safe behind their desks, in guarded offices inside guarded buildings. I-SAW is a bureaucratic conglomerate of multiple nations from multiple planets in multiple star systems that have set forth guidelines on how you can wage war. Ethically." He lilts the word with derision. "When I was civilian military, we were beholden to their recommendations."

"I'm sure they're very ethical," Santa Cruz says. He is approaching the intersection and slows down. Takes a knee. The Knights stop and assume defensive postures. "Whatever you think, Nonnatus."

"I'm checking, but probably to the right." Nonnatus examines the schematics in his Visuals, and his on-board system starts drawing paths. "There's a small network of corridors here, but it looks like they all access the same few rooms and mostly outline all of them. There's a number of different ways that thing can come right back here." He looks up and around. "Behind us, too. We should go to the right, I think."

Brigid turns and considers the way they've come. "It might behoove to backtrack to those two ZZH we encountered. Nonnatus, what's the direction you're looking at?"

"Security offices. Intel agreed with Brother Cleopas's father that's the most probable place they're holding the archbishop."

Brigid gives another look behind. Pulls up what Nonnatus is looking at. "Head that way, then. Maybe we can loop around."

Nonnatus says, "I'm recalling the drones."

"Copy," Brigid continues. "The 20de9, it's an alien hunter/killer drone, the 20de9. Nothing more. It's patrolling. I imagine the ZZH bought it black market and put their leash on it. But those things are known for biting their masters."

Santa Cruz says, "My Visuals has a very limited profile on them. *A malleable configuration weapons platform.* Great sales pitch language."

"I agree." Gonzaga says.

Brigid says, "It's a dumb killing machine. I stress *dumb*. But, I also stress *killing machine*. There are these devices you wear that broadcast a signal the 20de9 recognizes as friendly. It'll shoot literally everything else."

"I wonder if those two ZZH back in the room had them?" Gonzaga says. "We might want them."

"That's a good—" Brigid starts and Nonnatus says, "It's coming!"

The three drones come rushing into the T intersection, stacked on one another like each one is willing to run its partners over to escape whatever is behind them. Those brilliant blue lights start up. All-consuming in their luster. A flash of thin red laser cuts through the air and the drones each plummet severed in half to the floor. Red hot glowing edges where they were cleaved by concentrated light.

"Move, move," Brigid urges as they fall back. Gonzaga trips and stumbles to the side. He rolls into an open hatch at his rear on the right side of the passageway. Brigid sees him but Nonnatus and Santa Cruz do not. The 20de9 comes around the corner, a flowing tube of mechanically undulating cubes. All black as its intentions of indiscriminate murder.

Missing Gonzaga's stumble, Nonnatus and Santa Cruz withdraw into a hatch on the other side of the passageway. Nonnatus grabs Brigid by the shoulder and pulls him in as the combat drone reconfigures itself.

The blue lights begin again.

Gonzaga rushes to get to his feet. His eyes lock with the commander's as the passageway fills with an explosion of gunfire. Their gazes hold even as Nonnatus lunges forward, slams the hatch door's controls. It cuts them off, and Gonzaga reflexively slaps his as well. He can hear the 20de9 approaching in a smooth hurry. The hatch seals. The spray of gunfire stops.

Gonzaga steps back. Knows better than to follow his base urge and go out the hatch. He turns, runs the other way.

†

The three Knights pause at the closed hatch and hear the particular sound of the combat drone outside. Brother Nonnatus grabs a manual lock under the hatch controls and twists it. It clicks into place and he steps away. Commander Brigid backs up and pushes his remaining two warrior-monks with him.

"We need another way out of here," he says.

"We left Brother Gonzaga," Brother Santa Cruz says.

Nonnatus says, "We have to go—" and then a super-heated weld mark from a cutting laser pierces through to their side. It begins a draftsman straight line that starts carving a new door inside the door that is locked.

"Blast this mess!" Brigid hisses. "Go." They turn, run the other way.

To be Used

She watches through a ruptured grate over a ventilation shaft as the Knight re-enters the space. A whole gaggle of them, an infestation even, had come and gone minutes ago, and then all she heard was a violent thumping. Bodies hitting the floor. If they're here, she knows she can only expect one thing. Murder.

She knows her friends were those thumps. Killed silently, probably from behind. The Lord Jesus had been able to see his murderers. Speak to them should He have wished. But these Knights from this heretic Order, not them. Being Roman soldiers is above them.

The muzzle of her rifle fits just between where two ribs of the grate have been damaged by earlier gunfire. A bevy of impact holes above her where someone's—hers or the disguised shock troops they sent first—fire had cut through the vent and bore in. Came to rest. Burrowing little lead insects. She tracks the Knight as he investigates the electrical cabinet with the axe wound in it. Then he ducks down to inspect a shaft where cables new and old disappear into its gullet.

To the gravitational anomaly engine. This whole mission is shot. Over with, and only she knows it.

The Knight bears the distinctive markings of Those Washed in the Water and Blood from His Side. Heretics. She knows that for certain. "No good," she whispers to herself and eases the weapon back. "No mercy from those like him. I know all too well, sister."

She uses a single finger to trail a strand of hair off her cheek and behind her ear. Uncovering it just makes the panting sounds behind her louder. She turns—as much as one can inside the cramped duct—and aims the rifle there. Slowly shakes her head. "It won't save you."

The whimpering calms down to a barely controlled hyperventilation and she is satisfied. Turns back to the Knight. He seems his mind is made up. He ducks and enters the space. Travels through its mouth and vanishes inside. She knows the tables have turned.

Father Loognar said they would come.

She is thankful the Lord guided her here, now. By some Divine providence, somehow skirting the infiltrators and winding up in this maintenance closet. She has a single grenade. She could roll it after him. Raise the alarm. He won't be injured. Not in that suit. Maybe they could have a glorious last stand. Get the 20de9 drones over here. But something inside her pushes back against that plan.

She knows it to be the Holy Spirit, setting a third path before her. It's always the third option with God. Stone the adulteress woman in accordance with the Law of Moses or argue against it and therefore argue against the Patriarch? Neither. Christ presented a third option. He who is without sin may do this. Run and save His own life or face crucifixion and die? Neither. He chose to come back to life. Reunite the twelve tribes and crush His enemies, or let all of mankind fall off into sin and darkness and death? Again, neither. He chose to make all of mankind the tribes and conquer the real enemies of sin and darkness and death.

Begin a last stand and die, or cower and try to escape? She chooses that illusive third option.

She adjusts her respirator some, turns to the Mariol woman behind her. Bound and gagged, stuffed in here and shoved back by the sole of her boot as she hurried to get inside herself.

"They're here," she says, flat and disgusted. The woman behind her tries to chew the gag out from her mouth to respond. That gag, wet in the two spots from under her eyes, the Mariol housekeeper shrugs and keeps up her act. "They're finally here, and it's pathetic. We knew you'd send reinforcements, especially after you failed."

The Mariol woman does the thing they all can do where their eyes, floating in sockets too big for the actual organ and the muscles suspending them contact and expand in exaggeration. The eyes asynchronously rotate all around, like a marble rolling in a cup. Fear glazed over them, radiating. "Don't give me that act. That's even more pathetic."

She maneuvers inside the duct to face the woman fully. "Evolve, would you? Just one of you, *any one* of your kind, please? We brought you Jesus. We brought you the Truth, and still. Your race didn't have much more than the wheel and agriculture before we showed up. I know all about Mariol culture—I went to seminary with two of them. But it makes sense the 1513 would use you like this. Trained apes. They. . . you know you're being used by them, right? You have to by now. They're. . . the 1513 sent you and your teams here in this—" she motions to the jumpsuit the woman is wearing, that idiot alien logo on the breast pocket, "—worthless disguise. We saw right through it. Right through it."

She stares at the Mariol woman as a mix of deep pity and depthless rage boils at the back of her throat. "Mankind finds a tribe of humanoids. You. Tribal. We educate you, evangelize you, try to work with you just as God did with the Hebrews and Israelites throughout the ages to train you out of your caveman status. To make you like us. Better. And you get just good enough to be allowed, well, like I said. I went to seminary with two of your kind. But you're still so stupid as a species that the 1513 can use you as mining canaries. Sending you in first to see if you—simpletons, mind you—can fool us."

The Mariol woman's skin goes from that slate pale to a fiery mix of oranges and reds and browns. Her eyes begin to move even faster. Her nostrils flare.

She shakes her head violently back and forth, her face screwing up into a terrified cowl.

"It's a good act, this right here." She says as she aims her weapon at the Mariol woman. "If I didn't know the truth of you, I'd believe you were really just a cleaning lady and your story about this husk of an asteroid was reopening. It's a good story."

She huffs and thinks about her third option. "The Knights sent you here to die. You knew it when you took this mission. Somewhere deep inside, you *knew* it. A disguised assassin. A test, maybe? A Mariol team trying to prove to the Knights they too can be effective murderers for that heretic branch of Christianity?"

The Mariol woman starts to weep. The tension in her body slackens and she slumps down. Defeated.

"They used you, and they forced my hand," she says as she sets her rifle down. Withdraws a knife. "The longer you're alive, the shorter I am alive. I hate the Knights for this so much."

She moves over to the Mariol woman and envelops her. "I will pray for you, my mongrel sister in Christ. But I must use you too. Seems that's your lot in life now."

In Isolation, Pleasing Odors to the Lord

Brother Pio's headlamp light stabs through the darkness of the shaft and pushes the shadows up against the close-fitting walls like cowering prey animals. So far it feels endless. Every which way he turns the pools of black shift, but everywhere is little more than smooth-bored rock with an assemblage of cabling running like a trail of breadcrumbs deeper inward. Tight.

"Saint Pio, I wonder if this is what it felt like to be in one of your cells," Pio wanders aloud to his namesake as he crouches, shuffling ahead. Alone, left to his own devices, Pio finds comfort in rambling to the cloud of witnesses that stand at the feet of God and intercede for those still making their way. Always praying. Gun forward, feet rolling heel to toe in a smooth motion. Making haste to the little package at the end of the line with the bite strong enough to squash their plans and everything within a few kilometers of them. "I've seen pictures of those old Italian cells. Feels cramped like this does."

Pio uses his Visuals to measure the distance he's traversed. He dropped a waypoint in that position as he entered the access hatch. Coming up on half a kilometer. Half more to go. "Thereabouts," he mumbles.

The smooth-bore tunnel, as Brother Cleopas described it, is simply a drilled shaft to the center of Stake's mass. "I wasn't here when they did it, but my mom was," Cleopas said. "She said they literally just drove a boring bit the diameter of the tunnel straight into the proper depth." Cleopas held his arms out to encompass the size of the shaft, large enough to accommodate Pio in his full frontal assault armor and the cabling running in to the GravCore. But little else.

Cleopas continued, "Said there was almost a kilometer of spinning metal drill bit just sticking out there into space as the crew drove it in, centimeter by centimeter. By the time it was done, the whole length of it was in Stake. I guess some goofball on the crew labeled the machine the *Prostate Examiner*. I didn't know what they meant for years." Pio laughs at the thought.

He tries to move a bit faster, feeling the invisible hands on his back pushing him with urgency. "Blessed Saint Pio, please intercede for me and for the team. Pray that Cleopas gets that woman to the surface, and she can be taken to proper medical care. Bless my mission here to get to the GravCore before the ZZH try and trip it into destruction. And bless my other brothers who are not only down two of their number but need me to get here before they get discovered. Through our Lord and Savior Jesus Christ, King of all Glory, forever and ever."

Another twenty meters down the shaft and Pio's light hits a blue and green glint on the sidewall near his left temple. He looks at it and sees a vein of EcoPassage crystal captured in the rock. Next to it in old, fading ink is a handwritten warning stating, "DO NOT scratch this."

Pio's mind goes to Cleopas's story of the caustic centipede species whose eggs were embedded in the crystal. His imagination runs wild with flashes of visions of those multi-legged things appearing from every crevice and searing through metal with their nightmare drool.

"A plague Egypt would have endured if they had those things," Pio says. He doesn't see anything resembling eggs inside the crystal—no way the miners would have left them—but he gives it as wide a berth as he can. Which is essentially putting his other shoulder against the tunnel wall and sliding by. Keeps moving.

The next several hundred meters are full of prayers for blessings and intercessions. A rolling, bumper-to-bumper sentence of praises to the Creator and requests for divine assistance. Asking the saints above to add their prayers to his own.

"And to you, the twenty-four elders from the Book of Revelation, I humbly ask my prayers be carried as those golden bowls of incense you offered before God Himself. The smoke wafting up, as Moses was instructed in Leviticus, a pleasing odor to the Lord. And on that smoke, my requests. Most Holy of Holies. Jesus Christ, I love you."

Suddenly the shaft widens into a dugout large enough to accommodate his entire team if they packed in here shoulder to shoulder. And there in the center of the floor, a strange metallic device at the end of the cabling, like a child and umbilical.

"Gravitational Anomaly Engine." Pio says as he kneels beside it. "I need a favor from you pretty badly, and I hope you like sweet talking. I didn't bring anything else."

The first thing he sees is the device the ZZH hastily wired into it.

Wearing Blackened Burns

Brother Cleopas's Visuals flood with an overlay of transparent red markers as it detects motion in the thickening pools of shadow behind the ZZH soldiers. Their shoulder-mounted flood lights glare off the crystalline fauna around him, creating a spectacle of jewelry glints in the space between. Nearly blinding.

"There's something in here with us, you have to listen to me," he says, backing up slowly. The MedSled follows with him and the movement makes the soldiers tense.

"The Spirit of God is in here with us," one of them says. He leans into his weapon's sights and aims at the MedSled.

"All around us," the other says. "Now, whatever this contraption you have here is, it better stop inching forward right now. I'll destroy it and kill you, no problem."

Cleopas's hands come up, placating. "Don't shoot the MedSled—that's what this is. Mobile gurney—"

"We know what a MedSled is," one of them says with derision and offense in his voice. "We come from a first world too."

"Okay, sure. There's a woman inside there. An injured woman. Innocent." Cleopas uses a rear-facing camera to see where his Visuals pinpointed a thin spot in the ceiling. Targets it. "But what I mean is, there's a lifeform in here— an aggressive centipede-type lifeform. They have a caustic—"

"One of the bad actors you sent, you mean?"

"Bad actor?" Cleopas backs up a little more.

"We know the Knights 1513 were going to mount a rescue of this heretic we've got. You sent a entire platoon pretending to be janitors and miners. What do you think we are?"

Cleopas huffs as the revelation hits him. "They're not ours. The company is reopening this asteroid. The timing was just—"

"The *company?* Whoever owned this rock decades ago and then legally abandoned it in orbit? You know what? I've had it with the lies," the one with the medical port says in that bizarre interspliced voice of feminine and masculine. "Backup is around the corner. You and whatever other enemies you came in here with, your time is up. You move one more nanometer and you're dead."

Cleopas sees the way the light at the other end of the EcoPassage flickers in the hatch. Hears more voices. Someone calling. The two ZZH here with him respond. One of them puts a hand on a stalagmite, pushes off in the weak gravity. Makes a bold move towards him.

"I'm telling you, you've—" Cleopas says as he sees the first ZZH soldier duck under a damaged stalactite. As he does, a centipede drops on him.

He screams with an earsplitting pitch and spins in panic. In the half g, his flailing is like in water. Writhes, limbs wrestling with nothing as his higher-level thought functions evaporate. Basic instincts now. The centipede has wrapped around his face. He slaps at it with his free hand. His gun still in his other hand, swinging wildly. Shrieking. Tendrils of smoke twirl, becoming thicker by the second.

The other soldier starts to yell and the backup come running in, yelling also. The man with the centipede on his face drifts to his knees. Three more swarm him from nowhere.

Cleopas takes a huge step backwards. The one with the medical port orders Cleopas not to move, but his attention is so divided between whatever is crawling over his partner and the Knight, he can't contain himself.

"What did you do?" He bellows at Cleopas in that chopped up voice. "We're Christian just like you! More so!"

The first ZZH reflexively fires his weapon. Mashes the trigger down, wildly spraying the EcoPassage. Ricochets spark and zing everywhere. Crystalline fauna shatter and collapse. Dust clouds pluming. They cloud the air, refracting the flood lights in a trillion sparkles. The second ZZH begins to franticly slap at his legs as a centipede moves up it. He falls, hollering at Cleopas, "More so, even! We are what Christ—" he lays over and as he does a tide of centipedes lunge from the darkness.

Their floodlights swing about erratically. In the adjusted gravity, the explosions of dust and color float like clouds. The flashing lights everywhere become an enemy all their own.

Muzzle bursts from forty meters away spring to life like a handful of fireworks. Cleopas turns and runs. He takes aim at the spot in the ceiling he needs to breach. The ZZH's spotlights swing wildly about the room, refracting in the crystalline dust motes in the air. Strobing—blindly brilliant and then shadows filled with after-effects of the light. Drawing lines all along the colorful cavern.

Lifting his rifle up to the ceiling, Cleopas sees a centipede on it. His barrel begins to smoke as the thing drools its caustic mess on it. He smashes the gun against a stalactite and the centipede wiggles fiercely. Another one races up his arm. He grabs it by its shell-encrusted head, scissoring jaws snapping at him. Twists and decapitates it.

The body slips off, limp. Cleopas rotates the hand with the head in it, sees another centipede scurrying up that arm towards his helmet. He slaps at it. Smears it across his armor. Whiffs of errant smoke climb off where it left its juices. He looks down and sees so many more.

He aims his gun at the teeming mass, but a small voice in his mind says something else entirely. He swings up and cocks the secondary fire on the rifle. It launches a small projectile at the thin spot in the roof. It strikes and explodes. The ceiling fragments in a spiderweb crack and few bits fall before a *pop!* resounds through the space. In his shipboard training, Cleopas was conditioned to hear that sound and know what was coming next.

Worse than taking on water on a sailing vessel.

†

"Atmospheric blowout," his instructor called it. "I've been in two of them. Both happened on starships during combat. I was the only survivor on that deck in the first one. I don't talk about it to this day. If you want to know about it, look it up. In the second one I got sucked out into space with everybody else. I was blessed by our Lord Jesus Christ the rescue unit was alongside us when it happened. I was only actively dying for nineteen seconds before they snatched me up. Nineteen seconds. What suffering it was. And although I offered it up, I'm a selfish man at heart and I won't go through it again even if others may benefit from it. May the Lord have mercy on me for that, but it's the truth."

†

The few bits that fell reverse in gravity. The spiderweb crack heaves outward with that *pop!* and a hole exposes to the eternity of space. The bits fly upwards in the force of the new vacuum and out the hole. Everything all at once lifts and hurls towards the hole.

A reverse rainfall of writhing centipedes rushes up past him. Meet the stars outside. Tentacles of black smoke begin to whip along, swirling him like dark souls in some nightmare. The spotlights still spinning, dizzying, like dropping a hundred flashlights down a well.

Whatever the new ZZH soldiers coming in through the hatch were thinking, they've changed their minds now. As the atmosphere in the EcoPassage escapes, the hatch leading into the maintenance artery slams shut. Emergency procedure.

Cleopas catches himself on an impressively thick base of a broken stalagmite. He activates a setting on his suit for the vacuum.

He grabs the MedSled as it slings by and fights against the pull. He groans, knowing as soon as the atmosphere is gone, everything will ease up.

Clusters of centipedes fly by as well. Long and black, casting about as the temperature drops to well below freezing. Without their eggs embedded in the fauna to protect them, the convection of heat from them into the void of space is too much.

One lands on Cleopas's arm. Frozen in its death throe. He sees it, fuligin segments with a gorgeous, lush shamrock green streak under where the carapaces overlap. It is wrenching itself as backward as it can, its array of legs in rictus. Its mouth, more like a lamprey's maw than a single set of mandibles, stretches wide open as well. A drop of its caustic mucus draws off one of its mouthparts and settles on Cleopas's forearm. A sizzle and a whiff of instantly dissipating smoke drifts off. He shakes his arm and the thing floats off. A thousand more like it listlessly sail by as the last few gasps of the atmosphere trickle out.

A dead ZZH soldier comes by as well. Pockmarked by burns from the centipedes. Ruined, wearing blackened burns like animal spots.

EcoPassage3 empties of any atmosphere at all, goes eerily silent. Cleopas settles himself down from his bracing against the stalagmite trunk. Eases the MedSled off to the side, sees another dead soldier in a lazy spiral as he drifts. A layer of centipedes on him, dead but still connected like leeches. His face is horrified, frozen in that reaction.

Yet another comes drifting.

"Lord, have mercy on them. Eternal rest, grant unto them, O Lord, and let perpetual light shine upon them. May they rest in peace, O Lord. I know they believed they had Your full Truth, and if they did, please let my heart be open to it. And if they did not, please extend Your just mercy. You know their hearts, Lord. I love you. Amen."

He crosses himself and gets down to business. As more detritus and bodies float his way, he leads the MedSled over to the hole. Manages it outside and follows it.

As he emerges onto the surface of Stake, he looks around. Not too far from a grid cannon. He activates his beacon for the *Saint Eligius* and goes to disarm the weapon before it shoots down their means of escape.

The Grand Cardinals

The UnZerre FulZzhea WarHeight have made their universal headquarters in the city of Xewl. Xewl, a sprawling mega-metropolis home to multi-millions of citizens. It is a nation unto itself. Sovereign in every respect. A veritable colossus of a single city.

Its citizens represent dozens of species from throughout the galaxy, and dozens more religions. Xewl is located on the primary continent of the planet Cavvzeliton, fourth from its sun and one of seventeen celestial bodies orbiting it. Without Xewl, Cavvzeliton is little more than two oceans and three continents, mostly forested. With Xewl, it is a power player in its solar system.

In the intervening years since the ZZH formally declared themselves the true religion of Jesus Christ, it has worked to copy the Catholic faith is most ways, rename its parts into more fitting labels and grow outwards. And while they have a few missions elsewhere, without their presence in Xewl, they would be relegated to little more than a footnote in the Church's history of heretical development. Something to be classified as anathema in a council once and then left to the grinding sands of time.

Their grandest temple in Xewl is attached to their Tiberian Council, a three-person ruling body in the place of a single pope. Those beings, so unisex after decades of transition, sit in the audience room of their shared living quarters.

A beautiful picture window reveals the titanic skyline beyond it. Xewl, situated on a forested expanse of land with multitudes of structures making up its skyline. The different architecture styles of its numerous species make for a hodgepodge view. A tapestry of buildings like a rag quilt. Clumps of similar styles shoulder to shoulder with clumps of a vastly different build. Draftsman straight lines of steel mix with curving stone. Living trees grown over centuries and carefully curated to bend this way and that so their gigantic branches can support mud and excreted resin buildings.

Grand Cardinal Dakon, the second eldest of three Grand Cardinals, leans in to hear the briefing from one of his attendants, absently fiddles with a control knob on a permanently attached hormone pump just below the ribcage. Dakon's utterly translucent skin shows the veins and vat-grown organs beneath the surface as they twitter with the release of some cocktail.

"Father Loognar, eh?" Dakon says. A voice so phlegmy it is a struggle to decipher words.

"Yes, Grand Cardinal, Father Amit Hiram Loognar," the attendant says. Currently female, the attendant has long blonde hair pulled back into a tight ponytail, a single streak of jet black dyed through the locks. New to this appointment, she was not glad when the former attendant died suddenly but wasted no time vying for the job. She shows Dakon the tablet again, with the ZZH priest's picture on it. "We have inquiries about how he was released from prison so early into his sentence."

"But that was four years ago, yes?"

"Yes, Grand Cardinal."

"No one has answered that in four years' time?"

"Well, it was around a violent protest inside the prison. That may very well have been his opportunity to—"

"And how successful has he been since?" Grand Cardinal Mowzer asks. Mowzer, like Dakon, is translucent. Both legs have been amputated due to complication with body augmentation throughout the years. In their place are fake ones, not that Mowzer has walked in a decade. Next to Mowzer's transport chair is a bank of support machines, numerous tubes running from it and plugging in up and down Mowzer's spine.

"How successful has Loognar been at… what, Grand Cardinal?"

"How many opposing religions have bowed to him?"

The assistant swallows. "One, to my knowledge. He's— he's taken on the Catholic Church now. He intends—"

"The papists will not bow," Grand Cardinal Fu Anito says. Fu Anito's head and spine have been preserved in a complex life support contraption. The head sealed around the neck by a metallic ring. It sits atop a tank of preservation fluids that contains the spine and thousands of nerve endings floating in the lightly pink suspension liquid looking like roots from a sophisticated tree. Fu Anito's voice is generated by a speaker that rotates and aims at the intended listener.

It disturbs the assistant.

Fu Anito says, "The only favorable light I grant them is they never bow. Satan protects them over all his other minions."

Dakon scoffs and it turns into a congealed messy sound. Spits a wad into a nearby bucket. "Our time is now, though. This Loognar has real promise."

Fu Anito laughs. "Loognar will be dead before we wake tomorrow, and you know it. The report says he took a Knights 1513 archbishop. The Vatican's assassins. Loognar is a fool." The head turns and ruminates, the grumbling sound through the speaker fills the room with a low unsettling.

Mowzer raises a finger as if to make a point. A wire trails off it to a monitor nearby. "If Loognar fails, we shall be blamed. You know this."

Dakon scoffs yet again. "Succeeds or fails, we shall be blamed. Loognar knows the process. We will disavow everything."

"Of course," Fu Anito says as if it is the most obvious thing in the room. "This Loognar. . . the report says there are already deaths. Destruction. We're not covering those expenses. Let the Vatican do it as a sign of goodwill. They have their gold, stolen throughout the ages."

Mowzer looks at the assistant and says, "Should Loognar succeed, we shall enjoy the fruits of his actions. Should he fail, we shall shrug and at as if he is simply evil and the ZZH condones nothing of the sort. Where is Bishop Mib?"

The assistant thinks for a moment, finger to her lip. "His Excellency should be the Citizenry Relations facility. Would you like me to summon him, Grand Cardinal?"

"Yes," Fu Anito purrs. "Bishop Mib will need a plan of action to spin this."

"That's his job," Dakon adds. "Get him in here."

Mowzer looks to the assistant, asks, "Has the Vatican attempted to contact us?"

"Yes."

"And?"

"Per our direction, we did not accept their communication."

Fu Anito makes another grumbling sound. One eye closes slowly. Too slow to be a blink. Then the eye snaps open and Fu Anito coughs. "Contact them. Tell them we disavow Loognar and all his actions. We will take responsibility for none of it, and we pray for those lost in this most egregious conflict."

Mowzer sniffs, adds, "We will also pray for a swift and just end where all sides can see the light of Christ and realize it is through Him that we are united."

The assistant waits to see if they add anything more. Dakon remains silent, the phlegm gurgling in Dakon's throat with every breath. She waits a respectful moment to make her think she gave them an opportunity to speak, but not too long. She's learned her lesson about giving them too much time. Someone will think of something to say if given too long.

"I will do all that you ask. Thank you, Grand Cardinals, and God bless you." She turns and leaves.

Outside their apartment, she starts walking at a fast clip. Another assistant, presently male, rises from where he is sitting and falls in step with her.

"What'd they say?" he asks, tapping on his own tablet. He flows through the hallway they're in, stepping around furniture and ornate, protruding columns with the reflexive memory of someone who has made this walk all his life.

"The usual," she says. "Publicly disavow Loognar, privately hope he succeeds because we'll reap the benefits. We hate Catholics."

"And we're not paying for his damage?"

She smirks, glancing at him in a knowing way. "I thought getting this position would be the most important thing I ever did. But going in there day after day, listening to old dottle-ing fools ramble on. . . all pomp and circumstance. There's no real authority there."

He nods. "It's the *mit Augen zum Sehen* that run the show. Religion by committee. Ridiculous, but the checks always cash and the influence we get is no small gift. God is good, after all."

"And the *smell*. . ." she says as they round the corner. Enter an elevator and leave.

Inside the apartment, the Tiberian Council remain where they were, too worn down by time and alteration to make much of themselves anymore.

Fu Anito ponders while looking out to the skyline, asks, "Loognar's finances cannot be traced back to us?"

Mowzer adjusts in the chair, groans. "No. Our old assistant took that secret to the grave."

"Then Loognar better as well."

Dakon runs a hand down a weary face, sniffs hard. "So what if he squeals? A terrorist whom we've already disavowed would be blaming the heads of his religion. No one will believe him and that's that."

"I don't like making deals with the devil." Fu Anito says.

"The papists make deals with the devil. Not us. This dog of ours was already foaming at the mouth. So what that we put some slack in his leash? The Catholics are outside our front door, doing harm. Let the dog bite them so they know the truth hurts."

"May God have mercy on us for what we've done for His truth."

"He will, He will. . ." Dakon says. "No one else ever has, but we must have faith that, though distasteful, this is His plan for us."

"And if not?"

Dakon stays quiet. To answer honestly is too much. So, instead he simply responds, "I must have faith, that this is His plan for us."

Disavowed Breaker, the Latest Butcher

"Your Excellency," Father Oopar Ifex says as he shuffles inside his carapace towards Bishop Tauthail.

The bishop sets down his water and rises from his seat. He takes a moment to straighten his sleeves and sees the ring on his finger, emblazoned with the suffering Christ on His crucifix. "Guide us, oh my Great Lord." He says quietly and hears his words in his head more than with his ears over the creaking of the old shell as it skitters along the stone flooring.

Father Ifex nears and greets Bishop Tauthail by clapping his mouth incisors twice, his species' version of a smile. What head spikes Father Ifex still has have lost their more lustrous colors and have settled into then matte black of Vunhor old age.

The priest hands Bishop Tauthail a sheet of paper, his own diocesan seal at the top. As he reads it, knowing what it's going to say but runs his eyes over it anyways, and asks the question to which he already knows the answer, "Did you send a copy to the official ZZH. . . governing body? Their version of the Vatican, I guess?"

"Tiberian Council." Father Ifex asks. "Yes. I have their return receipt already attached to the operation folder."

"Thank you," Bishop Tauthail reads on in the letter as the Vatican of the Catholic Church spells out its position.

"I'm assuming the official ZZH has disavowed Loognar?"

"Yes, Bishop. They strongly condemn his actions, he does not speak for their peaceful religion, et cetera."

"They will not assume responsibility for his actions?"

"None," Father Ifex says. He reaches to his mouth, a hand with spindly and exceedingly long fingers takes his narrow, waxy beard and sculpts it down towards his Roman collar. An absently minded gesture he is prone to. "They stressed they will not associate themselves with any of his destructions, murders, financial accruements." He laughs, a short bark that might sound like an animal's warning of aggression if Tauthail wasn't such old friends with his assistant to know the difference. "But they really stressed the financial aspects."

"They want to make very clear they won't pay for the repair bills he's stacking up, huh?"

"Repair bills, legal action over his murders, none of it."

"Who would?" Tuathail hands the letter back. Father Ifex takes it and folds it neatly in half using only one of his six hands. Tucks it into his cassock.

"Father Ifex says, "They suppose Loognar is trying to make a statement, however incorrectly, about their religion's truth claims. He will suffer the temporal effects and blame, while the ZZH religion can continue, receiving whatever benefit his actions might be."

"Martyr complex," the bishop says. "Pure and simple. If the universe won't recognize the greatness of the ZZH, he will make it."

"Maybe recognize his own greatness in the process."

"Why not?"

Father Ifex asks, "Let's suppose he's successful—and of course I know he will not be, but for the sake of a hypothetical. . . if we were to bend the knee to him as the LSD has, do you think he would stop?"

Bishop Tauthail narrows his eyes. "How could he? No Protestant denomination would follow our lead. If they did, they wouldn't be Protestants. And no other non-Earth religion would follow either."

"I imagine he discounts any non-Earth religion totally. They do not have Jesus—the ZZH version or ours—so he would convert them, I suppose. But not care if they respected him."

"But us. . ."

"He must break." Father Ifex nods.

"All right. Disavowed by his own people," Tauthail says as he looks at the clock. The two-hour time frame he laid on Loognar's shoulders has dropped down to seven minutes. "The Vatican will not recognize his heresy as legitimate, nor will they order an evacuation of Xewl to appease terrorists. Archbishop Hrutt is, as he always has been, in the victorious hands of Jesus Christ."

He turns to the tech, dutifully stationed at their makeshift comms table. "Any word from the team on Stake?"

"Sketchy," the tech says. He points a finger at a scrolling feed of info on one screen, moves the feed around a bit and says, "Approximately twenty minutes ago they requested emergency evac on a civilian. The *Saint Eligius* is responding. Apparently, the asteroid is set to be reopened for a water reclamation project. Maintenance and housekeeping had the horrible timing of arriving on Stake hours after the ZZH arrived with the archbishop. The team says it was a slaughter."

"Lord, have mercy on them, please." Tauthail says. He and Ifex make the Sign of the Cross over themselves.

"No word on the archbishop yet." The tech says.

Tauthail nods and runs a hand down his face. He exhales a stressed breath, trying to purge the tension. He looks at Ifex, puts a hand on his shoulder. "Not to date us too much, but you remember the good old days when it is was more about smoothing out differences between cultural interpretations of Jesus and not racing against time with butchers?"

Ifex laughs his clipped bark again. "It was always that, Treasach. Always. Since our Lord came to your ancestral home and revealed Himself. A race against time, at least on the faithful's part. He is in His time. We should be, too."

"I know," Tauthail nods and pats the priest before setting his arm down at his side. "It will be over soon in our time, regardless."

"Commander Brigid's team is a good one," Ifex says. "His men are humble men. Godly men. And, they have a secret weapon. They have a man who grew up on that rock."

"Their medic, yes," Tuathail looks to the tech. "And they requested an emergency evac? For a victim?"

The tech nods, "They did, yes, your Excellency."

Tauthail turns back to Ifex. "Then I imagine he's the one accompanying the victim. The team is on their own, at least, for now."

"So much for their secret weapon," the tech says. His mournful tone changes the air in the room.

Ifex waves it off. "They always have Jesus, and what more do they really need?"

"True, friend. Very true."

Ifex looks at the clock. "Now, I'll stay and be with you as you report back to our latest butcher, eh?"

Tuathail puts his hands in his pockets and rocks back and forth on his heels. "That'll be good, yes. But we've got a few more minutes, let's—"

"Your Excellency," the tech interrupts, "We have an incoming transmission from Loognar, sir."

The bishop and the priest share a glance, then cross themselves again. Tuathail goes to his chair and Ifex goes nearby, and the bishop says, "So be it. I'm ready."

The screen comes to life, and there Loognar is.

Designated by the Sword

"Oh, blessed Lord, it is a good idea, it is a good idea it is a good idea itisagoodidea itisagoodidea itisagoodideaitisagoodidea just let me get there, please." Brother Gonzaga frantically prays as he races back to where they found the bodies. Alone and so new to this work, this life-or-death struggle. "I ask your blessings on me and the entire team as we. . . fight for your holy archbishop. Just let me get to the— the device. Make friends with—"

Gonzaga rounds a tight corner. An alarm about his near hyperventilation in red letters scrolling across his Visuals. He feels his suit inject him with a cocktail to calm him. Can't do the Lord's work if he's gripped in a panic attack. He stops, puts his back to the wall.

"Stop being an idiot," he says. "You're trained up for this. You've been called by God Himself to this vocation. You've survived worse. You're wearing a suit of sophisticated battle armor that would have allowed you to cut right through entire armies of the past. Right through. There's one robot here, and technically you don't know much about it. The commander was freaked out but who knows. Maybe he just— maybe it's PTSD or something in him. But not you. *Not you.*"

Flashes of his childhood spring to life behind his eyes and he tries to blot them out. Enemy invaders assaulting his home city. Rendering him an orphan. Alone. The innocent light beige of Stake's hallway takes on that orange, rocky hue his home world had. At the edges of his vision, he can see shadows of crackling fires. Remnants of the attack. He begins to smell the salty air and old, caked blood and the sulfur of—

"Okay, there's *your* PTSD," he says. Interrupted, the experience vanishes like wisps of smoke in a wind that stirred the trees from his youth. "If that's even what it is. It's just a memory. Everybody has memories, and only a few have damage. You're remembering old stuff and you should be concentrating on the here and now stuff."

He moves again. His Visuals showing his target is right around the next corner. He clears it. Still alone. "Saint Michael, prince of Heavenly Hosts, lay your sword from our sovereign God on my shoulder and designate me for this fight. Through Christ, our Lord, amen."

Gonzaga thinks he feels the weight of the spiritual blade settle on his right shoulder. Then his left. The alarm from his Visuals disappears. Maybe it's the injection taking hold. Maybe it is the blessing from God inhabiting him. More than likely both.

"If I had to pick one," he says, "It's always You, Lord. Always."

He enters into the third office they cleared earlier with this one end table in the corner; a plastic top on four metal legs. In the doorway beyond the line of executed crew. Before him, two dead ZZH soldiers struck down by his hand. The Knights laid them along the corner of the floor and far wall earlier in what passed for a battlefront position of repose.

"If the two of you were just moseying around on patrol, you must have had these friendly devices the commander was describing. Must have."

He takes one step towards the dead men and hears the distinct and disturbing shuffling sound of the 20de9. Not from behind. From the second office.

Gonzaga bounds over, grabs the nearest ZZH. Runs a hand up and down his back in broad, pressing strokes. Remembering instinctively that Brother Cleopas wears the beacon for the MedSled at his lower back. "Maybe the device is here too?"

The smooth rotating sound grows so much closer.

Gonzaga rolls the man over in one fluid motion, checks his front. His tactical vest rattles under the inspection, and Gonzaga's tension triples. Ammo magazines. A small and chintzy knife.

Pocket-sized copy of the Gospels as translated by the *mit Augen zum Sehen* council.

A shadow falls along the wall and Gonzaga can see it through the open hatch nearby.

His hand lands on a box with a bizarre and narrow bulge in one corner. The surface is sleek, almost like glass. "Like the drone," Gonzaga says in relief.

He doesn't really notice that his gun is already up, aimed at what is coming. Instinctual response to the threat, knowing full well that the commander implied guns do nothing.

His Visuals alarm in the right corner of his view. Lethal danger there. He spins around, down on one knee, the corpse pushing over with his movement. The room fills with binding flashing blue lights.

There it is. The 20de9, hovering in the hatch. T formation, but instead of Gatling guns there is a swelling below its alien skin-like surface. A ring, almost pressing through. The ring undulates in size, expanding and contracting like an iris. Steady, like breathing.

It adjusts and readjusts, as if it is trying to fixate on him but there is some kind of obstacle in its perception. Trying to work around it. Gonzaga imagines it like camera lenses struggling, trying to focus; blurry then sharp only to delve into blurriness again. The entire drone shifts side to side.

Two minuscule curved arms like animal horns come out from underneath the ring, themselves emerging from the still-pond of onyx surface. Point at one another. They begin clapping together in rapid succession. Drumming, racing.

The ring begins to vibrate with the clapping. Gonzaga finds himself so perplexed by the action he is still. Frozen. Something inside him—the Holy Spirit working—nudges him. He feels the glassy box in his hand. He slowly pulls it out of the ZZH soldier's tac vest. Displays it like a shield between him and the 20de9.

The drone goes still. The clapping arms stop. No more blue light patterns, stabbing like knives. The ring continues to vibrate frantically, steady in its excitement. As if the clapping horns have charged it somehow.

Gonzaga breathes a bit easier, which through the tension of the moment—the entire room seems to have held its breath when this thing arrived—he finds oddly amusing. His entire body is ragingly taut. Flight or fight in every single cell. But the calmness of God has rested upon him. This little box, this friendly device, is working.

With a smile that trembles on a flood of almost-relief, Gonzaga says, "But I have trusted in Your merciful love; my heart shall rejoice in Your salvation. I will sing to the Lord, because He has dealt bountifully with me."

Gonzaga rises to his feet, arm outstretched with the box in hand. The 20de9 does not flinch. Does not track him. Flatline-still as if he just pulled the power on it. He steps off to the side and out of the direct aim—so far as he can tell—of the drone.

Two meters away from the bodies. Three. Almost four and his back edges up against the far wall. The 20de9 has not moved; it still faces towards the dead men. The one Gonzaga rolled over and plundered for the friendly device remains twisted and half-face down, his repose as peaceful as it can be.

Gonzaga starts to back towards the way he came when the outward arm of the rotated corpse slips and slaps its hand on the floor. The quivering ring on the 20de9 discharges with a loud bang in the thin atmosphere. Gonzaga can see in the particulates free floating in the room as a circle-shaped projectile, invisible if not for the path in the particulates it carves. The projectile hits the corpse and splatters it with a roar that deadens to nothing as it strikes.

"Sound weapon," Gonzaga says, astonished. He looks to the drone, then back at the mess. To the drone again, and swallows hard. ". . . absorb ambient sound, concentrate it for that, that concussion ring. Just like you must have absorbed ambient light and concentrated it into a laser against Nonnatus's. . . little drone guys."

The commander's comments about the 20de9 not carrying much ammo make sense now. It doesn't need to. "It makes its own," Gonzaga says as the combat drone reconfigures into a train of shuffling cubes. Whatever it fired through its Gattling guns, fine. Sound and light weapons, worse. Does it have other armaments? Does it need to? Hovering, it floats out of the office and into a passageway as if nothing happened.

Gonzaga watches it leave and turn a corner. "Praise God it left the others alone," Gonzaga says. "I just have to find them with this."

He goes over to the other corpse to get its friendly device. It was so close to the ruined body, it has suffered as well. Gonzaga finds an armor plate in the tac vest bent and curled from the sound ring's impact. Two magazines shattered. The bullets can't be trusted.

He digs around and finds this soldier's friendly device. Cracked wide down the middle, some light-yellow fuzz puffed out from the shell. He shrugs—no idea whether it might still work or not. "The commander may know," and he keeps it just in case. Armed with two of them, he doubles back the way he came.

In Isolation, there is the Deadman

"All right, I'm pretty sure these fellas rigged you to crush us all if I tamper with this, eh?" Brother Pio says as he scans the piece of equipment the ZZH wired in series with the GravCore and its umbilical cabling running a kilometer out to its controller.

"Okay, Lord, be with me as I do this here. . ." his scan complete, his suit's system gives its best guess based on preloaded schematics and designs from similar types of equipment. It shows him electrical flow and from there extrapolates its probable functioning.

He points things out to himself as he works through it. The first two wires, he motions to and says, "You're two legs of power. This third one here is the neutral. This fourth bundle must be comms—control signals and feedback. This is how they tell you to tune up or down on gravity output. The power legs increase or decrease voltage upon that demand. Easy enough."

He looks at the ZZH's device. All the umbilical cables run into it—must have been cut by ZZH and reattached here—and run out of it to the GravCore. "But then there's this wire right here," Pio says as he motions to a single new cable that only comes from the shaft and goes into the device. Not into the GravCore. "You're the ZZH's new wire. Their control. Deadman wire."

He looks at it. It is two individual wires inside a single sheath. "One is control, the other is a low voltage leg." Pio sits back on his haunches and snaps his finger. "Low voltage holds in a contactor, like on a motor starter switch. Just powers a coil to bridge the flow of electricity. But the comms wire is the tunable signal from the ZZH. Override wire."

He nods, pulls out his tool kit. "If I clip the ZZH wire, both the low voltage and the deadman wire lose the power to hold the coil. The coil faults in the open position and the power for the GravCore is severed. If that GravCore doesn't have power. . ."

✝

"The GravCore is alien tech," Brother Cleopas said. "I can't explain its inner workings, but I know this. Whatever power source inside there, it just is. *It's constant. And it's huge. Multiple, multiple gs of exertion at all times. The tech I do understand is the containment field. That's what we power, and that's what we tune. The field allows a constant ratio of gravity to leech out. We can make it stronger, and it lets out less gravity. We can make it weaker, and it lets out more. If the containment field loses power, it fails instantly. And then—"*

✝

". . . We're obliterated in an overload of gravity." Pio says. "So, that's not what we want."

He sets back again. "But I've got to keep *them* from tripping the coil, so. . . override wire?"

Pio puts a single power armored finger on the ZZH's device box and pushes gently. Watches it slid a few centimeters along the smooth rock flooring. No hair trigger on it. "Good. Good."

He tilts his head this way and that, says, "Somehow the ZZH were able to interrupt the power and everything long enough to splice their box in. If they could do it, I should be able to."

He takes the box and pulls it back to him, examines it for some way to open a compartment where the wiring must have gone into. "Hopefully you're a dumb device. No internal monitoring circuit or booby trap. . ." he rotates it, sees a few screw ports.

"Lord, please bless me with this all being basic, *basic* tech. Use Your hands to guide mine. I beg of You."

He unscrews the few fasteners that he sees. Pops open the plastic lid on the device. Sees the override and deadman wires going into terminals. He scans it for some electrical measurements, sees how much electricity the override wire is pulling.

"Well, Lord," Pio says, soaking up the information and making some calculations. "If I disable it, we're dead. So, that's a no-go. If I leave it alone, the ZZH can disable it whenever they want to. That's a no-go. But, if I. . ." he reaches around to his power sources' compartment and opens it up. Finds a battery for auxiliary processes and pulls it. Reads its label, says, "You'll do for the override wire. Deadman is pulling too much."

He withdraws a short length of wire from his kit and cuts it, strips the ends. Attaches the ends to the battery terminals. Looks to the terminal block where the override wire lands. There are other empty terminals on the block, so Pio cuts two jumper wires and runs them from the outgoing signals of the override wire into empty slots.

He positions his cutters over the override wires, jaws almost closed. In his other hand, he has the leads running from the battery pinched in his finger, ready to stab them both into contact of the open terminals.

"Press and cut, press and cut, Pio. . ." he whispers. Feels a bead of sweat, heavy as six Gs tracing down his face. "Lord, once more, You and me."

He presses and cuts. In the blink of an eye.

The GravCore makes a weird blip sound, then continues to purr as it has for decades. Stake does not crush Pio. He screams "Hallelujah," at the top of his voice. Drops the cutters, grabs his screwdriver and tightens down the new leads from the battery.

His Visuals scans the new setup, displays that with the current draw on the battery, it'll be depleted of the voltage needed in approximately thirty-two minutes.

"Got to hurry, then." Pio turns to exit, crosses himself and starts praying again as he races back into the shaft.

They Don't Care About Bullets

"Central Processing," Brother Santa Cruz says as he buttonhooks through an open hatch and into a space large enough that sets off a new alarm in his gut. Stake's manufacturing facility. "Corner-fed room, the expected obstructions," he says as he clears his first corner and starts rotating his rail gun towards the next one. Under the aiming reticule on the weapon is *3.0 power ratio*. Only three percent of the weapon's strength behind every trigger pull. Nothing more. Firing that low will ensure the station's integrity against space.

Commander Brigid is through the open hatch right after Santa Cruz, gun held at the ready and crossing the threshold at a diagonal to cover the opposing side. He sees the obstructions Santa Cruz mentions. "Big," Brigid says as he moves the corner he's holding.

Brother Nonnatus is last. Gun up as well, he enters the hatch and steps to his right, back along the wall. "Covered?"

"Best we can until we clear this machinery for threats," Santa Cruz says.

"Copy," Nonnatus turns around. All the hatch controls have been on the left side of the opening as one faces it; him entering to right puts him there. He closes the hatch, turns the manual latch underneath it. "eControls are disabled. God willing, that drone will get tired of cutting itself new doors."

Brigid turns and looks at him. "If only God did will that. As it is, cutting a new door only buys us a few extra seconds. Let's go."

"Any word from Brother Gonzaga yet?" Santa Cruz asks.

"I messaged him. Told him to hang tight. Not sure if he got it; the walls in the manufacturing space are providing a lot of interference with the encrypted signals."

"He's got a good Guardian Angel; he'll be all right until we double back."

"Yes," Brigid says. "I hope he has the same sense of it. Newbies, though. . ."

†

The expected obstructions dominate the room. The Knights flow through silently. Machinery owning the space. "Drones would be nice," Brother Nonnatus groans.

Commander Brigid points to the first huge machine, says, "Schematics call this a processor/separator." A huge square with two control stations, one on each end. A hopper on top large enough to receive boulders the miners cut out. A few pieces of scaffolding remain where a belt coming out of the wall once fed it. That shaft now covered; welded over with a single plate of metal.

"I guess a belt fed raw mined materials into the top. As it went down, it was ground up and came out the far end."

"Anybody hide in that thing?" Brother Santa Cruz asks.

Nonnatus scales the device by a ladder fastened to one side. Gun first, he swings into the hopper. Waves them off. "Nothing but rollers and teeth. No boogeymen." He drops back to their side and they move.

"Fines separator," Brigid says as they come up to the next machine. Connected to the processor/separator by the grinder's outfeed belt, this next machine has a belt composed of metallic runners above the outfeed belt. The metallic runner belt paces the lower one for several yards and then runs off at a ninety-degree angle to a second machine, also topped with a hopper. The second machine has a large belly cavity and several pipes leading to and from it.

"That's the smelter," Brigid says. "Brother Cleopas said one of their primary mined materials here was ferrous ores. The processor/separator grinds up all the ferrous and non-ferrous, transfers it out here. The metal belt is, I guess, magnetized and pulls out the ferrous stuff. Takes it over there and drops it into the smelter. The remaining material keeps going over here—" he points the next machine, which they all can recognize. "Compactor/baler."

Nonnatus swiftly moves along the other side of the fines separator, outlining the machine as he goes. "No real place for somebody to stash away."

He gets to the smelter, makes a round about it. "The belly opens on the other side," he reports, "but the doors are tac welded shut. Piping in and out looks like gas for firing the ore. Those don't appear to be rigged to blow, so far as I can see or scan."

"I imagine they'd be fed from tanks," Santa Cruz says. "Stored outside, probably. In case of a mishap."

"Agreed," Brigid says. "And they'd be drained and taken during idling. That stuff is expensive. Keep moving."

They stalk to the compactor/baler; a large rectangle on its side. Operator control on one end, a hydraulic ram on the other. The thing is open on the side facing the Knights. Nonnatus ducks inside and back out. "Clean," he says.

Brigid calls them to a hold. Examines his Visuals. "Okay, it says after this they loaded the bales outside on the surface for storage. Cleopas said some of the companies who mined here just let their tailings and debris float away. Nav hazards. This company bundled and hauled. Sold it."

"We at the end of it all?" Santa Cruz asks as he holds his position at the corner of the baler. Nonnatus covers their rear. Brigid steps forward, clearing the one corner far off that he can see.

Brigid shakes his head. "Of manufacturing. After this—" he rounds the corner past Santa Cruz and gunfire strafes up his armor. Somewhere hidden behind the angle of the machinery. Voices start shouting. Brigid falls backwards and Santa Cruz grabs him with his free arm.

"That's why I'm point, old man," Santa Cruz says as he pops out around cover. Ducks back in as more fire plinks off the metal.

"Six coming in hot—" an explosion on the side of the baler knocks Santa Cruz back, hard. His rail gun bounces off the flooring. Slides along, half-spinning. Nonnatus leans around the machine, fires a small burst, ducks back. Pushes Brigid away, who is still slapping at his armor while a single spot of it sparks and belches a whiff of smoke.

"Lord, be with us," Brigid says.

Santa Cruz scrambles up from where he fell. Drags his gun off the floor and hastily rolls it in his hands, checking it for damage. A few rounds strike him in the back as he does it.

Brigid says, "All right, we need to fall back to a defensible position until we can—" another explosion. Shears off the corner of the baler. A shower of hot shards and smoking bits scatters along them and out onto the floor. They begin moving aft. Making space.

"That hopper gives us the high ground," Nonnatus says.

"Will it hold up to those explosives?"

"Doesn't look like anything will."

Brigid says, "Santa Cruz, get up there and see what you can hit. Nonnatus, take the opposite side, try to sneak forward and around. I'll lure them out here so we can—"

ZZH burst from the corner, their position obscured by the baler. Six troops, almost at a run. Shoulder to shoulder, guns up. Their line, moving like a marching band, swings around like a gate opening. Muzzle flashes dazzling.

Rounds fill the space between them. Nonnatus braces himself and extends his left arm. In the middle of his forearm a circular device pops out of the armor and rotates, drawing an energy shield wide and tall enough to effectively provide all three of them cover.

Santa Cruz takes aim.

The rail gun's muzzle sizzles to life and a projectile hurls forth at the speed of sound, instantaneously connecting with the middle soldier as Santa Cruz pulls the trigger. The soldier explodes with an electric blue shock wave. The other soldiers take the impact almost as hard. All five of the others thrown off their feet with severe injuries.

Several meters behind the targeted soldier a discarded metal cart hurls off its casters and shatters. A shower of sparks blooms on its thick metal surface. Overhead in the stony corner of the cavernous room another shower of sparks. Chunks of rock fall. The smelter rings like a gong in the thin atmosphere, a smoking hole in its side.

The Knights squat down behind Nonnatus's shield, listening for more echoes of a ricochet. When nothing new springs up, they ease. Rise to their feet. Nonnatus retracts his shield, and they make towards the fallen soldiers.

The ZZH remain still. Just like that, the swarming assault quieted. Brigid's Visuals scan them for signs of life. "That. . . did it, I guess," he says. He looks to Santa Cruz. "Was that an explosive?"

Santa Cruz looks down at his gun. "No. Rail gun munition. I just— oh. I see." He rotates his gun over and shows its digital read-out to his commander. "When I got knocked down by that explosion, my gun struck the ground pretty hard. Jumbled the power settings. I had it at three percent power ratio inside here. didn't want to shoot a hole in the crust."

"What's it at now?"

Santa Cruz shrugs. "Uh. . . ninety-one."

Brigid flatly says, "Too much."

"Yessir," Santa Cruz is already adjusting his power ratio down. "Any more like that anyways and I'll all but drain the capacitor."

"Dead weight, my friend."

"Well, I'm thinking they know about us now." Nonnatus says.

"Somebody had to have heard that," Brigid says, moving around the corner to see where the ZZH were. "Were they waiting for us?"

The Knights follow him. Beyond the machinery near the next door are two tables set side by side. A few scattered meal plates. Some entertainment devices. A copy of their biblical texts. Other personal-sized equipment the Knights' Visuals identifies as hormonal treatments or support devices for their special organs.

"We've got to get through that door," Brigid points at the next step in their path. "Move on to what they called the morale strip. Before the 20de9 gets here."

Santa Cruz slaps himself in the back of the head. "It knows we're in here now. I'm sorry, brothers."

"Don't beat yourself up," Brigid says. "Nonnatus, check it, would you?"

"Yessir." Nonnatus sets off at a trot to the next door. "Welded seam. Give me a minute." He withdraws a cutting disc and starts to work his way through the beaded joint running down the middle.

"Commander," Santa Cruz says. "I've got the breaching foam."

"Save it." On the side of the door a faint light draws a line in the metal. Nonnatus groans and steps back. "Too late." He says.

The light turns brilliant, then liquid runners of metal stream down.

"Too late?" Brigid asks as he turns to his Knight. Sees the cutting line from the other side. "Lord Jesus Christ, King of endless glory. . . mount up and fall back."

The 20de9 cuts the door off the hinge and punches it out of the wall. Enters. Brigid looks back to the ZZH soldiers strewn about, races to them.

†

Fifteen years prior to that very moment a younger Brigid, as a First Lieutenant in the FedNet military was hunkering down with his squad of six soldiers plus their sister squad, now leaderless in the face of the enemy. He was on the surface of Jav'ir, a small planet that held not much more than sand and voluminous natural sculptures of stone. Hiding like game in burrows, a bloodbath all around.

Jav'ir was formerly one of seventeen moons around a much larger planet, Oli'tri, but its inhabitants desired freedom so badly they made a deal with an alien species to tow them out of the planet's orbit and into their own. They were situated on the same orbital axis around their sun, two AUs away from Oli'tri.

As astonished as Brigid was that something existed in the galaxy that had the power to tow moons, he had more pressing concerns. Jav'ri declared independence in an impressively extreme way, and that stoked the jealous fires of Oli'tri. Simply put: Oli'tri claimed Jav'ri as part of their sovereign ownership, and they were coming to take them back. To resist was a death sentence.

The people of Jav'ri chose death.

The species that towed Jav'ri to independence claimed neutrality in any conflict—as was their way, and never to be violated—and once their move was done, left. Jav'ri was alone and extremely overpowered by their former parent world. With slaughter bearing down on them, they appealed to the FedNet. An entire legion of FedNet military responded.

Not to be outdone, Oli'tri withdrew from its arsenal a hideous weapon. Swarms of 20de9 drones.

†

Commander Brigid reaches the first ZZH soldier and flips him over. While patting at the man's tactical vest, he looks to his Knights. "Search the bodies for a small black box."

He reaches into a pocket and pulls out shattered remains of what he's looking for. He holds a shard up, says, "Like this, but intact. Check this pocket on each of them."

Brothers Nonnatus and Santa Cruz dig through the others, thinking that as organized soldiers, they'll have a common outload on their uniforms. Certain items in certain pockets, universal. Each man comes up with ruins of their friendly devices.

Brigid keeps looking to the end of the machinery. To the source of the sound of the approaching drone. He checks the last man and withdraws a cracked device that he holds for a moment and shakes. There's no outward sign of it functioning—no indicator lights, no sound, nothing—and a piece falls off. He drops it.

"We need to go. Now."

They turn around and start to fall back, Nonnatus leading, Brigid in the middle and Santa Cruz calmly but with purpose rolling his steps backward, fully facing their rear. Rail gun up.

They reach the fines separator, and a new sound joins the tension. Boots slapping the floor. Coming from the same direction they entered.

"Contact," Nonnatus says.

Brigid, who's been watching their rear with Santa Cruz, turns around. Six more ZZH soldiers, guns up. He says to his Knights, "We need their devices."

†

Communications between the Oli'tri and the FedNet broke down immediately and war erupted. The Oli'tri army was skilled and disciplined. They were honorable foes. The problem the FedNet encountered was the Oli'tri government was willing to turn all of Jav'ri red.

"Oli'tri's attitude was that old covetous one: if I can't have you, I'm going to make sure nobody can." Brigid said, years later while recounting the story in the Order's commissioning academy.

The FedNet fought and seized the day. One morning while his squad was processing Oli'tri prisoners of war, they were outside loading them into transports. Against the sunlit backdrop of a sky shining with their victory, the FedNet and Brigid especially, looked up to the clouds and saw a ghastly black web fluttering down from the heavens. Night-colored dots strewn throughout random latticework. It was as if some continent-sized spider took its trap of a home and dusted it with globs and ash, and then let it float down to the surface. It lilted easily on the high breezes, fluttering. So innocent except for the onyx coloring. And the way the Oli'tri prisoners lost their composure.

Brigid as a First Lieutenant watched as the group of prisoners he was walking beside all looked up. Recognized what it was. One threw up. Another fainted. A few more went weak in their knees. Another begged to be shot.

"We're doomed," the one next to him said.

"Why?"

"Don't you know what that is? How did they even get them here without— your Federal Network has failed us! Failed you!"

"But what is it? A bomb?"

"A bomb? A bomb might as well have a conscience!"

Another prisoner broke free from the group and started to run. He screamed, "We don't have our protection units! They'll think we're with them! Someone give me my protection unit!" FedNet soldiers chased him down. He fought the entire time. Not because he was trying to be defiant; he was trying to escape that falling webwork.

Brigid looked to the paling, sickening Oli'tri soldier next to him and took him by the arm. They both looked to the sky and watched as the small black dots on the weave separated. Began their own insectile flight pattern, descending down.

"We have plenty of ammo," Brigid said.

"They don't care about bullets," the prisoner said in a voice that had already accepted his death.

"Fire, then."

"Useless."

"Explosives."

"They pass right through." The soldier shed a tear. "Maybe munitions from your largest shipboard cannons. Maybe."

Brigid looked up, weighed how the prisoners were acting. Grabbed his radio, started shouting for covering fire. The first of the 20de9 drones hurled at the surface and then swooped up a few meters before it struck. Soared right into their camp. Screams and death. Everyone started firing then, and it fought back.

†

"We need to get them between us and the drone," Commander Brigid says, moving towards the ZZH. He skids a smoke flare across the floor at them. The thing hisses forth and spews a thick cloud up and out. Drawing a line of cloud. The ZZH open fire.

Rounds ricochet off the Knights' armor and all three of them run into the smoke. Use their power suits to jump two and three meters high. In barrel curls they clear the ZZH and land on the other side. Nonnatus fires into the soldier closest to him and as the body drops he grabs it. Tears the friendly device from his vest.

Two soldiers scamper backwards as Brigid shoots. One collapses but the other racks the action back on a large-barrel weapon he has. Fires it at Brigid. An explosion at point blank.

Brigid falls back, can't breathe. Feels the punch reverberate through his organs. Even now, he shoves that hindbrain panic down, acts. Scrambles up as best he can. Nonnatus is within range of shot. The blast knocks the device from his hands. He leaps for it. Small arms fire peppers him all over.

Santa Cruz takes two wide steps outside and fires at three percent power. Another solder drops, a smoldering hole still glowing blue in him, his tactical vest shredded. And with it, the device.

"Oh, for the love of Saint Peter," Santa Cruz chastises himself. Slings his rail gun across his chest and withdraws a small semi-automatic weapon. He comes up on point, but no one is firing. He sees the three ZZH soldiers lined up, the last whiffs of the smoke flair swirling about them.

And from the cloud, a silhouette emerges of an ever-changing mass of squares that somehow floats like a silk nothing, arranging and rearranging. The soldiers stand there, guns up, smirks along their lips. The monstrosity behind them, looming like a demonic specter.

"Looking for the archbishop, eh?" One soldier asks.

The Knights stand at the ready, their guns up as well. "We are," Brigid says. "Care to point the way?"

"Down," the soldier says. "In hell, where all heretics go."

†

The officer who became Brother Brigid got a pain in his jaw. The forward sky had filled with those descending webs, cut free from time and space. Gently gliding downwards from wherever they were dropped. All the tumor-like black dots on them separating off. Zigzagging in intricate and random patterns.

Just the sight of them elicited screams from those who knew what was coming.

As that blackness, that bizarrely calculating mass of geometric wash got closer, a whine increased, so slight and high pitched he couldn't perceive it with his hearing. But it was there, a mosquito-like buzzing in his brain. His jaw hurt. Where it hinged up into his skull, a sharp, needling pain. He looked around. Others had it too.

Men rushed into the transport ships. Ungainly, unorganized. Like rats on a sinking boat. They pushed and shoved. Prisoners fell over, still restrained in shackles. "Stop!" Brigid ordered. "Act like soldiers! What is wrong with you?"

Two of the nearby prisoners, now without their armor, were stumbling. His own prisoner in his grip turned and vomited. "Hear that?" he screamed between wretches.

"Yes, but. . . no," Brigid said. The higher order of his brain didn't know what he meant. But his frantic subconscious did. "I feel it."

"Sonic weapon!" The prisoner shouted. He fell, and drug Brigid down with him. That small toss to the ground revealed how unstable Brigid was on his feet. His equilibrium shot through with that same terrible harmonic. Then his stomach seized. He began to vomit as well.

From the rapidly approaching 20de9 horde, brilliantly piercing flashes of blue lights cascaded at him. They tracked along his eyeballs, blinding him. "What?" Brigid rolled away from the enemy. Turned his back. So foolish and he knew it.

"Crowd control lighting," the prisoner said as he coughed and hacked. "All of it. Disorient— disorientating. Disabling. But we have to—"

Machine guns unzipped across the field. Kicking up straight lines of impacts in the soil, laser line straight. One passed right through Brigid's prisoner and the man didn't have to worry about throwing up anymore.

Brigid stood. Saw the slaughter. Jumped out of the way of another incoming line of fire and rolled. A transport ship exploded in a curling burst of flame. Two other transports swung their defense cannons towards the mass and opened fire. Explosions blew apart their undulating formation and luckily a few of the drones fell from the sky, spitting smoke and fire. Dead.

Men started shooting from the ground and Brigid saw the things rearrange themselves with lightning speed. Opening geometric holes and pathways in their body formations to allow the rounds to pass through harmlessly. Then they would swing laser beams across wherever the muzzle flashes were. Men fell in pieces.

Brigid looked around, sneaking glimpses from where he crowded up into. The drones were learning as they took fire. What their current enemy fought with. Anything smaller than a ship's cannon was useless spittle. All it did was draw attention to get killed.

"We need bigger weapons," he said. "Or we're all dead."

He ducked down, fighting the intense illness. Called for air support from the atmosphere. Lasers flashed everywhere and he saw man after man fall into smoking pieces. The smell of sickness cloyed from all around. Intense blue strobes reflected off whatever surface they found, multiplying the disorienting effect by magnitudes.

By the time he heard the first atmo-to-surface munition strike, the officer who would become Commander Brigid was curled up in the fetal position, surrounded and half buried by scrap and the dead, so consumed with the way his body was twisted from the induced, vile feebleness, that he barely heard the deafening explosion.

And then it rained in megaton blasts, but his ears were closed to their thunderous noise.

Smoke, Teeth and Magnets

Saint Jude, patron of lost causes, pray for us Commander Brigid sends the message across their Visuals and throws three more smoke grenades. They forcefully spew a growing cloud even before they hit the ground, immersing everything in pea soup fog.

The ZZH react, open fire. The Knights scatter, futile rounds sparking off their armor as the entire section of manufacturing filled with a thick dirty white smoke.

Through the cloud a fantastic ring blast comes punching out. A vicious sound wave forming the smoke into its own image as it rockets forth from the 20de9. It strikes the far wall behind them, shattering it into rock rubble.

"Unload into that thing!" Brigid shouts. The Knights can't see through the smoke, but small flashes of muzzle fire make darker parts into lighter ones like lightning traveling through storm clouds. They zero in on those and fire. A weak laser cuts out of the smoke and swipes, but the drone doesn't have enough ambient light to work with and the laser is weak.

"Commander, my suit is picking up some kind of audible weapon," Brother Nonnatus says as he moves towards the machinery line.

"Probably a sonic weapon. Unshielded ears get it pretty bad. Headache, nausea, the whole bit."

"Copy. I think it's affecting the ZZH—" Nonnatus sees a massive dark shape shift in the cloud and then lunge forward from it. He pumps an RPG at the drone as it bursts from the thicker smoke at him.

The RPG whistles toward the 20de9. The drone unfolds itself, allowing a hole to appear in its body where the explosive is about to strike. It passes through the drone harmlessly. Explodes on the other side.

"Not good," Nonnatus says as he vaults over a shorter section of machinery and changes direction.

Brother Santa Cruz moves into the smoke. It wraps around him, coiling about all his armor. Secondary firearm slung at his side, he withdraws his TechHaft and sets it to imitate a spring-loaded dagger.

Flowing through the blinding cloud, his sensor array picks up on where the ZZH have planted themselves, continuing to fire. He saw three of them carrying much larger weapons than what the Knights have encountered so far. Heavy enough to damage their armor.

He slides up to the first soldier, fumbling with a tripod on which to set the larger gun. He tags the soldier with the dagger, a flash of energy and the soldier falls. No sound. A second soldier is moving towards them with the gun itself. A flash and he's harmless. Larger gun in one hand, Santa Cruz detects three other soldiers trying to get out of the cloud with no luck. One is fanning the air about him, the other two keeping low.

Brigid stands on the edge of the smoke, firing at the drone. From his side, he sees three quick flashes of energy. Santa Cruz emerges with a heavy crew-served machine gun in one hand.

"Thought we could try this."

"Probably should."

The smoke wafts their way, much thinner than the impenetrable cloud from before. Santa Cruz jumps on top of the nearest machine. Shoulder mounts the gun and draws a bead on the drone, chasing Nonnatus and swinging a laser all around him. Nonnatus is ducking and weaving, then leaps to a short platform before jumping over into the grinder's hopper.

Santa Cruz opens fire with the gun, riddling the drone from behind. Its onyx skin ripples with impacts for just a moment, then reconfigures and begins reacting instantaneously by opening holes to allow the rounds to pass through.

It sweeps a laser at Santa Cruz, who drops as it careens overhead. It sizzles as it swipes through the smoke. He can feel a searing heat along the very top of his helmet. He rolls off to the side as his suit reports back he took a millimeter deep wound. Much more and someone else will have to man the gun.

Nonnatus pops out of the hopper long enough to fire another RPG. It strikes directly in front of the drone instead of aiming for it. The explosion causes it to unfold itself outward like fluttering open a bed sheet. Distributing the force. It fires back with a sonic ring. Nonnatus grabs the edge of the hopper and swings out on the other side as the ring hits. The metal is extremely thick to handle boulders of ore and ferrous metals. It bellows out with a low note.

Obscured by the drifting smoke screen, Nonnatus keeps low and moves back around to where the Knights were before.

The 20de9 swoops up in the air and comes down into the hopper, swirls inside it like a snake searching for warmth. At the bottom are two hardened steel rollers, each studded with interlocking teeth. The gap between them is just enough for pebbles and powder to seep through. The drone sends feelers inside it, checking for remains of its enemy.

Brigid lunges at a control panel with a disconnect switch in the OFF position. He throws it on and the grinder, as manual and robust as they come, turns on.

The steel rollers both turn inward. Snag the 20de9 and drag it down. It begins to try and reconfigure but the rollers' teeth and the tiny gap do their work. Nonnatus pops up on the other side of the machine, fires another RPG directly at the drone.

Its reaction to the explosion causes it to unfold again, giving that much more of itself to the grinder. The Knights watch as the drone fights against an unrelenting tug downward, pulling itself towards the ceiling as the massive machine eats.

The drone extends what might be an arm, some kind of insectile protuberance. The end flares to life in a dazzling dot of red. It starts to fire its cutting torch, and the Knights can see through the outside of the hopper as a straight line melts out through the inside.

Then the line begins to carve off to the side, zigging this way. Descending down towards the teeth, zagging that way. All at once it cuts off and the glowing hot burn line radiates heat and drizzles of smoke as the grinder devours.

"Nonnatus, keep a lookout," Brigid says. "Santa Cruz, check the other soldiers for those friendly devices." Brigid looks around. Makes a head count as the clearing smoke reveals Santa Cruz's handiwork. "Where'd that other soldier go?"

†

Brennan's rifle is slung around his chest. When the smoke hit, his eyes watered and his lungs burned. What a combination to be hit with, fire and water. Like some great Tao duality, he suffered both at once.

All the shots rang out but even then, he was already flailing blind and panicked. Slinging his weapon to him, he cinched the strap tight and moved off to the one thing he knew would stop the bullets: the machinery directly to his side.

Under the constant cavalcade of gunfire and whatever that dreaded combat drone was firing, he moved until he ran dead-on into the machine. He clambered up it, and then over. Shielded from the worst of the smoke, he let his eyes clear enough to see he'd escaped, if only by a few meters.

He found the conveyor belt—really it was two stacked on top of one another, running parallel until one took a sharp turn—and was crawling through. Then a massive engine coughed to life.

Brennan could hear the grinding wheels on the machine start turning, anyone could recognize that sound, and then a strange thing happened. His rifle snapped against one of the belts. It wouldn't let go. And worse yet, it was moving. Whatever turned on the grinder has turned on the production line, and he is caught in it.

"What is this, a magnet or something?" He struggles with it. Pulled so taut that the sling is cinched, tight as a constrictor knot. He struggles in sheer fear. The gunfight has died off. He can hear the Knights clanking around in their armor, speaking to one another. The shrieking pleas of that drone, squealing like a pig. Brennen can see from where he's at as the drone is being drawn down into the belly of this processing machine.

His rifle stuck. Him, nearly strangled inside its sling. He stifles a warbling scream. He grabs a knife to cut it and looks over once more. And he really does scream.

†

"Magnetized to the ferrous ore belt?" Brother Santa Cruz asks as he comes over to the ZZH soldier, who is nearly in shock from his panic. Santa Cruz's Visuals scans the soldier and reports back his elevated heart rate, lowered O2 levels from fast, shallow breathing. Core body temp is up. His rifle is strapped to his chest, and that is frozen to the production line belt. The conveyor is traveling at a slow pace towards the smelter, something Brother Nonnatus has already declared inoperable.

The soldier flails about at Santa Cruz. Screams, spittle at his mouth. He kicks and the Knight moves out of the way.

Santa Cruz can't help but laugh. Holds up a hand. "I'll help you, but you need to calm down. Don't try and kill me, got it?"

"What do you have over there?" Commander Brigid asks.

"That other ZZH soldier you were looking for. His gun is magnetized to the conveyor here."

"He's stuck?"

"Yes, sir."

"He needs to tell us where the archbishop is," Brigid says as he comes over. He points a finger, "You're coming with us."

†

Brother Nonnatus stands at the beginning of the belt, knowing Brother Gonzaga and more ZZH are out there. Gun up, he turns in circles, checking the area. No way anybody missed that gunfight.

He turns away from the discharge of the grinder. Listens for anything at the door they entered through, or now, through the hole the 20de9's sonic ring blew in the wall.

From the discharge comes a wire-thin stream of straight black cubism, extending out like a never-ending nightmare. It bends once, a perfect ninety degrees upwards, then again as it turns forward. Two more lines appear, then six. Then the entire discharge is filled with a thousand lines all no more in diameter than a pen. They begin segmenting into cubes the size of sand grains, frictionlessly sliding along each other, merging, forming new geometric patterns.

A small ring appears just under the skin's surface, begins pulsating. Two horns extend out underneath, start chattering against one another like clicking pincers.

"That sounds... unnerving," Nonnatus says. It dawns on him and he turns just as a sonic ring blasts forth. Hits him square in the chest. He goes flying down the length of the conveyor.

Brother Santa Cruz hears the strike, spins from the ZZH soldier and sees Nonnatus flying his direction. Santa Cruz braces, takes the brunt of Nonnatus hurling into him. "Commander, it's back!"

Brigid appears from around the corner, weapon up. He begins firing into the drone as it reconstitutes itself. It hits him with a sonic ring, and he collapses off the far end of the machine. It starts flashing its blue lights. The soldier starts hollering. Santa Cruz turns, grabs at the soldier's tac vest. Digs out the friendly device and tosses it to Nonnatus.

168

"Get to the other guys! Get theirs and come back for us!"

Nonnatus stands up as rough as he feels, nods and limps over the machine. Santa Cruz grabs the soldier's gun, yanks on it. It breaks, and then he pulls the strap free. "Stick with me, I'll keep you safe."

The soldier, eyes wide and lips trembling, says, "A Knight 1513? You're insane! I've heard about you! Loognar told us all about how you— you'll do worse than kill me! Get away!"

"No—" Sant Cruz gets hit in the back by the drone's weaponry. He goes flying, his suit screaming alarms. The soldier turns one way, then the other. Starts to run.

†

Brennan gets a sudden pain in his jaw. His eyes, wet from tears after the smoke, start seeing double. He tries to run but his body's center of gravity rolls, despite what his feet are doing. Doesn't line up. His stomach seizes and he vomits.

Falls over. He scrambles along the stone floor, looking for somewhere to hide. This isn't what he was promised at all. This isn't what—

A sonic ring hits him full on and tears a chunk out of the floor where he is. He gets it worse.

†

"Eternal rest gra—" Brother Santa Cruz sees the soldier's lightning quick end and starts to move as a laser sweeps past him. He dives under a small platform on the machine, watches as the laser slices cleanly through the metal around him. He rolls and fires a single mortar at the drone.

It reconfigures its body to avoid the worst of the explosion, then shifts off to its side as it brings its weapons back around to Santa Cruz.

"Other side!" Commander Brigid shouts as he comes leaping through the air over the machine. His TechHaft ignited, a tremendous Merovingian axe sculpted in brilliant energy. Held in two hands, arms over his head, he comes down on the 20de9 and swings with all his might.

The blade cleaves into the drone's front—what must pass as its head. The axe drives deep and the drone malfunctions for just a moment.

Santa Cruz scrambles up to his feet and climbs over the grinder machine. Sees Nonnatus with two more friendly devices in his hand. He tosses one to Santa Cruz. Brigid comes hurling over the machine, runs to them.

"It's mad."

Nonnatus gives him a device and the drone slithers in its perfectly smooth way over the machine. Santa Cruz gets his rail gun and they are essentially where they were when the fight began as the 20de9 comes down.

And six more ZZH soldiers come around the corner. They line up, also with a tripod-mounted crew-served machine gun. "Knights," one of them says.

"You the squad leader?" Brigid asks.

"That I am. This is quite a mess."

"For the record, we just wanted to sneak in and out."

The squad leader hefts his gun, "You snuck in, sure. You'll be leaving in a wet bag."

†

Charge that thing up to 100, Commander Brigid sends as a message to Brother Santa Cruz's Visuals. It scrolls along the bottom of the visor's view, and Santa Cruz's thumb covertly moves along the rail gun to the settings. *Hit that thing right in the face with it. It's our only chance.*

As Brigid watches the number readout on the settings speed up to one hundred, he says, "Well, gentlemen. You have us backed into a corner. Can we negotiate?"

The lead soldier snickers. "Our leader is already negotiating with your heretic movement. He's not happy."

"What about us, though? Just the few of us here?"

The leader turns and looks at the pile of bodies from earlier. "The work of the devil himself." He turns back to Brigid. "Not a fan of anything you've done here."

They all make a show of readying their guns at the Knights. The tripod crew bring their gun up, pull the charging handle. The squad leader asks, "Which of you did that?"

"Me," Santa Cruz says and fires the rail gun.

A fantastic blue film of light emerges from the barrel to the 20de9, and it explodes in a gnarly burst of black shards. The ZZH soldiers collapse with it, engulfed by the violence.

The Knights dodge off to their sides, brutally pelted by the ruins of the 20de9. After the detritus finishes raining down, they scan the area. Brigid clears his throat, says, "We need to move before another six of these guys magically comes around the same corner again."

"I second that," Brother Nonnatus says.

"Commander?" a voice from the other side of the sonic ring's hole in the wall behind them. The Knights turn, see a familiar man in white and red armor pushing through the crumbled stone.

"Brother Gonzaga?"

"Yes. I, uh. . . got one of those things you were talking about." He holds up the friendly device. "In case we need it. Right?"

"Took you long enough." Santa Cruz says.

Gonzaga looks around at the ridiculous destruction in the room. The ZZH, the smoking hulk of the 20de9. Shards of it embedded everywhere. The damage to their armor. Santa Cruz's rail gun, red hot with a swollen capacitor. He points to it, says, "Why is it like that?"

Santa Cruz looks down and sees the thing, distorted and shimmering with heat. "Ah, yes." He ejects it and it falls on the floor. He nudges it off to the side with his boot. "Spent. Damaged, too."

The capacitor explodes with a percussive *pop!* and the Knights all instinctively jolt. Brigid wags a finger at Santa Cruz. Then he simply says, "Move out," and they head towards the door where the 20de9 first attacked them.

A Gnat on Animal Hide

The surface of Stake is as silent and gray as it ever was in Brother Cleopas's excited, frightened memory. The black vastness of space extends in every direction as if he was at the bottom of an ocean. The floating sprinkles of sediment are stars. The Herculean globe of Asperity forever cresting on the near horizon, its swirling storm systems and clouds the size of continents so awe-inspiring that he forgets to breathe.

"Thank God, for Your majesty right there. Who can doubt You? Ever?"

Cleopas stays low, scanning. The surface is not as jagged as his childhood memory remembers. Exaggerated hills and slopes in a child's fantastic mind turn to mountains and gulleys fit for a lifetime's worth of adventures. Now, just gentle features. The still dust and small pebbles, coating everywhere. He swipes a handful up off the surface and watches it hover and spread so thin in the weak surface gravity. Still directly above EcoPassage3 and it is down tuned to a half g. It becomes a fine mist as the heavy bits sink. Much of the rest glitters in starlight and disperses. *I did that so often as a kid.*

And near enough is a single grid cannon, motionless like an immortal sentry standing guard. Waiting, decades as mere moments in its vast memory. The cannon sheds a shadow off to Cleopas's side. He turns to the MedSled and finds the control on the touch pad to dial back its luminosity. Best not to move with a brightly lit machine giving him away. Then to the shadow's deep and dark line. He sprints over to it, hoping the cannon doesn't detect his motion so near the surface. The MedSled follows him. Silently hovering.

He falls into the shadow and takes cover behind a rocky outcropping. Looks over it to the grid cannon, expecting it to swivel suddenly and aim its large-bore muzzle right at his forehead. He slaps himself on the helmet, chastising. He can hear Commander

Brigid's voice in his mind telling him to slow down his racing heart. His imagination. The gulf of years since he'd been here last has been showing in his self-reflection ever since he set foot back on his old home, and now is no different. He prays to his patron saint to intercede for him. The angels. Jesus to lay His calming hand upon him.

It won't shoot at me. There's got to be some kind of safety on these things, he thinks to himself. *Keep them from shooting too low and blowing a hole in Stake. That's not good protection otherwise.*

He makes the Sign of the Cross over himself and stands. Walks toward the cannon and it doesn't detect him. The MedSled behind him, they cross the distance and reach the foot of it. Ten meters tall, five wide. Metal treated with some kind of coating that was designed to survive long periods of exposure to space, now somewhere near thirty years old at least and sandpapered by micro impacts and waves of dust, lost to memory of the void.

He traipses around it and finds an access hatch labeled maintenance in several languages. All of them faded, chipped. Attacked by erosion where there doesn't seem to be anything that could erode. He kneels and has to use his suit's strength enhancements to force open the covering. Inside, a small cubby he can reach a single arm into. Maybe his other one if he wasn't in his bulky armor. A few electronic devices and wires. And a cheap but durable handheld device with an unplugged cable. He takes it and plugs it into the first porthole he sees. Presses a button. Nothing. Nothing from any button, or any porthole. He sets the handheld aside and examines inside the small open area.

His Visuals outlines the cubby in translucent lines, decoding and deciphering its make-up in real time. Figuring out how to disable the thing. He gets a communication scrolling along the bottom of his visor to hold while it processes.

He turns to the MedSled, sees that even though the Mariol woman is still as death, she is alive. Struggling, running out of time. Her vitals are low. Sedated, pain killers numbing her. But she needs real medicine. Real attention.

His Visuals come back with three different potential solutions. He turns back inside, allows his system time to re-overlay its diagram and it goes to work. The first solution is to use the dead handheld device. With an eye flicker he commands the Visuals to mark it off. The second solution requires a newer version of the model of electronics inside. What's inside is so out of date that it does not possess the software needed to make the changes he must.

Eye flicker. Crossed off.

The third solution presents itself. Last, simply because it's destructive. "I could have thought of that," he says. Loosen a particular screw, remove the live wire it's holding on to and touch it to another terminal whose wire doesn't want any company. Short out the guidance system. He smiles and clasps his hands, "I praise You, my God. Who art all good and deserving of all my love." He pulls out a small kit from a compartment on his armor and opens it. Inside, his newly acquired precision screwdriver.

Cleopas shuffles through Santa Cruz's precision tools. "This one is better than mine. I'm jealous."

"Jealousy is a sin."

"So is stealing," Cleopas says while sliding the precision tool in his pocket. "Those always come in handy."

"Comes in handy, indeed." He says to his memory from earlier. He uses it to remove the live wire, then touches it to the other terminal. A spark, a thin hiss of smoke. Shorts out the guidance system. Red warning lights come on in the cubby's electronics and Cleopas smiles. A digital readout inside it begins flashing with the word *fault*. "Who says Divine Providence isn't a real thing?"

He leans back, activates his comms. "*Saint Eligius*, come in, Unit 4 hailing. Come in, *Saint Eligius,* over."

"Come back, Unit 4, *Saint Eligius* responding, over." The scratchy voice of the ship's captain comes back.

"4, *SE.* Homing signal sent, ready for medical emergency evac, over."

"*SE, 4.* Homing signal pinpointed, en route. ETA, two mikes. Out."

Cleopas shuts the hatch and waits in the deepening shadow of the grid cannon. He looks to the MedSled and prays in thanksgiving to the Living God who has blessed him this far.

†

The surface breech hatch that sealed in EcoPassge3 from the outer passageway remains steadfastly in place. Loss of atmosphere can and will kill the living quarters in Stake, and its systems, though old, are dumb and robust. Nothing complicated. Complicated systems fail, especially when they're old.

Dumb and robust. Those don't need second chances.

The internal alarm about the breech was new. Unique. Worrisome. It deserved investigating, especially now that the hatch was not closed, but rather the environmental seal was in place.

A small and perfect square in the corner of the breech hatch burns to life. Maybe fifty millimeters on each side. Maybe. Sizzling from the passageway side. The light drawing into it a pale orange, blossoming into a vibrant red and finally a penetrating yellow.

The metal square falls inside. Instantly a perfectly formed black cube, featureless and glisteningly onyx fills the blisteringly hot hole. The 20de9 slides inside. An impossibly long, squared-off tube inserting into the EcoPassage as if it was a solid piece of metal being driven in by a piston. As it reaches the end of its formation, it unfolds a needle-thin armature that picks up the laser-cut square and puts it back against the door. Another armature tacks it back in place with a several lightning-fast blips of weld.

The javelin of cube begins to shuffle, reassemble. Becomes a thick swarm of barely connected boxes inside the rough terrain. Sweeping around dead insectile things. Bodies of friendlies. Under and over damaged crystalline obstructions.

Ahead it can see a shaft of starlight innocently splaying down into the cavern.

†

"*Saint Eligius,* Unit 4, confirm it's safe to make our final approach, over."

"4, *SE*, safe to approach is confirmed, over."

"*SE,* 4. Copy that. Making our final approach. Out."

Brother Cleopas looks out into the stars and watches for the black-as-the-void ship to approach. He doubts either his eyes or his Visuals will detect it before its right on him; it's not much of a stealth ship if he can see it easily.

The MedSled's control screen flashes a new warning. The Mariol woman's heart rate has sunk again from an already too-low rate. It pumps her with more fluids, an inert mixture to try and keep her veins full and her circulatory system away from that all-too-close precipice of death. Cleopas taps the screen, tries to make sense of the worsening situation.

"Lord, give us just a few minutes more, please. I beg of You."

Something catches the corner of his eye, and he looks up. The ship? So close to the surface already?

He sees something wiggling at the hole he breached into the surface. A caustic centipede, maybe. Huge for one, though. Too big. Detritus from the action below?

As he watches, a long, thick black shape, blacker than the space around it, rises. Under control of itself. Not floating aimlessly.

Squared off on every corner, featureless. A cube separates from its geometric body and shuffles. Rotates at an angle like a piece sliding along some three-dimensional puzzle. Then several more do the same. The entire thing, like a maze that rearranges itself. It folds, adjusts, slides in and slides out. All done under some intelligence Cleopas can recognize as such but not comprehend.

Like a caterpillar it rises out of the hole and lays down, unfolding different features and begins to move purposefully. So sleek and fluid it looks lazy, but with dawning dread, he knows it is not.

His gut takes over his thinking. That thing is patrolling. Lifeless, time has no bearing on it. It can outlast whatever it is searching for. And the search is all that matters. When it finds what it is searching for, that must be something else entirely.

His Visuals flash a combat warning. The bizarre creature is recognized in his system as a threat. A serious threat. He pulls back closer to the grid cannon, grabs the MedSled and pulls it hard. Tucks it in against the wall of the weapon.

"*Saint Eligius*, come in, Unit 4 hailing. Come in, *Saint Eligius*, over. Hurry."

"Unit 4, we're en route. ETA is fifteen seconds, over."

"SE, 4, beware. We've got company on the surface. My Visuals identify it as—"

The 20de9 spins. Instantly unfolds into a T shape and a single barrel extends from each cross arm. The muzzles glow hot in the frigid nothing about them, start tracking in the sky.

"Watch out!" Cleopas shouts as the 20de9 fires twin lasers. Long beams of heated red flash forth. He looks to where the beams slash high above. The *Saint Eligius* is there, so faint in its anti-detection coating and bizarre shape that it looks closer to a raindrop being smeared on a flat surface of the stars and black space.

Angry red lines tattooed on its skin, radiating heat. It maneuvers evasively. Spins. Barrel rolls. Fires back with two light machine guns.

Cleopas looks to the drone and sees it change its configuration in the blink of an eye. Turns itself into a webwork of holes more akin to a sponge than a robot. The rounds pass through these custom openings and dapple the surface of the asteroid. It fires those deep crimson lasers again.

"4, SE, come in!" The pilot's voice bellows over Cleopas's comms.

"Yeah, go," he says. Ducking behind the grid cannon, peeking over to see the 20de9 slithering, changing shape in a series of constantly undulating cubes. A thousand minds calculating a thousand different tactics to better position itself. Pouring itself out in solid blocks, flowing over each other and climbing towers of its old structure, each cube moving after it's been trodden over.

"Can you provide support?" the pilot asks. "We're not a combat vessel. We've got a few missiles and these guns it's dodging."

Cleopas takes stock of himself. If those shipboard munitions aren't doing the job, nothing he has will work any better. He looks up at the grid cannon, down at the surface.

"I've got this cannon here."

"Will that shoot a—" the pilot breaks off with a shout as the ship does another maneuver to dodge strafing lasers. "A hole in the asteroid?"

"Not necessarily," Cleopas says as he stares at the horizon. "I just have to aim it right."

"Well, aim it right, then. Because we're dead out here."

"Can you lead it away from me? Far away? Then double back faster than it can move?"

"I'll try," the pilot says. He races off along the surface of the asteroid and the drone refolds into a long tube. Charges after the ship. Cleopas watches the *Saint Eligius* try out his idea. No matter where it flies, near enough to Stake the combat drone seamlessly keeps up.

From the rear of the 20de9 a single stack of cubes mounds, and on its tip a weapon appears. Fires again. The *Saint Eligius* gets hit as it barrel rolls off to their starboard side, dives under the curvature of the asteroid.

"4, SE, no can do. Seems if I'm within a certain distance from the surface, it's going to track us and open fire."

Cleopas opens the cubby back up, leans in. "Roger, go ahead and get to where its safe for you. I'll let you know what I figure." He turns back and sees the Mariol woman, every second ticking off her life. The *Saint Eligius* banks hard and drops below the horizon.

He activates his Visuals again to try different parameters. Maybe something he missed last time. He turns off his mic, talks to himself. "Let's see, I fried out the targeting system, but if I. . . oh, maybe I can get the sights to work manually."

His Visuals re-examines the cubby's electronics. As it figures on what it can recommend, Cleopas takes a small wireless dongle from his suit's manual interface compartment and snaps it into a communications block on the cannon. On the inside of his left forearm a pad opens up, complete with touch screen and keyboard. The dongle makes good contact with the brains of the cannon.

"I praise You, Lord, for that. Please keep those little miracles coming." One hand reaches to the Rosary he has painted on his armor. A finger finds a bead and he begins praying as he works.

A warning pops up on his screen stating the cannon's auto-targeting system is off-line. Damaged. "Yes, I know." He says, flicking away the digital warning ribbon. "I smoked you out a minute ago."

He scrolls through a few directories and stumbles across a help menu. He opens it and there is a query tab. He starts to type and looks up. Sees the 20de9 come floating back, refolded and continuing its patrol as if nothing just happened.

"That thing is psychotic," Cleopas says. He stays down as much as he can and finishes his query. In response to *manual targeting*, the interface comes up with several topics. He sees one that looks promising and selects it. "Lord, guide my efforts."

A to-do list unspools, and he reads through it, smiles. Crosses himself. He stands up and peeks around the corner of the cannon, sees a high point a few clicks off. He drops a marker to it in his Visuals and sends the coordinates to the *Saint Eligius*. "Can you guys lead the drone to this point?"

"We've got maybe five minutes to give you before we can't make it back to the rendezvous." The pilot says. "Whatever it was firing has torn through our ship."

"It'll be tight, but it should work."

"Roger then, we'll lead it there, but we can't stay put for it to kill us."

"I wouldn't ask that."

"En route."

Cleopas looks back to his forearm interface, then into the cubby. He removes his precision screwdriver again and uses it to dismantle a small plastic covering over a side of an electronic device. It pops off and he sees three more comms ports for the handheld device in the cubby. He grabs it, following directions and plugs it in. The handheld comes online, and he starts to use a joystick to manually adjust the cannon's massive barrel.

Latitude and longitude coordinates begin to roll up and down on the handheld's small screen as he thumbs the weapon around. The 20de9 detects the cannon movements and comes up on point, weapons unfolding. It fires a split second of blast at the muzzle as the *Saint Eligius* crests the side of Stake near them, blowing into view and startling both Knight and drone. The ship banks hard and swivels. It races towards the peak, and the 20de9 follows.

Cleopas looks up at the grid cannon. The blink of an eye laser blast the drone fired severed the muzzle from the cannon. The angled slice is still glowing red from the heat of it. "Mother Mary, pray for us that this still works. No going back now," Cleopas mutters and continues to train the weapon on the site.

The ship and drone are moving fast, too fast for Cleopas. "Can you make a couple of swoops or something?" he asks. "You're faster than the cannon is."

"Those things were lightning fast when they shot at you earlier."

"That was auto control. This is manual. It's speed-governed or something."

"We don't have much—" the drone fires something else at them, no laser line this time, and the ship takes the brunt full-bore. It drops terribly in the starboard aft quarter, then raises back up. "Hang on," The pilot says.

The *Saint Eligius* fires its cluttering package. Designed to bombard and overload enemy tracking systems with light and noise, the package is like an explosion of blinding, deafening confusion. A literal box punches out the nose of the ship in the drone's direction. With a dazzlingly brilliant display of flare-like light, it explodes. Cleopas's Visuals react with throwing a shade over his visor to defend against the radiant burst.

Metallic streamers flutter. Even Cleopas's comms system is overloaded with incredible white noise and hissing. His ears hurt and he screams as the sounds dig into his brain. His suit reacts, but it is a split second behind.

His armor administers a medicinal cocktail to fight off the worst of the effects. "Got to stay on task, here," he says. He thinks he hears the pilot apologize for unwittingly hitting him with it too, but his ears are ringing with deafness. He refocuses on the handheld device, canting the cannon into target.

The drone seems to be stifled by the cluttering package. It momentarily unfolds into a flat, featureless disc. Cleopas sees it and thinks of a dance floor for some reason. Turns back to the handheld. The cannon is almost in place.

"Just a few more seconds," he says. He thinks he hears the pilot acknowledge and say something about leading the drone to the coordinates. Cleopas can't look at them and the handheld at the same time.

His eyes are doing better than his ears, and he sees another warning flash up on the MedSled. He can recognize it as another problem with the Mariol woman. He prays. The handheld has a small screen on it, and it shows a view through some sort of limited-range camera situated on top of the barrel itself.

"This is really, really manual." A small targeting reticule is drawn on the camera's view. The coordinate numbers run and finally hit where he wants it to be. He can see the rocky features of the rise along the bottom of the view. Space beyond.

"Ready," he shouts just to hear himself.

"Almost. . ." the pilot says, and Cleopas hears him more clearly through his ringing. He sees the *Saint Eligius* zip across the camera's view and the blackness of the drone enters it. He slams his thumb on a flashing red button on the handheld and the grid cannon shudders as it fires through its laser-cut barrel.

The drone evaporates from the screen as the cannon fire drives into it. Flicking a gnat off an animal hide, skinning the surface of Stake. The top layer of sediment of the asteroid underneath the combat drone is charred and hurling dust clouds in the rooster tail of the cannon fire. A puff of dirt flinging off into the cosmos, following the trajectory of the blast.

Cleopas drops the handheld, says, "Got it. Come get her, would you?"

"4, SE, en route. Thanks for saving us."

CARL MICHAEL CURTIS

"All praise and glory to God, my friend. But you're welcome."

For the Sake of All of Us

"Well, Bishop Tauthail, this is quite disappointing, but to be expected from all parties," Loognar says into his comms screen. He leans back and exhales slowly, running his fingers over his teeth as his eyes lose focus. Thinking.

"Then I will make good on everything I have promised you."

The bishop on the screen begins to speak and Loognar terminates the contact. A contact request comes through almost immediately, but Loognar ignores it. In a near zombified state, one arm reaches out to the cable plugged into the console. Unscrews it, drops it like trash. With the wire connection broken, the comms request disappears. With a blank void now where the negotiator was, Loognar simmers. Seeing his reflection looking back like some challenging bully, staring him down to do as swore.

Unblinking, he says to himself, "This is your cross, friend. Many of the people you've led have already lost their lives. Vengeance is God's alone, but it is through your bloody hands he shall have it."

He stands and rolls his head on his neck. "So be it."

He walks out from behind the desk he's commandeered—such a large thing in such a miniscule room—and takes up a control sitting on the end table near the door. He punches a code into its keypad, watches the small screen feed him back a list of numbers, then an error code.

He does the entire process over again, only to receive the error code again. He huffs, drops the control. "They're on Stake," he says. Surprised but not surprised. "And now I can't even adjust the GravCore. Damn them."

He stands for a moment in silence. Bows is head and prays. When he is done, he says, "My hand has been forced. This is God's will." He walks around the desk, careful to step over the severed Mormon's head still discarded on the floor. Sits back down at his desk and records a monologue on video. Transmits it and steps outside the office.

†

"Our Savior sacrificed Himself for us," Loognar says as he walks over to a medpod wherein the strapped-down archbishop lies. "And so shall you. The grand gift of His body, given up. He said so Himself. A sacrifice. I've done it, and I want nothing more than to bestow upon you the opportunity to actually be Christlike. Isn't it incredible?"

The room is small cafeteria, brightly lit by the windows to the outside. The few benches and tables have been folded up and stuffed into a corner. The archbishop, supine on his back, tied down, stripped of his cassock. Hunger and thirst have set in, with the amount of time since his kidnapping. He's begun to measure his captivity by the stickiness in his mouth that has now reduced to dryness.

"If He asks me to be martyred for Him, I will be so honored."

Loognar snickers. "I expect to hear this from you, a pious fool."

"We're to be fools for Christ, are we not?"

"What good shall it do with the wrong theology?" Loognar sits down near the archbishop's head. Takes a drink from his glass. "Do not the Phytom peoples from Wet Rock think they are pious for sacrificing themselves in droves on their holy days? That is foolish, and that is for their god. But it is useless."

"Our missionaries have shown many of them the truth—"

"Your missionaries sell them a better lie than what they're living with already. Not hard."

"And the ZZH is preferable still? To Catholicism?"

"How could it not be?" Loognar lights a cigar. Blows the smoke on the archbishop. "We have the fullness of revealed truth." He smiles grandly as if he has some great secret. "You should know this. You've flown so close to the sun of our belief. Just realize it. In his first letter to the Corinthians, Saint Paul states that until Christ returns, we are bound to see truth in a way that is incomplete, a mere reflection, as in a mirror, dimly. We are simply given a slight bit more light than you. That is how I know."

"What you mistake for Christ's light is nothing more than the fervent heat of pride."

"Unsustainable."

Archbishop Hrutt narrows his eyes. "Why would a god worth worshipping wait two and a half millennia before revealing the rest of his truth? You think Jesus, in the first century, was paving the way for technology that wouldn't arrive for all that time?"

"Yes. Of course He was."

"Why would God design man, call him very good, but still intend on him needing false organs and hormones to change his very creation into what that creation desires?"

"I will not answer for God. He will tell you. You might hear His voice following you down into the pits, but you will know."

"Never. My God did not make man and woman so they may be woman and man whenever they so feel. Your doctrine is one of confusion and immorality."

"Immorality?"

"How many people abandon your faith?"

"Less than abandon yours."

The archbishop scoffs. "Ours is tremendous. Yours is niche. At best. If there are a hundred million Catholics spanning across the galaxies, there are but a hundred thousand ZZH. And how many of those will leave every year? Let alone die due to your procedures?"

"We are constantly gaining new parishioners. We convert—"

"You gain embryos by the truckload and force them in. Ruining their genetic make-up from the get-go. They have no say in the matter; it's worse than brainwashing. It's a maliciously impressive leash you put on somebody when your religion reprograms their body and then threatens to withhold the constant and lifelong medical help they'll need if they abscond. Chained by DNA."

"They know the situation when they take their vows."

"Catholics are free to leave the faith and suffer no consequences from us. Their logic and reason may fail them, but our teachings do not."

Loognar leans forward and rests an arm on the glass over Hrutt's head. Places his chin on his forearm and exhales long and tired. "You're not stupid. Why do you deny the Biblical teaching we have embraced?"

"There is no such thing as a Biblical teaching to mock God's design."

"All throughout the Bible, there are passages that support our doctrine."

"Your retranslation? I know all you've distorted in order to justify your—"

"In Genesis, when God makes creation, does he only make the day and night? A zero and a one? Is there no dusk or dawn? No gradation at all? How about the land and the sea without reference to the wet, shifting shores, marshes, swamps? Sun and moon without regard to all the other celestial imaginings? How are there only two states? A binary? Are there not shifts between as part of the natural process? We must infer from this a spectrum of—"

"A false comparison and intellectual lie."

"With all the shades and subtle differences of humanity, how can they fit so neatly into binary terms? A blonde in a culture composed of black-haired folk? Blue eyes on a brown eyed continent? God loves variety. We are so unique, so incomparably unique, that to allow oneself to move fluidly through any definition into a whole person is nothing but fulfilment. A box was not meant to remain a closed container. Open it to see why it is there to begin with."

"The sun and moon, land and sea. None of it are made in the image and likeness of God. Only we are. There is no comparison there. You cannot say that because mid-morning and swamps exist that God intended us to be fluid in our sexes."

"Let us not forget about the role of sin in darkening our intellects. God's design was with our theology in mind. Your theology comes along and pushes us down. Makes us look like we're the sinful ones. But your sin caused this binary lie."

"God makes no mistakes. He made us complimentary in nature to mimic the Trinity. To be like Himself the best we can. One man, one woman, united in life-giving love to produce a child. Your way sterilizes more of your people than it does create life. The ZZH birth rates are extremely low because of your laboratory inventions, and you rely on conversions—"

"—they come to us in droves to be converted to the truth—"

"You grossly exaggerate. There are no *droves* of adult converts. Only a few lost and hopeless souls you take advantage of, to run through your rigamarole of excruciating hormonal treatments, organ replacement just to—"

"I see now why you're so obstinate in your denial of faith and truth." Loognar reaches to the medpod's touchpad and types in a sequence of commands. Inside, devices begin to whir to life. The archbishop flinches as a small articulated arm starts an IV on him.

Loognar takes a drink from his glass and says, "Deuteronomy 22:5 forbids crossdressing, but that is *crossing* genders and not *confirming* genders to oneself. This is one in a long list of things that, among other purposes, is to keep the binary roles distinct in such a rigorous culture. Woman cannot enter the temple, men cannot evade military service nor women should enter it, etc. Jesus did away with these. Why would Christ fulfill Moses's laws but allow this one to remain? Any "Christian" should answer that."

"How about proper worship, then? The duties befitting each sex as God designed them. He knew we were fallen, and men should protect women by entering the military, and fulfilling their drive as men to be protectors. Women need not be on the battlelines. Their cost is always greater than men's. And let's not fool ourselves into believing the ZZH fulfilled this Mosaic law. You distort it to justify your personal theology."

"Always with an answer, aren't you?" Loognar smiles, but it conceals deteriorating patience. "Numerous name changes occur in the Bible. This lends towards the affirmation of crossgender naming conventions."

"God changed their names in order to give that person a particular and powerful role in His work of revelation and salvation. Not to surreptitiously give a precedent for changing sexes."

"Yes, yes. I know. I know the Bible so well. From Abram, meaning *high father* when he was still childless to Abraham, meaning *father of multitudes*. Entering into covenant with God to have more descendants than there are stars in the sky. Jacob, meaning *supplanter* to Israel, meaning *God contends, fights* after he wrestled with an angel all night and through his progeny the Twelve Tribes of God's chosen people came."

"Simon to Peter, Saul to Paul. Sarai to Sarah. Our Lord gives new purpose, not new gender."

"Eunuchs were trans, or at least had the same experiences and therefore their distinctions become nearly moot. Deuteronomy 23:1 forbids a man whose testicles and/or penis that were destroyed to enter into the society, casting them out for this terrible accident. It is the first recorded bigotry towards us. Later, during the Babylonian and Assyrian conquering, two cultures who were more progressive in thought than Israel, they ordered eunuchs be made and allowed them to flow between binary positions. This is true egalitarianism as it allows them to be who they know they are."

"Matthew 19:12, Christ announces the three types of eunuchs: those by force and thus made eunuchs, those by intersex and thus born eunuchs, and those who do it for the Kingdom. And this is the voluntarily celibate. You know good and well in their time they castrated males to serve their female royalty without fear of rape or infidelities."

"And what of it?"

"Those born with a genetic defect are no less children of God. They're not automatically a sign of your religion. And Christ Himself was describing the celibate priesthood—"

"If you will not be convinced by God's word, what do I have for such a man? Surely you will ignore the lifestyle, then? How we are free to be fluid, to see experiences through the eyes of men and women. Have you never wondered about the glorious pain of childbirth? The matronly care of young, something masculinity by its nature does not feel so deeply?"

New sources of searing pain begin entering the archbishop's body. The medpod at work. Still, in the conversation, Hrutt is flabbergasted. "No. If I were to marry and we were blessed with children, I would know the masculine experience of protecting. Providing. My spouse may know the feel of a preborn child twirling in her womb, the birth, the beauty of nursing. Not me."

"I have successfully birthed two children as a woman."

Hrutt studies him for a moment. "Tell me, what were you born as?"

Loognar taps on the glass with a single finger. Smiling with his lips closed, almost ruminating on his younger days. "Female. Though most think I was male for some reason. Why do you ask?"

"Whenever I'm having a dialogue with a ZZH practitioner, I always just like to know. What was your birth name?"

"Amelia. And as a male I am Amit."

"I see. Tell me, why did you murder the Mormon but keep me alive?"

Loognar leans back from the glass. Runs a hand back along his hair from forehead to neck. "They were more of a test, really. Yes, of course I despise them, but we ZZH don't consider them Christian at all. They took the names from the Bible and made a new story, whole cloth. A complete reimagining. But somehow, they persist."

He leans forward, staring intently. "I do not care what their temple authorities think of us. But they're annoying on Xewl, and I needed to give my followers an exercise. Before that portion of our mission, they were strangers. Newly assembled. They had no camaraderie. They needed to go into battle together. To be *tested* as a team." He leans back and claps his hands. "And it worked out. The LDS is leaving Xewl."

"How did they not complain to the authorities? Run it up their ladder to their temple authorities?"

"Xewl doesn't care. Plain and simple. You know that."

"The secular authority is overburdened with day-to-day problems, yes. But to lose an entire segment of their population to your action of force—"

"ZZH were some of the original founders of Xewl," Loognar says. "We have, what would you call it? Precedent? We're given slack?"

"But us? Me?"

"You, I want to win over." He assumes a possessed look; eyes unblinking, burning from within, lips sealed over the tops of his teeth. Even the cords in his neck stand out. "I want you on my side. Catholicism's greatest evangelist against us, to be for us. Think of the sweep of influence. The conversions. The legitimacy. How far we can reach."

Hrutt shakes his head. "No." A small word in a quiet voice. But it obliterates with the power of the sun all that in Loognar's consuming stare.

Loognar's face goes blank. He sits back almost as if he was pushed in the chest. Places his hands together, trying to find something to do with them. Lets a minute pass.

Loognar leans back over, says, "I know of a concept you all have. A *hell shelf,* as it is sometimes called. For the scholarly, it means a bookshelf in your study where you keep the religious texts of other religions. The Gnostic gospels, the Quaran. The New World Translation of the holy scriptures. The Book of Mormon. Let alone the texts from all these other worlds we visit, their species and their religions. And our book.

"It must be a heavy shelf."

"You worship it." The archbishop says, and his voice sounds hollow through the glass.

"Only one tome on it. Where you have filed away God's Word with all that blasphemy." He lights a cigar and drags it until the cherry glows yellow, then uses it to point at the archbishop. "I knew from the beginning your Order would send a rescue. Of the two of us, *I'm* no fool. I'm sure you have men right now, combing Stake looking for you. Mercilessly slaughtering my soldiers as they find them. Serving Christ through bloodlust. I want that, you know. I fear, as an imperfect human, the Lord needs me to have it."

"Why want your own men to die? When I'm not even there?"

Loognar smiles viciously. "So, I may die a martyr for the truth, and you will live on as an example of it." He begins pushing buttons on the container's touchpad. "God asked Moses to sacrifice his own son for His sake. God sent his only begotten Son to die for the sake of all of us. And now, I'm asking you to live for the same reasons."

Even the Darkness

"Schematics say that's the back way," Commander Brigid says as he points to where the stairwell disappears into the ceiling.

A metal ladder—two strips of flat stock steel with rungs welded between them, scraps of grip tape wound around them and now worn down to ribbons—leads from the floor of the maintenance closet up into a circular hole above. The closet is little more than poured-in-place concrete with a single drainpipe extending floor to ceiling. Bits chipped out of the walls, leaving pockmarks. A few dark stains on the floor. Rust rings from buckets long gone stored inside. A single dirty rag tossed in the corner and forgotten when it was all said and done.

"That should lead to the morale center," Brigid motions to the hatch in the ceiling. He turns to Brother Santa Cruz, his point man. "Once we're up there, it's all train-car style. One compartment leads to the next in series. But, along the outside of them there is a passageway that runs the length of them, with a door into each. We can use it to skirt the whole thing and drive straight to the security office."

Brother Nonnatus nods. "And that's where they're hiding the archbishop?"

"Intel and Brother Cleopas's dad thinks so," Brigid says. "Built-in holding cells. Comms and security systems center. Mantrap on the outside, one way in. One way out. And it's within fifty meters of where they moored the Huskvar, albeit through an exterior wall, but maybe they made a hole somehow. It'll be a firefight. But, if we hit them hard and fast, we might be able to overwhelm them."

Santa Cruz puts one hand on the ladder. "Fatal funnel once we're through this. Train-car style can't be anything else."

"I know."

Santa Cruz doesn't wait for any pity. He doesn't want it. "Good thing my guardian angel goes before me in all things." He asks, "How many does that Huskvar seat? We've already hit how many of them?"

"Almost twenty now," Brother Gonzaga says. "And that's just us." He looks at his fellow Knights and says, "The rest have to know we're here. Especially after back in there."

Brigid nods. "I'm sure. So, we move fast."

"Roger," Santa Cruz says as he heaves up the ladder. His dead rail gun slung across his back; he leads with his small arms rifle.

Brother Nonnatus grits his teeth as he thinks it should be one of his drones first. An unnecessary risk as his brother goes blind into what might very well be a fatal funnel. Shredding him. They'd all know what is still left of the ZZH. Maybe not this one moment, but maybe the next. And the security office is no doubt some armored stronghold. A last stand. Their final pitfall. Not to mention an awaiting 20de9 drone.

"Clear," Santa Cruz says over the comms. Brigid goes up next, and fast.

They hold the dark space as the others join them. Fan out. Brigid sends a message via their Visuals reading *dance space and bar. Passageway to our left.*

Before them on their right is the blank remains of a large wooden bar top. Spots on the floor where stools were once mounted are now empty; chairs unbolted and taken somewhere to all their unknown futures. Garbage or repurposed, leaving only their circular imprints and anchoring bolts as traces of them ever being there to begin with.

The bar top is flat and long enough to seat ten people. Plundered of any drinkware or spirits. Even the taps are gone except for one which is obviously broken and laid over. A great stretch of mirror remains behind the mammoth slab of wood. Spiderweb-cracked and coated in dust. Someone has used their fingertip to scrawl *God's truth is transitionary* in the coated grit.

Twenty meters forward is the opposite wall, and if the schematics are to be believed somewhere in there is a door. That wall serves as the back wall for the next train car in the morale center. Above there used to be lights. Now just girders and conduit running to electrical boxes that stand empty. The floor in front of them is tiled, with a riser off towards the front on the opposite side of the bar. A few standing tables remain like giant mushrooms. Discarded for reasons only those packing up the shuttered mine know. One table—a circular top on a stylishly thin pedestal toppled over. The surface cracked like a fault line. Still in its center is an old candle sconce, missing its light source. Attached to the surface of the toppled furniture somehow.

Santa Cruz follows the rearmost wall, which has a door in it that leads from the mines or the earlier explored part of the settlement. It is composed of two sliding portions that retract into the walls surrounding them, their seam in the middle of the doorframe. It is welded shut running up and down. The ZZH did not use it.

The Knights move to their left, leaving the small maintenance closet in the dance floor to their right. Covering the dark room, a cavern in its own right. No movement. No sudden explosions. No assault.

"My scans have nothing," Gonzaga says in a hush. "No people, no traps."

"Tactics point to the passageway," Brigid says. "I want to check it out—much easier to clear than to keep going through big dark rooms with debris, oddly located doors. All that."

"Great place to get pinned down," Santa Cruz says as he reaches the corner of the far wall and the rearmost one. "Straight ahead on our left, correct, sir?"

"Correct."

"On it."

Santa Cruz flows forward, giving a hand signal and dropping a marker in their Visuals as he meets the steps to the dance floor riser which is a meter higher than the floor they were just traversing. He makes it to the door which should lead to the passageway beyond. A hall that runs the length of the morale center so they can skip the boxcar-style strip of vacancies and go right to the security offices. Right to the Archbishop.

"No door at all," Santa Cruz says. "Welded plate."

Brigid comes up to it. The door has been removed—the empty hinges in the frame testify to that—and replaced with a sheet of metal welded in place. The commander inspects it, says, "Weld bead around the entire thing. Not just tacked up here."

"It was the same with the main entrance back there," Nonnatus says. "I wonder if they sealed this whole place off from the surface of the asteroid."

"Open space on the other side of this plate?" Brigid asks with a faint knock of his knuckle on the thing. "I wish there were some windows we could look out and see for ourselves."

"Schematics show they used to have a line of high-def screens connected to exterior cameras." Gonzaga says.

"Like on ships." Nonnatus says. "Windows into space, especially on an installation like this would be a silly hazard."

Santa Cruz huffs a laugh. "Can you imagine dancing with a drink in your hand, enjoying the view of that gas giant only to have the window bust out and you're sucked into space? All dressed nicely and whatever?"

"Gives a whole new definition to the phrase *going-out clothes*, doesn't it?" Gonzaga asks.

Brigid grunts. "Quiet. We do this the hard way. Go."

They cross the rest of the dance and bar and move towards the far wall. The door that leads into the next section.

They reach it and find it still in place. "The Lord is merciful in His kindness," Brigid says. "Other side is games and theater."

"Wide open room," Santa Cruz says as he moves for the door.

"Just like this one." Gonzaga says. "Better than the mine."

Santa Cruz pauses, feels Brigid's hand on his shoulder. They stack up and the commander slaps his point man once, hard. Santa Cruz yanks the mechanical knob and pushes through. He gets two steps and stops rigid, gun up.

The others push through the opening, find themselves face to face with a solid wall of white. They look up and down and see dark slits at both ends. Everything else is blocked off just as they come inside.

Santa Cruz peers down at his feet, says, "Oh. Duh," and withdraws a blade. He slashes the wall in front of him and it unzips with a sound of fabric tearing. He yanks the knife to the floor and shoves through. "Movie screen," he says.

They go through the cut and view a sea of empty seats. Theater, indeed. On the outside wall there is another high riser floor with numerous bare electrical conduit drops form the ceiling. The riser is empty except for a lone rectangular table, low enough to be seated at.

Brigid says, "Games, arcade. Move to the right and follow the stairs."

Santa Cruz leads the team up a gradually ascending flight of stairs that runs the length of the room. Same conditions as the dance and bar; girders in the ceiling. Skeletal remains of whatever grandeur the miners could muster up in a temporary structure to take their minds off the fact they lived and worked in the same place. A floating rock with no escape.

"I wonder how many movies Cleopas watched in here as a kid?" Nonnatus says.

"Probably impressing the chicks over there on that riser when it still had arcade games," Gonzaga says.

"I wish he was with us," Brigid says. "I want my guys together."

"Might be best he's outside," Sant Cruz says. "He'd be too far down memory lane with all this. Distracted."

The stairs have little dots in their corners that once must have been lowly lit. A guiding path in a blackened room. But now even those stay as dark as the air. As they pass each row of empty movie-goer seats, the Knights cover down the walkway running from wall to wall. Maybe some ZZH soldier laying prone with a machine gun, just waiting. Maybe a trip wire. Nonnatus looks to where the ceiling meets the wall they're heading to, where the projector's booth would be.

No booth, but the remnants of scaffolding that used to hold up the projector mounted on the wall opposite the screen. Just one more thing his drones could have examined, cleared.

Santa Cruz reaches the zenith of the steps, holds their position. Gonzaga, bringing up the rear, has ten more steps to climb and trips. He stumbles into the seating, seeing something move in the shadows down the walkway to his left. He falls, shoulder hitting into Nonnatus and squeezing his trigger. A burst of rounds shatters the illusion of their silence and eats holes in the flooring.

"Contact location?" Brigid shouts as he spins, takes what concealment he can from the backs of the final row of seats.

Gonzaga curses, shoves up to move. "My left, that row I tripped at," he glances back, determined. *What did I trip on?* "I swear I saw something move about halfway down."

Brigid snarls. "Santa Cruz, hold the door. Nonnatus, you've got overwatch. Gonzaga, get up here."

Gonzaga scrambles to move next to his commander. "Take the side we just came up. I'll take the far wall. We clear as we move down, aiming inward. Concentrate on your half. I've got mine. We move together. Go."

Brigid rushes down to the far wall and gets into position. The two Knights take their corners in the top intersections of the room, begin to move down the rows of seats quickly but surefootedly. One long stretch of chairs, then the next. Their flashlights cutting through the darkness and laying bare anything that might be hiding in the shadows.

They get to where Gonzaga tripped and see something small lying on the floor. "Hold." Brigid says. He studies the item in the light of their beams, cocks his head off to the side. "Check it out, Gonzaga. I'll cover you."

Gonzaga shoves awkwardly though the tight rows of seats. Theater designers wanted one more row of ticket buyers in here, not an already large man wearing bulky armor. He gets to the object and considers it for a moment. Then bends over and picks it up. "A doll," he says as he wiggles it in his hand.

A pink rag doll, stuffed with batting. Two arms and two legs, a head with a stitched smiley face on it. Sky blue buttons for eyes and pigtail hair streamers cascading down both shoulders. Stained black by the years of lying there, lost in the dark by its young owner after watching what must have been the final program this theater put on.

"Found your mascot," Santa Cruz says.

Gonzaga can hear his brother Knights amused sounds, less than laughter but mirth all the same. He squeezes the doll all over to make sure it's not masking a dangerous surprise somehow. "Nothing in her but stuffing," he says. He tucks the doll into his armor.

"We finish this, then," Brigid says. They continue clearing until they get down to the level with the projector curtain, then come back up.

"I'm sure I tripped on a stair and my fall shook this thing off the edge of her seat," Gonzaga says.

"Probably," Brigid agrees. "Just in case, when we go into the next section, we secure that door behind us."

Santa Cruz nods, turns to the door. Brigid walks up and puts his hand on his Knight. The other two stack up on him, and their commander says, "Last boxcar. Strip club."

"Follow in the footsteps of Christ, my brothers," Nonnatus says. "And don't step into anything sticky."

Brigid slaps Santa Cruz and he opens the door. Flows inside and off to the right. The commander follows off to the left, Nonnatus and Gonzaga follow.

"Even the darkness is seedy," Nonnatus says as they move through the space. Again, the ceiling has nothing to offer but bare girders and open graves where the lighting used to be. Down the center of the entire room there is an elevated platform with a polished surface. Studded the entire length down are mounts where the dancer's poles must have been, matching braces on the platform and on the metal girder above.

The entire room is covered in mirrors in all degrees of viability. Some have come unbolted from their fasteners and tipped or totally fallen. Those that only tipped have an edge shattered on the flooring, ruining their square symmetry and forcefully sprinkling the ground with shards. The fallen ones are little more than a mess of jagged ruins.

Another cocktail bar stands along the closer wall, and just like the much larger one in the dance room, this one is missing all its stools. All its glassware. All its refreshments.

Whoever emptied this space left behind three tables. Where there would be high-def screens showing off the outside reaches of space, there are instead private cubicles.

"Check behind the bar, then we need to open all those privacy rooms," Brigid says.

Santa Cruz leaps the bar, scans about and says, "Clear," and leaps back. They move in single file across to the far side of the boxcar-style compartment and begin tossing open each of the private dance room doors.

"Little bigger than the maintenance closets," Gonzaga says. "Space is at a premium, I guess."

"Elbow to the face in there," Nonnatus says. "Count me out."

Brigid stays quiet for a moment, looking around. "There's got to be a dressing room tucked away around here," he says.

The men look around, and Santa Cruz calls up his Visuals, has it overlay the schematics onto the room. He taps his helmet, calling their attention. "Over here," and he leads them to the far base of the platform where it curls a slight U shape. He takes a knee and grabs a hold of a latch. "Get ready," he says and pulls up.

The latch opens a door. A bell tied to it dings wildly as it bounces on its lead, made off to the lifting door. The Knights dodge backward, guns up. No attackers rush out. No explosion from within the compartment.

They spin, forming a circle. Ready. And as nothing comes to them, the darkness eases back out from the tension. Santa Cruz looks at the bell, says, "This is brand-new. The cord it's tied to the door with is also. This isn't left behind by the miners."

"ZZH."

"Got to be."

"I've been waiting to see a booby trap around here," Nonnatus says.

Brigid asks, "How big is the compartment down below?"

"Schematics show a dressing room for three people, looks like. Three of everything. Make-up desks, dressing counters, three showers."

"Clear it." Brigid says. Santa Cruz nods and looks to Gonzaga, then drops inside. Gonzaga takes point by the open hatch. By the sound of Santa Cruz inside, it's tightly packed. Gonzaga looks down in there and sees his brother's light flashing over everything. Slicing off odd sections of shadow as he clears the space.

Finally, "Coming out," Santa Cruz says and emerges. "Empty. Except for this," and he holds out a note. A fresh sheet of paper with the words, *keep looking* written on it. "It's signed by that Loognar guy."

Brigid grimaces and takes it. Folds it once and puts it in his suit. He points to the far wall where the security office is supposed to be. "Taunts. They knew we would mount a rescue. Keep going."

They clear the strip club in a single file line, heading straight to the door marked *security*. Its passcode locked with a card reader next to the pad. They pile back up, one directly behind the first, Brigid's hand on Santa Cruz. Santa Cruz sends a message to the others, *this door is open,* and with it a screenshot of where the door almost meets the jamb but not quite.

They acknowledge, and Brigid slaps his point man on the shoulder. Santa Cruz opens it, and they go inside.

Not Her Blood

She checks herself over as best she can without a mirror, waiting unarmed, dry-mouthed and with her heart raging just under the surface. "Calm yourself, Benedict," she says out loud, and half the reason is to check and see if her voice has shifted to the feminine enough to sound authentic.

"Just keep following as the Holy Spirit leads." That sounds good enough.

Scratchy footfalls shuffling towards her. Glints of a flashlight start cutting their way through the darkness at the mouth of the tunnel the Knight went down earlier. He's coming. Game on.

She turns and runs her hands down her figure one more time, feels the hormone pump on her waist. "Stupid, stupid stupid. . ." she grits her teeth and unzips the jumpsuit with its idiot maintenance company logo on the breast pocket. Starts breathing heavy but shallow. Fast. Tries to calm herself again—the spirit is willing, but the flesh is weak—and she disconnects the pump from the port in her side. Pulls it out and tosses it down a passageway whose entrance is a meter from her.

She crouches down in the corner, then lets her jangled nerves get the better of her. "Act the part," she says. And to her amazement, a tear streaks down her face. "Thank you, Lord." More follow.

The Knight emerges from the tunnel, dirty with its dust and grit. She holds up her hands, blubbers. He turns to her, gun ready to shoot her but not aimed. High ready, trigger indexed along the receiver.

"Please, don't kill me. . ." she stutters. "Please don't hurt me like those— those other. . . people. Please I'm begging." She lets the sobs come forth. Her chest hitches and she falls to her knees. She ran a near overdose level of a mostly-estrogen cocktail from her pump barely ten minutes ago. Something their physicians warn sternly against, but the rush of such hormones under these stressful conditions certainly elicits a physical response she could use right this second.

"I'm not going to hurt you," he says as he immediately relaxes some. "We're here to help."

"Are you?" she mumbles and hopes he takes her question as that of a distracted, tormented survivor and not how she really means it.

"Yes, of course. I'm with the Order of Those Washed in the Water and Blood from His Side. The Knights 1513. Are you hurt?"

"I don't—" she starts but sees where he is pointing. At her. She looks down and sees the Mariol blood on her jumpsuit. Her eyes flick to the ventilation shaft, the punctured grate she replaced after she got out. "—eh, notice. I didn't notice, I guess."

"Do you need medical attention? Can I get—"

"No. No, no. Please, just get me out of here." She clears her throat and rises out of her cowering squat. She's thankful the jumpsuit is long-sleeved; her forearm hair is still thick and dark and wiry. It's always one of the last things to go in her shifts.

The Knight looks her over. He seems to be sizing her up. Determining pity or wrath as his response. She'd been worried he was sent out on his own because he was an especially effective killer and didn't require an entire squad to have his back. But after pondering it for a moment he had to be some kind of technician if they sent him to the gravitational anomaly engine.

"I can make it," she says. "I knew as soon as I saw your armor. . . the insignia. . . you'd be able to keep me safe."

He can't help but stand up a little straighter at that. She brushes a lock of hair behind her ear, then thinks it won't hurt to brush behind both. She tries to give him a smile. Tries. It's hard acting to encourage a heretic and bloodmonger to compassion.

"I'll do everything I can, okay?"

She lets out a half second burst of laughter. "I knew it," she says. "Come with me. We've got to meet up with my team."

She runs over to him and grabs his arm. "Anywhere." And she keeps up with him as they move out.

Servants

"Hit it like Saint Michael did, clearing the foul from Heaven," Commander Brigid orders as they reach the security door. The Knights stay four meters back as Brother Santa Cruz nods. Steps right up to the main outer door. Ejects a spray nozzle from his gauntlet. With a click it spumes a thick froth, like a sealant foam. He traces the entire door frame in two seconds and gives the hand signal for *incoming*, then steps back. The froth reacts with the air and its surface boils. Changes color from a milky tan to deep purple in the blink of an eye. Smokes.

A few white-hot sizzles and then it bursts into metallic flame like an ignited flare. The metal of the door glows a fantastic orange. Santa Cruz steps forward and front snap-kicks the door in. The entire space encircled in his froth outline caves forward, clattering on the floor. They rush forward through the haze of smoke.

"Go, go go!" Brigid says.

The entrance is a mantrap—a small antechamber with one way in, one way out. Only one door may be opened at a time. In part that is because the outer door runs into the room by sliding into the right side of the wall. On the right wall, there is the second door, which also slides inside. If one is open, it physically blocks the other from opening also.

Santa Cruz hits the operator controls for the inner door. A gamble, but one they feel confident in since the outer door isn't registering in the system as open.

"Of course," Brigid had stated earlier, *"all bets are off if the ZZH rigged something. But being this close with the foreknowledge we're coming; we have to stomp through. Dynamic entry."*

"Overwhelming force," Brother Gonzaga added as they stacked up to make entry.

"Always," Brother Nonnatus said.

The inner door opens for Santa Cruz, and he pitches in a flashbang. As it explodes, flooding the room with overpowering light and sound, they move forward.

The security office is a square, three meters by three meters. A desk, two empty chairs. A laptop computer that is too new to have been left behind by the miners sits on the desk, powered up. Something flashing across its screen. Santa Cruz pushes through the office and into a narrow hall. Two open doors on their left side. Holding cells.

He makes it to the first, gun leading the way. "Clear," he says and goes to the second. "Clear." He says again. There is no more. Two concrete walls; one at the end of the hall and one on their right side.

"They wanted these folks to have no illusions about the comforts here," Brigid says.

In sharp contrast to the comforts of the morale cars, the security post was a metal lockbox and the only difference between those who governed the space and those who were incarcerated in it was a few degrees. Nothing more.

The Knights inspect every corner for anything, and Santa Cruz uses his rifle to point into the second cell. "Commander."

Brigid comes up to him, looks inside. Archbishop Hrutt's miter is on the bunk, laying on its side. A streak of blood in it. Brigid considers it for a moment. Goes inside the cell, squats down. Looks at it, has his Visuals scan it for any kind of trigger or trap. Sees nothing. He picks it up and holds it upright, shakes it. A piece of paper flutters out and down. He picks it up, reads it aloud. "Laptop." He twists his wrist and the note faces them; the Knights can see the single word printed on it.

They move back through the hall into the security office. Gonzaga motions to the computer and Brigid nods. Gonzaga taps the keys, and the screen comes to life.

The ZZH leader they know as Loogner appears. He is seated in a brightly lit office. A bookshelf to his left is loaded with binders and a series of books. All the binders are white with large black printing on the spines. The books, all the same caramel brown with the same large font title on them. A sequence of numbers on the bottom of the spine.

Topping the shelf is a used lamp. Ornate; a single metallic spiral. The shade is geometric and four-sided. Each side is a different color. One white, the next two different blends of blue. The final one red.

A picture window behind him displays swirls of gorgeous color. Waterlike in their quality, the colors are really clouds of what might as well be an artist's palette. Meeting, mixing, birthing new hues and shades only to peel apart. Pure again. Churning like a mass of ideas in the mind of God Himself, fixated on what wonders He can work next.

Loognar appears tired. His features seem to even now be shifting between male and female as he prepares himself to deliver this message.

Brigid walks over and grabs the device by its screen. Turns it towards himself. "On pause. Pre-recorded." He clicks on the touchscreen. The frozen Loognar comes to life.

"Knights, I assume?" He wags his eyebrows and looks off into the distance while the parade of colors goes on outside. "Mounting a rescue mission as opposed to dealing with us as Christians. I figured as much and am proud to say the Holy Spirit led me this far. As you can plainly see, your heretic archbishop is not on Stake. Every movement . . . every decision I make . . . I pray for guidance. I have it in spades. Just one more piece of evidence Jesus is with *me*. *My* mission for Him. If you've made it this far, it is not so much by the will of our Lord and Savior, but by the will of violence you seem so well adept at calling God's. The will to murder anything you disagree with."

Nonnatus smirks and says, "Not like you at all, terrorist."

Loognar leans back in his chair. "Two things, Servants of the Diabolical. Only two. One, Hrutt is beginning to see things my way. He will preach my gospel—the Lord's true good news—or he will pass on to his judgement. And two, by playing this video you have triggered an overload of the GravCore on Stake. Give it thirty seconds. It will max out its exertion and obliterate you with it as the entire asteroid crushes inward to the size of a human head."

"That's. . . not what I want to do," Gonzaga says.

"I will pray for your souls," Loognar says. "But know your kingdom is of this world, and the Lord will not recognize your names in the Book of Life when it comes to His kingdom. It is finished."

He reaches forward and kills the video recording. Brigid reaches forward and slaps the laptop shut. "We'll know in short order if Brother Pio accomplished his mission."

Santa Cruz points at the laptop. "Those rainbow whirls behind him—"

"Sure looks like Zaffre Asperity," Brigid says.

Gonzaga claps his hands in frustration. "Oh, the gas giant. He's on the gas giant. Good. I thought this was going to be hard. Silly me."

"Don't despair, brother," Nonnatus says. "We're not allowed to worry. God says so."

"I know. I just. . ." and he trails off.

Nonnatus holds up a finger. He opens the laptop and examines the data tag on the video. The other Knights look at him expectantly. "This video is very recent. Within a half hour or so. And here—" he points to a log in the laptop's system, "—this is another video sent earlier. But it's been deleted. Replaced with the one we just saw."

"Re-recorded a message for us?" Brigid asks.

"Looks that way."

"Interesting."

"But. . . Two things, Servants of the Most High. Only two," Nonnatus says with mirth. "One, it's been at least thirty seconds and we're not being crushed yet, so I think Pio pulled off something in our favor. And two, I've got my Visuals blowing up a still image from Loognar's little pep talk there. He's shown his hand."

"What do you mean?"

"That lamp on the shelf, notice that?" The other Knights nod. Gonzaga shakes his head. "I was focused on the pretty colors."

Nonnatus shrugs and says, "It's Carhovian. They're a human species—not a huge population by any means but they made their mark in this neck of the woods with their management capabilities and. . . their décor. They get hired out by all kinds of species and companies to run their operations. It's like, a genetic trait in them, almost. Besides that, they're well known for their furniture, decorations, artisanal stuff. Anyway, that lamp style with the white, red and two blue shades, the swirling metal, all of it, is symbolic of their culture. And the only people who possess those lamps are top dog managers. CEOs, stuff like that."

"So, he's in a CEO's office somewhere." Santa Cruz says.

"Not *somewhere*, a Carhovian office on Zaffre Asperity."

"Does that narrow it down?" Gonzaga asks.

"Hang on," Santa Cruz says. "I'm blowing up the image also. Those books. . ."

"Exactly," Nonnatus says. He's only half in the conversation because his other half is concentrating on examining the books in the picture. "Operating manuals." He says in a voice that has revelation in it.

"Operating manuals for Platform 841, sector AAB." Santa Cruz says. "They're marked for that operation."

Brigid raises his firearm into the ready position. "We'll have Command get in touch with the Carhovians and get us the exact coordinates for the platform. Let's go. We've got to get off this rock."

Part Three:
From Gray Rock to Rainbow Skies

Guardian Angels Can Fly, Too

"All units, rally in the hangar," Commander Brigid says over their comms. "We're moving out to a secondary position to complete the mission."

Brothers Pio and Cleopas acknowledge. Brigid leads his group back through the morale sections at a fast clip. Through the processing room and the gunfight there. Past the offices. Get to the hangar.

"Approaching from the exterior, anteplanet side," Cleopas says. The team watches as their brother approaches the open hangar's force field from the outside. A silhouette against the brilliance of the laser line that outlines the bay door—a vast rectangular opening in the side of the hangar—and tests passing through it with the muzzle of his weapon before committing his whole body. He comes in and Brigid tosses him a waypoint in his Visuals of where to come. Cleopas joins them.

"I ran into this crazy drone thing. Solid black boxes that kept shuffling around. Impressively armed."

"We did too," Brigid says.

"I was hoping they only had one," Brother Gonzaga says. "Now. . ."

"Two is one, one is none," Brother Santa Cruz says. The wisdom of weapons, be it concealed on your person, what you carry into battle or just as a rule, two weapons equals having one. Only having one equals having none. Too many things go wrong too often to only be armed with a single item if a person can help it.

"Didn't know that rule applies to combat drones," Gonzaga says.

"It applies to everything," Santa Cruz says.

"Not to God," Brother Nonnatus says. "One God."

"In three persons."

Nonnatus nods, considers it. "I'll give you that. Two is one, one is none. *Three* persons is one God. Doesn't really work."

Santa Cruz shrugs. "But it does, though."

"Knock it off." Brigid says. "If they had two combat drones, we've got to consider the possibility they still have more."

"Commander, while I was out there, I watched the Huskvar take off."

"You did?" Brigid asks. "Send me the video."

"Copy." Cleopas has his Visuals transmit the video feed of what he observed, and all the Knights watch in a small pop-up window. From Cleopas's vantage point behind a small outcropping, the Huskvar's engines ignite, and the ship lifts off, then tilts on its axis towards Zaffre Asperity and its thrusters engage. A cloud of asteroid dust and even some small rocks are kicked up under the plumage, cast about.

"Nonnatus, calculate its trajectory and send it to HQ. The guys figuring out which platform has the archbishop could use that."

"On it, sir."

Brigid looks around. "Now, where's Brother Pio?"

"Should be him right there," Gonzaga says as he lifts his rifle to cover a shape coming their way.

"Not a regular Knight silhouette," Santa Cruz says as he arms the mortars on his suit. The Knights prepare for another battle, and Santa Cruz says, "It's not geometric, though. Looks like two humans, or at least humanoid."

"Pio, report in," Brigid says.

Pio's mic comes on and they can hear him panting in time with his footfalls. "Almost to. . . the hangar now." The sound clicks off, then comes back on, "And I. . . I found a survivor."

"Praise God," the Knights whisper. As they give glory the Lord, the blob-silhouette enters the hangar chamber and materializes into Pio and an unarmored woman. She looks alert, frightened. But she also carries herself with a strident determination that betrays any thoughts of weakness.

"Survivor indeed," Brigid says. He tosses Pio the waypoint and he pauses, shifts his course. The woman moves with him. They jog over to the team as Brigid rises from his guarded position to meet them.

"Brothers, this is Bee. Bee, my commander, and my brothers in Christ."

She smiles and looks to the floor. Waves with a small gesture. "Thank you for your help."

"Wonderful," Brigid says. He looks her up and down. Exhausted. One old scar on her cheek going to her chin. An ill-fitting jumpsuit from the maintenance company, complete with hastily sewn-on patches and plenty of old stains to show off against the new grime. And blood. Outfits like that are always racing against their bottom line. Tossing a ragged jumpsuit at some new employee seems to check a box in the savings column. "You hurt?"

"Scared," she says, bashfully. "Beat up. Nothing worth worrying about. Promise."

Brigid motions to Cleopas, "He's our medic. We'll get somewhere safer, less active, and he can look at your wound."

"No," she says in a voice that sounds guarded. "I don't— it's nothing." Brigid looks at her, and she takes a deep breath. "I— I don't like being touched."

"Copy," Brigid says, nodding his head. He looks at Pio. "You hurt?"

"No, sir. Mission went off without a hitch. We've got—" he checks the counter on his Visuals and says, "Approximately twelve minutes before my bypass on the GravCore gives out. Then this whole place is toast."

"Twelve minutes, so be it." Brigid ruminates as he turns to the blasted fleet parked in the hangar. "Cleopas, I received word from the *Saint Eligius* that their little stunt getting the Mariol woman off-world cost us our transport."

"Yessir, that drone thing ate them alive with its firepower."

"It's out of commission, though? The drone?"

Cleopas makes the universal gun sign with his hand. Cocks his thumb up and down. "Yessir, sniped it with a grid cannon."

Brigid looks to Bee, says, "I know your company suffered heavy losses today."

Bee looks off in the distance. From a dark place, she says, "My people have suffered today, yes."

"But one woman survived when the ZZH executed an entire group. I don't know her name. We got her out of here. Brother Cleopas risked his life for her."

"You shouldn't have."

Cleopas makes an embarrassed gesture. "It was no problem. I act for Christ, please give Him your thanks."

The woman nods slightly. "And there was a drone, you said? Those black things hovering by the— other people here?"

"Yes. Two of them, at least." Brigid says, studying the hangar. "We've got to go."

†

The facility is quiet. Every metric it scans for is flatlined. While on patrol, twice it has come across deceased remains of numerous organic beings. Once it has come across recognizable materials from the same manufacturing facility as it. Damaged beyond repair.

As it randomly chooses a patrolling pattern, it scans gravitational anomaly variations that are slowly but steadily becoming more erratic. And stronger. Those readings feed into its survival matrix and computation programs. A need arises—as much as it can have a need—to create distance between it and the source of those fluctuations.

It begins a non-randomized course. Near enough is a flight deck. Typically, the organic material it has been assigned to for service use craft on that flight deck. Traveling away computes as the most effective solution to the problem. Create distance between it and the source of those gravitational instabilities.

The closer it approaches the flight deck, the more its sensors pick up whisper-quiet sounds that correspond with full accuracy to vocalizations of organic material.

†

Commander Brigid looks at a small craft, probably a crew transport from a larger mothership. Not built for long voyages on its own, but for transferring crews and equipment. No damage as far as he can see. "That one looks intact and about our size."

The Knights move to it. The transport is little more than an open box with sets of removable seats bolted into the cargo hold. The cockpit is cramped for its three seats—pilot, copilot and navigator. The navigator chair is stacked so closely behind the copilot they better be friends. Little more. No fancy accommodation of any kind. The wings on the ship are retracted along the starboard and port sides, like a bird folding its wings.

"Bee, did you arrive in this ship?"

She looks confused for just a moment before her eyes light up. "No, no. I. . . I, uh. . . arrived on a different one."

Brigid nods. "Understood. Are you a pilot?"

"No. I'm unskilled, as it were."

"I'm sure you have plenty to offer. Brother Pio, can you get this thing off the ground?" Brigid asks. "You're my luckiest guy with things like this."

Pio studies the inside of the cockpit, touches a few controls, steeples his fingers in thought. "Yeah, with my guardian angel's help, I think I can."

"Guardian angels can fly. I like that. Get to it."

Brother Nonnatus leans over. "Saint Bosv of I'thall could fly too, remember. Might, you know, implore his help."

"His people have wings, right?" Pio asks absently as he sits down at the pilot's controls.

"The ones that lived in the trees, yeah. But they had some aquatic folks too, and they had—"

Brigid clears his throat. "Less jibby-jabby, more flying. We've got five minutes, maybe. Go."

"Roger," Pio says as he turns the power on. The transport groans much more than hums as its electronics kick off and it immediately rises a meter in the air. Jostles. Pio startles, shoots one hand out to a series of controls boxed in by a thick green line. "The real pilot must have left the auto-hovering on. Let me see. . ."

"Turn this bucket a hundred and eighty degrees and out the door." Brigid says.

The transport jostles again and Brigid looks back to Pio.

Pio has his hands in the air. "Not me."

"GravCore?"

"Maybe. I'm not seeing any alarms on this bucket of bolts but that doesn't mean it wasn't damaged in the firefight from earlier. I'll get it moving."

"Good."

Pio looks at the controls again and places his hands on them. Throws a switch, taps a read-out gauge. "Just registered more weight for some reason. I think the GravCore is affecting us."

"Out the door, then." Brigid looks behind him and sees Brother Gonzaga helping Bee buckle in. She gives him a sidelong glance; it's obvious he doesn't know what to do but wants to help and she doesn't want help. She finally lifts his hands off the buckles and shoos him away. Finishes it herself and leans back.

Brother Santa Cruz laughs at them as he shuts the crew hatch.

"Secure it, people. We're out of here." Brigid says, and buckles in.

His Knights sit down, and Pio keeps the transport stationary and wobbles it around in a half circle. He aims the nose at the hangar door and crawls it forward.

Nonnatus looks up and says, "Sir, just got word back from HQ. We know the location."

"Let's hope it's better intel than what we did have," Santa Cruz says.

"Get it to Pio," Brigid says. "Set course, brother."

"Yes, sir—" The hangar's ceiling suddenly crunches down hard. Like a slap from a giant outside, the roof caves in. Debris rains down. "GravCore!" Pio shoves the thruster controls forward and the transport blasts out of the collapsing hangar. Santa Cruz stumbles but catches himself on a railing. Gonzaga isn't so lucky and falls onto a seat face first. Bee bursts out laughing as the other Knights catch themselves in one degree or another of tumbling down.

The transport kicks out of the hangar and its hindquarters waiver in the pull from the suddenly expanding gravity behind them. Pio adjusts a few controls and gives the transport more power, taking his right hand off the controls just long enough to make the Sign of the Cross over himself.

The transport creaks and groans a moment more and then heaves forth as if it burst from a bubble. "Thank you, Lord Jesus Christ," he says. He flicks a few switches, and a monitor turns on in the cargo hold where the Knights are strapping themselves in. "Sorry, Cleopas," is all Pio says as they watch Stake eat itself.

The asteroid collapses into itself in great thrusts. Subterranean caverns draw their surface layers down like sinkholes exposing. Avalanches of free-spilling dirt and rocks suck down into those sinkholes as the outer crust is devoured in thunderous claps. A few mechanical explosions and mineral materials burst forth in plumes before being captured by the gravitational well. They fly right back to Stake and become part of the tremendous effort to reduce the asteroid to a pebble.

Cleopas watches his home get smaller and smaller. Breaking here and there along rapidly developing fault lines. Caving inward in spasmodic lurches. Reduced. All his memories of it, a mountain of experience that formed him into the Knight he is now, a servant of God and defender of Truth. The snowcap on that memory mountain is this view now as he bears witness to the end of such mortal things.

"I'll have it again in Paradise with Our Lord," he says. Stake disappears in the space it formerly occupied. All that is left is a dense cloud of dust particles, some larger chunks thrown far enough to where the gravity cannot reach, and a new view of both the blackness of the void's canvas as well as twinkles from distant stars.

†

It managed to unfold several segments around the bottom of the travel vessel. It had just risen in the air by approximately one meter, preparing for flight. By rearranging itself to be very thin, it coated with near completeness the underbelly of the vessel. Adding its weight, yes, but the vessel successfully flew. It continues scanning, and the first and most obvious thing it detects is the gas giant planet before it. The vessel is on a steady bearing towards it, with decreasing range detected every moment.

Combat programming recognizes travel that will insert the unit into an atmosphere. The assumed outcome will be that it is being delivered either to storage, or to war. So, it waits.

†

"Praise God," Commander Brigid says, staring in awe of the vanished spectacle. "Praise be to our Lord and savior Jesus Christ, we made it, and that Brother Pio ran into Bee here, so that she might make it too."

"Amen," the Knights say.

Bee makes a non-committal gesture and looks away. "I had prepared myself to die there," she says. Runs a lock of hair behind her ear. "But you came along, so. . ."

"I'm glad you're with us," Brother Nonnatus says.

"They'll think I'm dead, with all the others," Bee says, almost to herself.

"If God finds it good to allow the other woman to pull through her injuries, we'll have two of you. We'll get you back to your company, your family. Whoever you have waiting at home for you." Brigid says.

"Of course," Bee says. Turns to Brigid and stares at his helmet. "Thank you." She sounds hollow, but she's just lived through a terrible battle. She clears her throat and says, "The other people. . . they were convinced the maintenance folks. . . were disguised soldiers. Come to fight."

"No," Brother Cleopas says. "That asteroid has been idled for decades, but somebody bought it. They were going to reopen it. The maintenance crew was there to get the ball rolling."

Bee glares. "Seriously?"

"Yes. What terrible, terrible luck."

Bee huffs. "Why would God send all those people to die like that? Screaming? Executed? And why would the other people be so stupid?"

"I don't know." And no one offered her a better answer. She looks away, and in her heart, she feels a stab of hatred towards both the ZZH and God himself. Can't help it.

They sit silent for a moment, and then Nonnatus says, "Boy, Pio, that didn't feel like five minutes left."

Pio says, "Approximately five minutes. It was a little less than two."

"Less than two does not approximate five. FYI."

"I got us out, right?"

"Get us to the platform," Brigid says. "I've sent a message to Mobile HQ. We need the calvary on the way. This little transport isn't going to get us much further." He looks at Bee, "We're going to have to do something with you, though. I'm sure you're tired of fighting today."

Bee gives him a smile and shrugs. She makes the Xewlian gesture of rubbing a thumb and forefinger along the top row of her teeth. Finally she answers, "Life is war. If we made it any other way, God wouldn't have had to spill His blood for us."

What Deposition Storm Means

"Stay right in front of the storm, Brother Pio, we'll need the cover." Commander Brigid says as the gorgeous upper atmosphere of Zaffre Asperity swirls around them. The atmosphere is teeming with gigantic storms, and as they dive in from space one is directly behind them. The Carhovian platform they need is a minuscule pinpoint ahead, and the storm is chasing them to it.

The undulating ribbons of color have grown tremendously larger now that they've breached the outer layers of the atmosphere. What from Stake looked like mere rivers of spiraling colors are now expansive lakes and seas. In stark contrast to the bleak and dirty asteroid, the relentless expanse of black space, this is paradise.

It is beautiful as the thick clouds break over the nose of the ship. Swimming in a color wheel. Driving through the clouds, forcing them up and over the external cameras that serve as viewports to the sky before them. Pio watches closely on his range finder to make sure that the vast mass of newborn storm behind him stays where the commander wants it. Such a titanic disturbance on their enemy's RADAR will mask their approach. A pinhead versus an avalanche.

"I'm hoping they think we're dead back on Stake," Brother Cleopas says.

"With any help from God, they do," Brigid says. "But that won't last as soon as their RADAR differentiates between us and that monster conflagration back there."

"They got RADAR? Monitoring it, anyways?"

"I would," Brigid says in a dark tone. "Plus, I imagine they've also got the Huskvar by now. If it came here at all. They might have boogied out, but I have to assume it came here. Which means they had at least some folks we didn't run into. Who knows what they've outfitted the Huskvar with. Especially now that we're certain Loognar planned on us mounting a rescue."

"Why not just kill the archbishop, then?" Pio asks.

"No doubt he's got something viler in mind," Cleopas says.

"I'd bet my paycheck on it." Brigid says, leaning forward and studying the instruments as he has one hand above him, clinging to the overhead. He turns quickly to see his men one more time. The woman, Bee, strapped in and calmly watching them in the back. All of the Knights at what Brigid always thought of as combat ease. That ability to take a few minutes in lulls of warfare to unconsciously unwind. Build back up for the next fight. He smiles inwardly, thanks the Lord for these brave souls and turns to the front.

"Well, that Huskvar seats somewhere less than ten people," Cleopas says. "Even if they made adjustments to it and dumped everything they didn't need inside it. Stood heel to toe, they're not getting more than. . . let's be super generous and say twenty soldiers."

"And these platforms aren't big," Pio says. "I'm starting to get a clearer picture of it now on the RADAR. They can't outnumber us too much."

Brother Santa Cruz pats his rifle. "Five to one? That really means one to one, with us." He turns to Brother Gonzaga and slaps him on the shoulder. "Well, two to one for this new guy here."

"Please," Gonzaga waves him off and peers out the rear monitor. He groans as the storm behind them, more a colossal gathering of numerous volatile gases as big as a continent on some worlds, bears down on them. "Uh, Commander, I'm pretty sure this is one of those bad storms we don't want anything to do with."

Brigid coughs out a laugh. "I'm absolutely sure it's one of those bad storms we don't want anything to do with. But we're not leaving without the archbishop. The storm will have to deal with us."

"Hey Pio," Santa Cruzs says, "This thing got any way to see what those clouds are made of?"

Pio shrugs and checks his instrument panel. "The basic sensor package, I guess. Don't want to wander into acid vapor or something extreme on some strange new world. Let's see. . . Water, ammonia, methane, a few things most other worlds don't have. Why?"

Cleopas turns to Santa Cruz and says, "Well, one of the big deals about Zaffre Asperity is the atmospheric mixture. It's rich in valuable diversity. I imagine the Carhovians' platform is here to filter out various gases and bottle them. There was a huge rage for all that when I was a kid."

Pio gives a glance to Santa Cruz. "That answer your question?"

Santa Cruz is eyeing the darkest lip along the bottom of the formation, itself a veritable beachhead in length. It shimmers with glinting dots. Hefty sparkles refracting their sun's light against the backdrop of the menacing cloud lip. "Not really." He turns to Pio. "Just keep it behind us." His helmet in his hand, he rubs his face, then looks up. "Or under us."

Brigid raises an eyebrow and holds his arms, palms up. "Care to share?"

"It's raining, whatever it is."

"Pio said it had water, some other stuff."

"Yes, Commander. Water shimmers, but not like that." Santa Cruz rolls his head on his neck and grabs his small arms rifle by the buttstock as it dangles across his chest. "Jewels do, though."

The entire team groans. Brigid looks at the monitor, then back at Pio. "ETA?"

Pio taps on a small readout pad on the controls, looks up and out the monitor serving as a windscreen. "Less than five mikes."

Brother Nonnatus smirks and says, "So, really, we've got less than two mikes."

A small pinpoint dot on Brigid's Visuals flashes and the words *receiving/downloading transmission/trusted source* appears. Brigid sees the sender from 1513 Command, and he snaps his fingers. He uses his Visuals to flick it over to the others. Santa Cruz puts his helmet back on and watches the report in a thumbnail viewscreen.

The transmissions takes life and there is Brother Steks, an IT guru and member of the Ploytu species. Brigid's team had completed a minor mission on the home world of Ploytu 7 in the recent past. A few weeks before Gonzaga joined them. It was a neat coincidence to see him now, with his people so fresh in their memories.

Brother Steks begins in his high-pitched, staccato voice, "Greetings, my fellow brothers in Christ. I've only just received this information so bear with me as I read. I'll skip over the technical specs as we look to what will most vitally influence your mission." He holds one of his two elegant and very long fingers to his mouth as he scans whatever data set is in front of him. He gestures between a readout and the air as if he was making points during a lecture.

"Uh, here it is. Here it is, yes. The schematics about the Carhovian Platform 841, sector AAB are as follows: it is an atmospheric gas refinery, concentrating mainly on. . . oh, doesn't really matter. . . duh duh duh. . . nothing flammable, volatile, et cetera. . . small crew complement of five including the platform manager. . . seventy-eight percent of platform real estate is dedicated to machinery processes and therefore unavailable for occupation by crew. . . a single square plot dedicated to vertical landing and takeoff vehicles on the bow. . . hope you're traveling in one of those. Duh duh duh. . . gravity generation is slightly less than one g but is essentially negligible, hull layer shield generator specifically designed to repel geminized. . . what is 'geminized?' Some Carhovian term, I assume. Anyway, *geminized* clusters of atmospheric gases and products. And—"

Brigid pauses the playback. "Hang on," He quickly cross references a few things in his onboard computing, says, "Our term for *geminized* is deposition. Deposition, when gases directly turn into solids."

"Gem storm," Santa Cruz says, and crosses himself. "We're going to be doing this in the middle of a jewel storm."

"I hope they're diamonds," Nonnatus says. "I just like those."

"I don't like anything from a hulk of a rain cloud that is going to hurt us."

Gonzaga says, "Yes, but the platform is protected from that. It said so in the report. There's a shield or something."

"Brother Steks said *hull layer shield generator*," Cleopas says. "That's a few centimeters off the skin of the ship. That's all. We'll still be fully exposed."

Gonzaga starts to say something, then stops. He nods and flaps his hands in an *oh well* manner. "It was a good life."

"Will be tomorrow, also," Pio says. "We'll beat it there. *Now* we're less than two mikes."

"I'm resuming," Brigid says and the report starts playing again.

Brother Steks unfreezes, says, "And the rest appears to be mostly technical specs. Most of the interior is taken up by machinery. There is a cafeteria that doubles for everything else besides sleeping quarters. Sleeping quarters and the manager's office are side by side, accessible immediately through the cafeteria. Other than that, there is a mechanical office on the underbelly of the platform and a few access closets throughout. I would imagine if the archbishop is there and still in the medpod we saw in him earlier, it would have to be the cafeteria."

Brigid pauses that, says, "I'm sending the schematics to you all. We make a straight line there."

Brother Steks unfreezes and continues, "I've looked at this a few different ways and I have to assume the ZZH was hoping to keep you occupied on Stake. This platform has very little in the way of tactical advantage once you set foot on it."

Brigid pauses it again, says, "Looks like the ZZH were relying on being sneaky. Kill us on Stake. I'm going to—"

A single pop strikes the top of the ship. Incredibly sharp and heavy in sound, a small divot pokes down into the cargo space. On the viewing screens, the storm has raced forward enough to begin to overtake them. Raindrops of solid jewels start to plink down all around. They look marvelous in the light of the atmospheric colors still radiating from ahead.

"It went through the outer hull," Nonnatus says as he runs his hand over the divot impressed into the inner hull just over them. "That's forceful. Still less than two mikes?"

Pio goes back to the readout pad on the instruments and then startles. He shouts and yanks the controls. As he does the forward monitor lights up with strafing fire. "There's the platform!"

As the swirling atmosphere before them thins out enough to see some distance, Platform 841 emerges from the glory of the clouds. The ZZH Huskvar is there, settled on the VTL port, an aftermarket cannon on its roof. Gattling munitions at the Knights.

Flashes of muzzle fire. Tracer rounds embedded in the onslaught. The platform fades in through the remnants of thicker clouds and the Huskvar blasts away. "They know we're here," Gonzaga says.

"If you hadn't said anything, I wouldn't know." Santa Cruz says as Pio's evasive maneuvers throw him around.

It takes the rest of the Knights off their feet as well. Bee Rampart screams as she rattles violently in her seat restraints. Brigid slams up against the starboard bulkhead and Brother Steks' report begins playing again.

"—storms are common at the heights you'll be operating at, so be mindful, please." He freezes in still frame again as Brigid pauses it.

"We've got a bullet storm too," Nonnatus says as he pulls himself up off the deck. As he does another impressive whack strikes the overhead. The divot it makes is deeper than the first one.

"Keep telling me it'll be a good life tomorrow, please." Gonzaga says as a third divot jams its way right over his head.

A fourth impact drives right through the inner hull and into the deck under Cleopas's heels. Still on his back, he sits up and sees a translucent gem, streaked with gold filaments and brilliant orange specks. He remembers the fathers of his friends would come back from trips to Asperity with handfuls of these as gifts. Little trinkets. How heavy but astounding they were. The one that just drove through rolls over the deck and touches his boot. "Just like home," he says and picks it up.

A fifth hits, then a sixth and then several more. "Protect her!" Brigid shouts, pointing at Bee. Gonzaga moves over and poses over the woman. He is very close to her, and he nods bashfully.

"This is just, uh, to keep you safe. It's—" the overhead is punctured several more times. It strikes the Knights and the gems ricochet off, bouncing through the cabin. The moving white noise of the weighty jewels rolling around inside becomes deafening as Pio dodges gunfire.

"I'm willing to let you die for me," Bee says. "Especially since you guys were kind enough to take an unarmed, unarmored woman on your little combat raid, here."

"We didn't—" Gonzaga begins but then a flurry of gems peppers the overhead. One strikes him on the crown of his helmet and flings off. Enough punch through in one spot to tear a hole large enough for a fist to go into. "You'll need an atmospheric suit," he says, lost in new thought.

Bee begins to choke as the contained air inside the ship rushes out. Whatever is in the higher atmosphere of Asperity isn't what Bee breathes.

"Cleopas!" Gonzaga shouts. "That suit! Right there!" He points to a small white case mounted on the portside bulkhead. There are five, and Cleopas grabs one. Tosses it to Gonzaga. He opens it up and dumps a universal exterior exposure suit on Bee's lap. "No time to waste. Put it on. I'll shield you."

He takes his helmet off and slips it on over her head. At the base of his neck there is an expandable tube that he pulls on, then hooks it into the helmet. Bee hears air hissing into the helmet, takes a deep breath and looks up at the Knight giving her his supply. His lifeline. She ponders taking long enough to let him asphyxiate but figures this clumsy brute will just pull the helmet off her if he needs it. She can't resist his power armor.

She undoes her restraints and a line of fire cuts through the top of the ship. She screams but thrusts her legs into the suit's lower half. As she dresses, Brigid calls out, "All right, listen up."

The Knights do what they can to stabilize themselves inside the rapidly deteriorating ship. Pio swings them around to the rear side of the platform, away from where the Huskvar remains landed. The deposition storm continues pelting them.

Bee finishes getting into her suit and Gonzaga, cheeks puffed out from holding his breath, takes his helmet back. He exhales inside it and breathes in deeply. The smell inside the mask—Bee's breath—has a peculiar scent to it. Not bad, per se, but almost chemical in nature. They're all under stress. Maybe that explains it. Maybe it was gas trapped inside the helmet as they switched it around, something invading from outside. He puts the idea out of his mind and turns to his commander.

Santa Cruz points to the rear monitor, damaged with a single bullet hole through the screen but still projecting. "Make it fast, that rain is about to quadruple in intensity." The beachhead of cloud lip is impossibly darker than it was before, and the rainfall much thicker.

Brigid says, "Pio, get us up close, we need to find cover. We bail out the back. Gonzaga, stuff the girl someplace out of the way. The rest of you, you're on me. We're making contact. We're leaving with the archbishop, or as witnesses to his martyrdom."

"Saint Michael protect us," Pio says, and makes his end run to the platform.

Party Crashing

"That's a ship, not a platform," Brother Pio says as he guns the engines and charges straight at Carhovian Platform 841, sector AAB. P841 is cigar-shaped with a stubby but significant super structure sitting atop, covered in numerous pipes and surveying antennae. Running down both sides are several catwalk-like constructions, more piping and boxy protrusions. A smaller substructure about half the mass of the super structure extends off the belly and features two wing-like projections to either side.

On one end are thrusters, the other has a series of three lights and the landing pad where the Huskvar has landed. As Pio approaches at breakneck speed towards what appears to be the aft end where the thrusters are sitting docile, a small line of dots appears moving along the catwalk.

"ZZH gunmen," Commander Brigid says. "Our first stop."

The dropship is canting badly to one side. The thick cloud coverage of Zaffre Asperity is penetrating through every puncture wound in it. The continuous hail of jewels pelts along the craft, deafening the men inside. Even their comms, designed to filter out external noises and concentrate on voices and what their onboard programming deems necessary are being washed out. Confusing noise clutter.

The rear hatch opens and drops partway down. The rush of incoming weather whips into the cargo hold in misty loops. Buffets the Knights. Brother Santa Cruz shouts, "Door must be damaged. It's jammed coming down."

"Unjam it." Brigid says as he readies his rifle into his shoulder and comes back.

Brother Gonzaga's eyeline follows where the ambient light from outside limns the doorway. Sees a dark break in it where the metal must have been rent and causing the jam. He grabs ahold of the frame for stability and stomps the door right at the spot. The enhanced force of his strike shoves the door down with a hideous shriek of metal. It flops down, boneless. It bounces and shudders the whole craft.

"Unjammed," he says and gives a thumbs up. He turns to Santa Cruz and motions at the door.

Santa Cruz nods approvingly, says, "Not bad for a new guy."

"I know."

"Still two on one odds, though." Santa Cruz says and walks down the limp door, and as he does the dropship maneuvers up, revealing P841 beneath him. As the line of ZZH soldiers appears below them, guns lighting up in muzzle flashes, Santa Cruz jumps.

"Let's go, Two to One," Brother Nonnatus says as he races past Gonzaga and out the door.

Brother Cleopas and Brigid come up next. Brigid takes Bee by the arm and pushes her into Gonzaga's chest. "Someplace as safe as you can find. Then get in the fight." He leaps off, following Cleopas.

Gonzaga looks at the woman shrugs. "Okay, then," and he sweeps her off her feet with one arm. Catches her behind the knees with his other, cradling her. He jumps as well. Bee screams as they fall twenty meters to the skin of the platform.

†

Brother Pio swings the dropship up high and off to his port. He rolls the ship to where its belly is to the platform, curving out. The 20de9, still along the bottom of the ship, painting the belly a solid black. Exposed. A single jewel falls and strikes the drone in its side that lines along the starboard. It registers the impact and computes the dangers of the storm. When a second jewel comes at it through in the onslaught, it reacts nearly instantaneously and reconfigures a tunnel through itself to allow the jewel to pass harmlessly through its whole form. The more that come, the more it learns to react.

As soon as Pio makes what he thinks he can get in the outward curve, he swerves hard right. The bow of the platform comes into view. The landing pad. The Huskvar's aft end. Pio shoves the throttles down to their maximum and aims directly at the Huskvar.

The after-market cannon on top of the RV craft begins to rotate towards Pio. "This'll be close," Pio mumbles. "Lord, Your will be done. Not mine. But, if You're in the mood, let me pull this off."

One hundred meters. Pio, so nervous that he has a hard time concentrating, runs his eyes over his controls one last time. If the dropship slips under or over the Huskvar, this end run is futile. The cannon is nearly on target.

Fifty meters. The swirling colors buffet the windscreen cameras, smearing freckles of the Lord's rainbow in a dazzling display. Such beauty with such violence right behind it. A new bucketload of raining jewels peppers the dropship and Pio sees that he's being pummeled down, off course. The cannon clicks onto target. The barrel starts glowing.

Twenty meters. Pio slaps the control stick up and turns to run aft into the cargo hold. With a prayer more felt than formed into words, he runs. The cannon opens up and a stream of projectiles hammer-smashes the exterior cameras feeding the windscreen view. Chew through the forward exterior and ricochet all around Pio as he races to the open back hatch.

Five meters. Pio takes a single step down the hatch, and it bounces under his footfall. He leaps off to his left, towards P841. As he hurls through the air, he sees a bizarre gesticulating mass of onyx black unspool from below the ship and latch onto the platform as well. Even in that split second, he can see it opening holes all throughout its body as the storm jewels fall through it. He instantly feels the blast pattern of gems rain down on him. He hits an exterior wall and dents it in as he collides with the platform.

One meter. The dropship misses the Huskvar entirely. It rams into the landing pad and the square of metal squeals as it tears off the side of P841. A single ZZH soldier comes spilling out of the Huskvar, running to the body of the platform. Pelted with diamond-esque rain, the soldier spasms once in a great jerk and falls over.

The weight of the Huskvar on the pad exacerbates the tearing, and with a sudden snap the entire thing tears free. Jagged edge and all. The Huskvar keeps firing as it drops towards the surface core of Zaffre Asperity, nearly two million kilometers down.

"I knew You'd deliver me, Lord. I love you so much," Pio says as he forces himself up. His hand rests on the platform surface, and there he can see a forcefield extending off the surface about fifty centimeters. "That's all, huh?" He looks up and sees the storm raining down on the P841, but its shield is only enough to protect the literal surface. Standing outside of it is of no consequence.

There is a small lip of protection above him; a single large pipe wide enough for him to stand under and mostly be safe from direct hits. A deluge of gems pours down the port side of the platform, and Pio races aft towards his brothers, trying to keep something above his head.

†

"Father, the heretics are on board here with us," a ZZH soldier says as he enters the space Loognar has been occupying. The ZZH priest doesn't turn towards him, but rather continues inputting some kind of protocol into a medpod in front of him.

"And?" Loognar asks, half distracted.

"Well, sir. . . a 20de9 drone came with them. And we— we don't have any, you know, of those devices that tell them we're friendly."

"Where are they?"

"On Stake. With the soldiers that needed them."

Loognar presses a final button, and the screen turns into a green square before flashing back to whatever it was displaying before. He turns around. "Avoid it, then. And if you cannot, try to lead it to the Knights."

"We'll all die, Father."

"As God wills it, then."

The ZZH soldier looks defeated, despairing. He stiffens up, nods curtly. "We knew this when we embarked on this mission."

Loognar smiles. Walks over to the soldier and makes the Sign of the Cross. "To be martyred for Christ is a great honor, and testament to the faith. Go, and do not be troubled."

The soldier smiles. His Adam's apple is betrayed by a peculiar softness around his eyes. His hair in a bun perched atop his head. He turns and moves out.

Loognar watches him go and then removes a device from his suit. It is of the same design as the friendly devices for the 20de9 but shaped differently. Almost cylindrical, he grasps the two ends and twists a quarter turn. It opens and both ends slide out, revealing their inner contents. He presses two buttons simultaneously, and then enters a code on an alien touchpad made of crisscrossing slashes of various thicknesses.

It vibrates four times in quick succession. A single light on it begins flashing silently. Loognar pockets the device as best he can inside his jacket and turns to the medpod.

†

On the exterior of the platform, the 20de9 has collapsed itself into a column alongside the outer wall. A single lip feature above it deflects the storm gems in a great torrent. Along its secluded control board, a line of lights flashes four times in quick succession. Another single light comes on and remains. The drone begins to move, creeping along with determination.

†

Loognar gets to the side of the medpod and peers down through the transparent glass that wraps around the top of it. "Both of us will be martyrs. Not equal, but the same. You're so important to me, Archbishop Hrutt. So important to the ZZH. To the truth of Christ."

Inside the medpod, the archbishop lays on his back, straining against all that is occurring. Tubes run into several parts of his body. Sweat pools all along his sides. Even his legs. He bares his teeth in agony. His eyelids have squeezed so tightly that they have begun to swell.

"It's a calculated risk, giving you such a hefty first dose," Loognar says. "Being an older man, not having the centuries of proper breeding as we do. And like this," he waves his hand over the medpod, then around the room, "Not exactly ideal. We have impressive facilities in Xewl. But you're very close to our standard converts. This is a bigger dose, and with that you're also not getting the recommended intervals between treatment cycles. But I truly believe the Lord is with us. His hand is at work everywhere. Such graces! Once you heal from this, you'll need a few of our lab-grown organs, as we all do. And a pump, like this." Loognar pats his side where he has a small contraption mounted on his belt.

"Nothing a few surgeries won't fix. We have to work fast, of course. While I dislike the term *forced conversion*, I do think there's something to be said about walking a mile in our shoes. Maybe this is closer to transplanting our feet onto you, but it works. Shoes, you can take off. Lose your feet, and you become something less than you once were. And when the great preacher against us becomes *for* us, becomes *one* of us, what an incredible witness you will be!"

The archbishop tries to raise a hand. The muscles in his arm convulse and he stiffens, then lets his arm settle back down. He coughs, moans, "Playing God. . . does not. . . make you. . . godly."

Loognar gives a trite smirk, barely more than a twitch of his lips. "We are to be like Him," Loognar inhales through his nostrils and snorts like a bull. "Even if you don't want to be."

He turns and sees in the doorway a shadow like a wall. Perfectly geometrical. Cube upon cube upon cube, all metallic night, constantly shuffling and rearranging. Loognar touches the cylinder inside his jacket and closes his eyes. "Thank you, Lord, for delivering unto me this blessing. I shall not fail You."

He holds one hand out to the 20de9 and makes a *come here* motion, flapping his fingers. "Welcome," he says. "Welcome, indeed."

†

Archbishop Hrutt can already feel the process easing up, but only as much as the tension on a ship's anchor eases as the tide turns favorably with it. Still taut, still ever present, but a slight relaxation none the less.

He hears Loognar speaking to someone, his back to the archbishop. Hrutt can lift his head just enough on his neck—all cords burning, all veins thrumming like over-taxed pipes—to see the ZZH priest. He extends his arms out to his sides as if he is assuming a cruciform position.

Something tremendous and the color of desolation engulfs him. Swallows him whole.

The Explosions and the Pauses

Brother Santa Cruz gets hit twice by gunfire as he plummets onto the catwalk, lands on his feet with such thunder that it rattles and somewhere off to the side he hears a bolt break. The small caliber rounds make a *plinking* sound off his armor as he raises his own weapon. Lays down covering fire for his brothers.

He moves and follows as his Visuals identifies hostility. But even if he wasn't wearing a helmet with an onboard computer overlaying the battlefield onto his view, he'd know where the muzzle flashes are coming from.

All the ZZH in their light armor, a bland industrial gray against the rainbow backdrop of the gas giant is so starkly contrasting they might as well have beacons on. Their firearms are all variants of the Darvian LM1157, a rudimentary but reliable semi-automatic rifle. "Terrorist melee guns," Santa Cruz says as he sends a volley of rounds towards a cluster of engaging enemies. "Let's hope that's the heaviest thing they got."

"Heretic knight—" a soldier shouts as he unloads a fully automatic weapon at Santa Cruz. He spins, takes a knee and draws a bead on the soldier, hits him with one solidly placed burst. "Okay, proven wrong as soon as I spoke," Santa Cruz says. The soldier collapses, the gun an attractive item for Santa Cruz to claim as his own. He grabs it up and checks its load. "Got a CJ1541. Might come in handy."

As the others pound onto the catwalk, Santa Cruz hears more bolts breaking. Even the sporadic gunfire of the soldiers doesn't cover it. Three more ZZH soldiers come around the bend in the catwalk and open fire. Santa Cruz sweeps the 1541 across them and they fall on the metal.

A second group comes around, one soldier maneuvering from positions of cover while the rest lay down covering fire. A volley of blasts ricochets off the catwalk and Brother Gonzaga grabs Bee, spins around with her in tow just in time to absorb the fire along his armored back.

"This isn't a safe place, you incompetent goof!" she shouts as she pounds her fists on his arms.

"I know, I know. We're heading that way." He says and lets her go. In the distance, a single *pop* accentuates the stream of bullets and Brother Nonnatus sees a trail of smoke fling up into the sky.

"Incoming!" He shouts and pushes his brothers forward. They continue to return fire as the explosive arcs high in the sky and comes back down.

Santa Cruz activates his suit's built-in mortars. A flurry of finger-thin contrails blast off from him and mingle in the air above. Forming their own arc at the enemy. The ZZH's explosive detonates midair in the cloud.

A second ZZH explosive fires off at a much more direct angle. It explodes against an outcropping nearby them. The Knights send a barrage of gunfire across the catwalk and strike three of the soldiers. Santa Cruz jumps up on the platform side of the walk and lets the 1541 loose. It chews up the metal between them and lays across two other soldiers.

A huge explosion sends a ball of flame out away from the platform. Two soldiers careen down off the platform in a hail of flaming debris. "Struck their supply crate or something," Nonnatus says as Santa Cruz gets down.

The explosion causes the catwalk to surge and tilt back in a violent dip. The single rail keeping the Knights from falling over the edge and down towards the planet's central mass isn't very inspiring to safety.

"Get off this," Commander Brigid says as the Knights rush to one side. Off the catwalk, he turns around and sees just how much lower the outside of the walk cants down than the platform. He crosses himself and turns to Gonzaga, says, "Get her into a spot where she won't be hurt," as he points to Bee. "The rest of us, push to clear the crew spaces. There can't be too many more soldiers, but it'll only take one to off the archbishop. Move, and may Christ bless us."

As they begin to move forward, a terrible calamity echoes back from the bow of the platform. Everyone looks that way around the curvature of the structure. See a gush of black smoke roiling outward on the starboard side. Some flames belch as well. Broken pieces of metal, and then the edge of the landing pod jerks downward the same way the catwalk did under their feet moments earlier. It snaps off, and the Knights loom over the edge to see everything including the ruined dropship and the Huskvar crumble down into the vast depths.

Brigid dials up his comms. "Brother Pio?"

"Yes, sir?"

"Are you still with us?"

"Yes, sir. Just, ah. . . making my way back aft towards my team."

"We're starboard side, near the aft corner. ETA?"

Nonnatus can't help but chuckle. He sends his brothers a message that scrolls along the bottom of their Visuals. *Two mikes.*

Pio says, "Two mikes."

Brigid laughs at that. "We'll head your way. I'll send you a layout on the schematics where we're going."

"Copy."

The team sets in, and Gonzaga looks around for the nearest corner to tuck Bee into. "Come with me," he says as he takes her by the arm and leads up a small set of stairs that lead to what looks like it could be an exterior workstation. Off another walkway, a small square pad with a podium on one end. The podium has a single touchscreen and interface terminal on it.

Gonzaga looks around, sees that the square pad is both covered and blocked on three out of its four sides. The open side has a small expandable half gate that extends across. He puts Bee inside the workstation and draws the gate closed.

"Not great," he says, "But I think if you stay down below this, you'll be fine. The bad guys are going to run towards us. You stay put and we'll be back when all is clear. Got me?"

Bee scowls. "Oh, yes, sir."

"Thanks." Gonzaga gives a half-wave and starts off after his team. Bee watches him go. The walls around the workstation are not there to enclose it, but rather features of the platform that can be considered walls at all. An exterior feature running higher than the workstation pad, a series of large diameter pipes and conduit running up and down, mounted so closely that there are only finger-sized gaps between. Bee watches as Gonzaga turns a corner and races towards the back of his last teammate as they make entry into the platform through a side door.

Bee also notices the controls on the workstation. She grabs a lever and twists it, feels the pad under her shudder and lifts upwards. "Oh," she says as a smile crawls across her face, "This workstation can be elevated, eh?"

†

"I think we're the last," Gruber says to the other two soldiers as they keep low and watch the Knights run around the starboard quarter and inside the platform. Smoke is still curling into the air from where the Knights destroyed their RPG battery. Wisps of it get in Gruber's eyes as he watches. "Loognar is all that remains besides us, and the priest is dealing with the process."

Jov curls a lip, lifts the breathing apparatus and spits at their feet. "Loognar knew this would happen. One must know anyone who crosses this heretic order pays for it in blood. We knew that and we were foolish enough to do this anyway." He surveys the dead nearby, pushing down the hurt. His ears still ringing from the RPG explosion.

Gruber scoffs. "We *believe* in this. We—"

"No, no. The Mormon operation made it look easy," Spawngower says. "They just. . . did as they were told. The Knights 1513— Jov is correct. Look what they've done to everyone else besides us. We had dinner with our siblings last night on Stake and now we're all that's left."

"I refuse to admit some collection of militant Christians somehow fooled us," Gruber says. "We knew this mission was a one-way ticket. We did it for the ZZH. We did it for Christ's truth."

"We did it because we were under Loognar's spell, and it got everyone killed now—"

"We knew the costs. The risks. Loognar will be a martyr right along with us. We sent a message today."

Spawngower grimaces, shuffles a heavy sniper rifle from resting on one side to the other. "I've been thinking, Loognar wanted us to be recognized as Christ's Truth by the Catholic Vatican. You know they never will, just as our Tiberian Council will never recognize them as the fullness of truth. I saw a communication that the 1513 spoke with the Tiberian Council. They've disavowed us. *Us*. We're. . . considered a terrorist break-off from the church."

Gruber scoffs again. "The Council. . . weak. They're all weak."

"No, have you—"

"Yes, they are. They will most certainly enjoy the fruits of our sacrifice today. Bringing our doctrine into the light across the galaxy. Revitalizing our conversion efforts. Displaying that Christ's Truth is worthy of dedicating one's life to. Of dying for! The Tiberian Council will sit back on their worthless, weak, fat laurels and enjoy all those things purchased with the lives of our siblings here today. Yes, they will denounce our methods, and I'm sure they'll do it publicly. But they're more worried about reimbursing that husk of an asteroid, or the ships those 1513 spies came on. The life of this worthless archbishop we stole. I'm sure the financial institution of those Romanists have already requested restitution for our damages. An itemized bill, even. That's what they're worried about."

Spawngower looks down the way they were headed before they ducked away from the Knights. "We need to get back to the Huskvar. It's our only chance."

Gruber slices a hand back and forth at the neck, says, "Negative. The Knights crashed their own ship into it. It's destroyed." The other two look stunned at the news. "It was that loud explosion from the bow of the platform. Just a minute ago. How did you two miss that?"

"All the gunfire. . . we were running. I guess I. . ."

Jov asks, "How are we getting off here, then?"

"Is this platform space capable?"

Jov thinks. "I seriously doubt it. It's not a ship—I mean, it looks like one, but it's really just a hunk of workspace with machinery all through it. I doubt it can propel itself enough to defeat gravity with all the weight it has. Or if it's even atmosphere tight if we did get into space."

"So, we're stuck."

"What you mean is, we're stuck with *them*."

"There's got to be a way—" Jov begins.

Gruber says, "The Knights destroyed both our ship and theirs in one fell swoop. They must have more coming. Any moment. But we don't have any backup. They're all dead. Our religion has disavowed us. The most violent enforcers in the galaxy are here, mopping up. Best I can imagine is we get executed right ion this platform. Or we get taken prisoner. And I have heard stories from our siblings of what the heretics do to prisoners."

"I'm not giving up my rifle," Spawnbower says.

"Then they'll take it off your corpse."

Jov looks around, "But Loognar says the Knights don't take prisoners. They only let their side of the story get out. Prisoners equal two sides to a story, you know?"

Gruber shrugs and slaps their shoulders. "The stories I hear may just be stories. Boogeyman stories, I don't know. Then we go down fighting what we came here to fight. Oppression. Injustice. False truth. The enemies of God."

"They just cut through everybody. *Everybody*," Jov says with a forlorn melancholy, inhales deeply and huffs. The weariness is like a long note on that one breath. "I'm almost out of ammo. I have no provisions. You?"

Gruber shrugs. Pulls the action open on the LM1157 in hand. "One in the chamber and a magazine with—" ejects the mag, looks in it, "—three more total."

Spawngower pats the sniper rifle. "Two eight round magazines."

Jov wipes away a single tear. The other two try to act tough, but the raw emotion has its effects. Jov remains silent for some time, staring distantly into the sky. The percussive patter of the jewel storm drowns out the few sobs escaping. Finally, "Do either of you want my gun?"

Both look confused, and both shake their heads. "Why?" Gruber asks. "Didn't you say you had almost no ammo?"

Jov nods pitifully and sets it down at their feet. Points to it and says, "It's there anyways."

Jov turns and walks over to the edge of the catwalk, then shoves over the rail. The other two shout as their friend plummets down through the rainbow swirls, being pelted by the storm until after a few moments, Jov disappears into the rich color and violently active storm.

"What in the Great Name was that?" Gruber asks.

"Despondency," Spawngower says. "Jov knew the risks, and when faced with the consequences, the devil stole any faith left. Without faith, there is only despondency."

"Well, I'm not killing myself."

"Nor will I." Spawngower gives Gruber a nod, trying to communicate they will die together. A sound travels to them, weaving about the concussion of the storm. Slicing through the veil of slow-dawning horror they're experiencing. There it is again, and both soldiers prick their ears to it.

"A voice?" Gruber asks.

"I could swear. . ." Spawngower mutters quietly. "Sounds like. . ."

Spawngower looks up cautiously, fearful a headshot will ring out as soon as the killer spots a target. No gunshot. But a waving hand from the other side of the ship. Spawngower squints, dares to let a smile break. "Rampart?"

From across the way, Bee is waving, calling. Beckoning them over.

Finding One Another

Brother Pio rushes out from under an overhang and spends a moment being berated by the storm before buttonhooking into the door his brothers just entered. He focuses his comms in a directional manner—hard to transmit through the hefty clutter of the storm and the walls of the platform—and says, "I'm inside."

Commander Brigid's voice comes back to him and says, "Ten meters in. There's a single left turn in the hallway, then us."

"Copy."

Pio moves at a hustle and crosses the distance. Ten meters of narrow, nearly blank hallway. There are a few posters that strike Pio as the basic corporate safety awareness type of thing. Photos of Carhovian men demonstrating team lifting and wearing proper personal protective equipment. All in language he doesn't read.

"Coming around the corner now," Pio says and slows down. He doesn't want to startle his brothers. "Brother Gonzaga, don't get jumpy and shoot me."

"I'm not."

"Here I come," and Pio turns the corner. There are the other Knights holding a defensive position just outside a door. Brother Nonnatus and Cleopas facing his way, guns out. Gonzaga in the middle as the others watch the closed door. On the wall looks like some kind of weekly dining menu by the format of it. Pio still can't read Carhovian. Over the door is a word on display, ornately painted on a slab of wood.

"Stack up," Brigid says, and they make a single file line. Each with his hand on the shoulder of the Knight in front of him. Brother Santa Cruz at the head of line, all his focus on breaching the wooden door before him. Their commander takes a breath and says, "Move."

Santa Cruz kicks the door handle, and his armor enhances the strike. The wooden door collapses off its hinges and caves inwards.

He flows in. Brigid is second, and even before he passes through the frame, Santa Cruz says, "Contact."

The team gets inside, and it is quiet. Peaceful. The fact that there are no gunshots, no telltale sign of whatever contact Santa Cruz called out is unsettling.

"Mess hall," Brigid says. The room is tight, all things considered, but obviously a cafeteria for the platform's crew. Four rectangular tables bolted to the floor, each with fold out circular seats. On the opposing wall is a serving window with an empty metallic well for hot food trays.

Overhead lights. A window looking outward into that gorgeous swirling atmosphere. A few posters. And a medpod containing Archbishop Hrutt.

The Knights move over to it. Cleopas taps on the touchscreen display and begins reading for the processes it has done and the one it's currently engaged in.

Brigid goes to the glass and sees the archbishop grimacing. Tubes snaking into his arms and legs. Five different small, rectangular devices laid all over him, each beeping and whirring as they perform whatever their function is. A single tube into the archbishop's nostril, a neon green fluid filling it.

"Archbishop Hrutt?" Brigid asks. "Can you hear me?"

The archbishop nods, opens his eyes to slits.

"I'm Commander Brigid from the 1513. We're here to retrieve you, Your Grace."

"They've been... hard at work." The archbishop groans. "Hard at work."

Brigid looks to Cleopas, who nods. He says, "Commander, these logs state the ZZH has been administering dangerously high dosages of chemical cocktails, hormones, the whole nine yards." He taps on a button and says, "They're making him a selective hermaphrodite."

"They're making him ZZH?" Gonzaga asks.

Cleopas says, "Their condition, anyways."

The archbishop coughs. "He. . . he thinks if I'm. . . like them, I'll . . . I'll advocate for them. He thinks, *my enemy becomes my friend by— by being forced to become— me.*"

"Can we interrupt the process? Put it on hold?" Brigid asks.

Cleopas runs through a few menus, pulls up a list of dialogue boxes, switches back and forth between a few screens. "They've gone so heavy so fast, the stress on his body, his actual genetics, it would most likely kill him if we withdraw it. The best bet is to let it continue; that's serving as life support."

"Can he not receive life support without continuing the process?"

Cleopas continues to search, cross reference. He sighs. "No. This medpod is of ZZH design. The process *is* the life support."

Gonzaga swears. He steps forward, says, "Wouldn't it be better to just withdraw the process then?"

Brigid and Cleopas both shake their heads. "No. That's mercy killing, and it is still morally evil."

"But the archbishop is—"

"Simply suffering is not a reason to take innocent life," Cleopas says. "Assuming he survives the process at all, he'll have whatever life one can expect, just as the ZZH do. This can open new doors for the archbishop's ministry against this ungodly process."

"Or," Brigid says, "He can enter into a contemplative stage in life. Write. Offer his struggles for the salvation of others. There's so much."

"Until God. . . or my brothers in Christ need. . . need me to. . . to lay down my life," the archbishop says, "Let me retain it."

"Of course," Gonzaga says and turns away.

Santa Cruz says, "I didn't see any other transports. Whoever is left from the ZZH is crawling around here. We've got to go."

Brigid nods. "Get the medpod out of here. Through the window if we need to." He activates his off-world comms, says, "Commander Brigid of Special Operations Unit #7-1a reporting. Primary objective accomplished. In need of evac. Entire team plus two additional, one of which is inside a medpod. Home in on my beacon."

He activates their position to transmit to the Command Center. Nonnatus and Cleopas examine the window, Gonzaga and Pio retrace their steps through the hallway to see where they can keep the medpod safe from the storm. A return transmission comes through.

"Unit #7-1a, command acknowledges. Rescue is in route to your location from the staged area in orbit. ETA, ten mikes. RADAR shows a severe storm in your location. Confirm, over."

"Severe storm confirmed," Brigid says. "It's raining literal gems. Visibility is limited to ten meters; the downpour is very heavy and damaging. Over."

"Copy, #7-1a. We've got cloud seeding capabilities on site. That should clear up the storm enough to do an I3 Rota extraction. Over."

Santa Cruz claps. The others groan. Gonzaga looks confused. "I3?" he asks.

Brigid holds up a hand. "I3 Rota, copy. We'll be ready. #7-1a out." He closes the comms and looks at his Knights. "Well, you heard them. Get ready."

"What's an I3 rotor-whatever?" Gonzaga asks. "They never trained us on that."

"Ieiunium Rota, is what it is. I3. Latin for *fast wheel*. Back in the old days it was called a Fulton surface-to-air-recovery system. Or STARS. It was also called a Skyhook. Our ships are the *Angelic Thrones* class."

"The what?"

Santa Cruz says, "It's wheel-shaped ship. Thrones were depicted as being like wheels covered in eyeballs. This is simple stuff. They come swooping in and—"

Brigid cuts them off. "Get the archbishop outside. We've got ten mikes to finish this gig."

Nonnatus laughs. "Unless they count ETAs like Pio does."

†

Spawngower and Gruber have to rush over the stern transom being pelted by the gem storm since the catwalk which did go from them to Bee fell off during combat. Each successive gem strike on their poorly armored backs and shoulders like an icepick. Each, just one more crack of the whip driving them forward. So, so many.

Gruber gets there first and dives under an overhang, instantly relieved with the shielding. Spawngower shoves in next, and they huddle for a moment, savoring the break.

"I'm sure I'm covered in bruises now," Spawngower says, rubbing a hand along everything struck.

"I'm worse off," Gruber says, showing the damaged hormone pump and a single gem lodged in the top of it. The status lights on it still glows, but a single red light flickers on and off steadily. A fitting for a hose is smashed, canting the plastic tubing off at an angle and allowing out a slow seep of fluid. "That's a problem."

"We can get another one," Spawngower says. "I hate to say it, but maybe we can even take one off a dead sibling back there."

"All those siblings have been laying out in this storm for the last ten minutes at least. They're ruined for sure." Gruber looks over and sees Svolt, dead and face down in the storm. "Svolt there was transitioning female. I'm going male. Even if we find one, if the process is wrong, I'll get the Opposites. I don't want that."

"I understand. I had a former mating partner that mistakenly did that. Took mine instead, on accident. It was three days before we figured it out. The Opposites are bad."

"Yeah. No thanks."

"I might have an old one," Spawngower says. "Back in our stuff." The sentence trails off as Spawngower looks over Gruber's shoulder to where they need to get to see Bee. "Speaking of an old mating partner, I think Rampart is back in there," he motions to the workstation just past where they are.

"Might have some idea of what to do next." Gruber fiddles with the hormone pump and then with a scoff of frustration tosses it down. "Rampart was a former mating partner of yours?"

"Yes. Last rotation when she was male, and I was female. We couldn't pair."

"Terrible."

"It was very hurtful," Spawngower says, rubs a sore hand where a circular purple bruise is rising. "How'd she even get here?"

"Good question."

"Let's ask," Spawnbower looks up and down the path, then darts out towards the workstation. Gruber sticks a hand out from under the covering and is immediately struck by a falling gem, then huffs wearily and follows.

As they cross around to the workstation, Spawngower calls out, "Rampart?" and is answered by a forceful but hushed bark to stay quiet. They round the bend and there she is, squatting down. Her body is facing away, but her head is turned.

"Silent, fools. They'll kill you."

The two crowd in with Bee under another thick run of piping and Spawngower asks, "How did you make it here?"

Bee looks them up and down with a calculation that bothers Spawngower. He remembers that look from their pairing attempts. No matter the state of their gender evolution, the eyes never change.

Maybe it was the soul behind them, but whether it's the windows themselves or the view inside, Rampart reveals it. Spawngower knows the gears are turning.

"How, I asked?"

Bee inhales deeply. "Prisoner. I was captured by the Knights 1513 when they killed the siblings I was with."

"But not you? You lived?"

"I'm female. Maybe that's the difference, I don't know."

Gruber sneers. "These heretics don't care, and they certainly don't *think* you're female. We're all deviants. But to that point, say they do think you're female. We had other females, you know. Svolt back there. Knox and Fellenfiffer on Stake. If you think—"

"—I don't care." Bee says. "Besides. They didn't bother to tell me why I'm not dead yet. I am a prisoner."

"Lies," Gruber says. "Father Loognar says they take none. Even Jov said he's heard if they do, it's a fate worse than death. You're no prisoner. Maybe you struck a bargain."

Bee holds her arms out. "How am I to escape? They shoved me here, went off to kill or capture the rest of you."

Gruber looks out into the storm. The raging clouds overhead have cast a pall over the otherwise brilliant color display. The swirls continue to pirouette around them but muted now. Shot through with glittering jewels like meteors.

Bee regards Gruber with contempt, then turns to Spawngower. "You're armed still?"

"A bit, yes. But certainly not enough to take on a squad of armored Knights." Spawngower turns to Gruber, "It might be that we should allow them to take us. If they haven't hurt Rampart yet—"

"Never." Gruber says. "We must be as defiant now to these heretics as our forefathers were when the Church demanded we stop preaching our truth, back in the beginning."

Spawngower pulls the rifle's strap over his head and lays it along a short wall. Then turns to Gruber. "It's suicide."

"It's martyrdom," Gruber says. "I will die for Christ and His truth in the ZZH church. We—"

A shot blasts out from behind them. Spawngower feels a spike of blistering heat travel through. Watches Gruber take a gut shot and fling backwards. The force of impact propels Spawngower forward, collapses face down on Gruber's limp body. The gem storm instantly begins pelting them. A hand grabs one ankle and drags Spawngower off to the side. Spawngower watches as Rampart strides into view and takes Gruber by the straps. Lift enough of Gruber up to haul over to the platform's edge.

Gruber is coughing up blood, trying to curse. To protest. To accuse Rampart as she coldly slides the soldier off the edge. Down into the rainbow abyss, a forever eddying current of beautiful colors. Then Bee turns around and jogs back to Spawngower, one hand over her head against the falling jewels. Out of the storm. She kneels so close to him she can smell his blood.

Spawngower can barely form words; the point-blank shot to the lower back has ruined all the organs there. The exit wound is hideous. As blackness surrounds Spawngower's vision and creeps towards the center of view, Rampart sets the rifle back against the wall and shrugs.

"Gruber's right, you know. Neither one of you complete idiots looked at my clothing."

Spawngower's eyes feel so heavy. He sees the exterior suit Bee is wearing. The maintenance company logo stitched on the arm of this one as well. He shifts as he can. Just one more time.

"They think I'm a helpless victim."

Blood spills out Spawngower's mouth and weakly utters, "Traitor to us all. . . to me. . . we—we were mating. . ."

Bee Rampart huffs with a tired, sad lilt. "Mating partners, yes. And you couldn't conceive." She leans forward and pats Spawngower's hairy cheek. "But you birthed that round into Gruber so very well. Finally, there's one thing I can't complain about your performance."

A blinding muzzle flash from near her knees. Searing pain through her entire head. Bee falls back on her hindquarters; arms dart out to support her. She instinctively rolls off to the side. Raining gems pelt her over and over. She scrambles to her feet, immediately runs into something metal. The shock of her eyes overloaded by the gunshot's flare instantly turning her already racing heart into a blistering engine.

The brilliant spots in her vision die back. She can feel blood running down her face. Hand to her left ear. It's gone. Ruined skin in its place. A nasty cut running down her face. Long, as long as the lies she's been telling.

She screams with rage. But the man who shot her, her old mating partner, the small frag gun in his hand, it shakes. Drops. Too weak now. She wants to run over and kick him. Turn that gun on him. Instead, she just hunkers down under the awning she's found nearby, the agony of her head wound consuming her.

Spawngower can't move. Tries to think. Begins a small mental prayer, but before any idea of what to really pray for occurs, it all goes dark.

Such Thunderous Noise

Commander Brigid finishes reading the latest message he's received from Operational Command and turns to his Knights. "Just got confirmation they've begun the cloud seeding op. Once we start to see the rain break up, we need to start scanning for the I3."

The Knights all nod. They've removed the window from the crew cafeteria wall. TechHafts made short work of the welds that held it in place. Set off to the side, they've made an opening big enough to haul the archbishop inside his medpod to the outdoor rescue.

"Make sure we get the equipment it's attached to over there," Brigid motions to a smaller box-like stack of devices that are connected to the medpod by cables.

Brother Cleopas starts moving it towards the window opening. "Auxiliary life support machinery," he says and sets it down. "Pretty good setup, too. This will take care of a lot of stuff the pod won't by itself." He looks out as a dark patch of swirling comes by, aggressively pelting an area near the window opening to the point where several gems strike and bounce through the opening. "Lord, I wish we had this with the Mariol woman. I wonder how she's faring."

"Much more comfortable now, brother."

Movement from inside the medpod catches Brother Nonnatus's eye. He leans over it and watches, then nods. Looks to the commander and motions him over. "Sir, the Archbishop wants you."

Brigid approaches and leans over the viewing glass. The archbishop raises an unsteady hand with one finger extended as if to point. "Beware. . . Loognar, he. . . is still about . . . with some kind of . . . large black device. It . . . consumed him, but. . ." the sentence trails off, too weak to hear.

Brigid considers his warning and thanks him. "Large black device. That can't be good."

"Our Savior be with us if he brought a 20de9 with him." Brother Santa Cruz says. "Brother Gonzaga, you still got that device you took off the ZZH?"

"I do," Gonzaga holds it up. "Want me to sit on top of the medpod? Leave it with the archbishop? You think that would be enough to keep him safe?"

"Worth a try," Brigid says. "Yes. We can move, fire, all that. But if—" a distant popping sound from outside catches his attention. From far away, high up. He turns to look and sees a bright spot appear in the storm. "Cloud seeding has arrived. Five mikes and we're out of here."

The cloud seeding missiles are small, needlelike. Each carries an onboard payload of a chemical medley that disperses and renders inert the mixing gases in Zaffre Asperity's atmosphere that combine to form the gem storm. Holes begin appearing in the roiling clouds; gaping spots that push back the violent gray mixture and allow through the sun rays. Portals in the storm, from where beyond the amazing greens and reds and yellows of the atmosphere can peek through and dazzle with their patterns. It allows through hope.

"Praise God," Brigid says so warmly those two words glow.

"Yes, praise Him." Loognar says from one of the doorways leading into the cafeteria. From nowhere. The Knights spin and raise their weapons. The ZZH priest stands as an onyx-black wall so great in height he ducks to enter the room. Bizarrely geometric shapes like armor all over him. His face exposed through a helmet-like opening in an otherwise massive, boxy chest. "Always praise to our God. He delivered you unto me, as He promised to deliver the wicked to the righteous throughout the testaments."

"Nice armor," Santa Cruz says as he maneuvers between Loognar and the medpod, gun up and mortar hatches open.

"Your archbishop will carry our gospel forward. Your feeble rescue attempt is too late." Loognar says. "I will offer you the same grace I offered him. If you submit, I will hear your confessions and offer absolution before sending you to our Lord. Otherwise, you will be reduced to red smears, and I shall simply disappear into the night. So, what say you?"

"You're not getting off this platform," Cleopas says. "You've got no transport."

Loognar smiles. "Arrangements are simple enough."

The Knights have fanned out, covering their fields of fire. Brigid sends orders to scrawl along the Visuals of his Knights. Battle plan. "Your sacraments are invalid," Brigid says. "Good enough answer?"

"It is."

Brigid fires directly at his face. A thick finger of black extends out faster than a thought, and the rounds ricochet off as the doors to Loognar's helmet close. A single red cycloptic eye alights in its place. He has two arms in the 20de9 suit.

"Cheap but expected." Where the hands would be, there are two undulating rings pressing up from just below the alien skin. Expanding and contracting in size. "My sword is merciless."

"Sonic weapons," Gonzaga says, recognizing the rings from earlier. Each Knight realizes just how loud it's been with the gem storm haranguing the platform.

"Such thunderous noise outside, isn't it?" Loognar asks. He starts to laugh and Santa Cruz fires all his mortars at him.

The explosion is immense. Loognar fires his sonic cannons a split second later, and the sound waves send surges of flame and small debris back at the Knights. Cleopas engages his suit's shield from his forearm and takes the brunt of it. Gonzaga grabs the medpod controls and races to the window. Nonnatus and Santa Cruz lay down covering fire as Brigid helps Gonzaga drag the archbishop through their opening.

Loognar emerges from the smoke and errant flames, firing a second round of sonic pulses. They hit Cleopas and knock him off his feet. He scrambles while gunfire erupts from around him. Loognar swings his arms wide open as if to embrace them all at once. A grand group hug. Projectiles strike and bounce off his shadow-made-solid armor. He laughs.

Cleopas makes it to his feet. Brigid sends a message that they're outside. *Fall back.* Nonnatus and Santa Cruz send a second volley of mortars and move to the window. Through the new explosion Cleopas sees the 20de9 fritz and try to disengage from Loognar, but somehow whatever leash Loognar has on it he forces it to stay in place. Take the hit for him.

"Thing has a survival instinct all its own," Cleopas says to himself as he moves to cover his brothers with his shield.

"Let's go," Nonnatus shouts to him. Cleopas makes it to the window and gets hit with another sonic blast, throwing him out and back. The downward heave of gems immediately begins pelting him all over. He holds his shield up against the rain and regains his feet. Moves out of the way just as Loognar cuts a section of the wall with blistering lasers and comes outside.

†

Still with fury racing through her veins, Bee Rampart examines the rifle her siblings left behind. With it, two magazines worth seven rounds total. One magazine with four rounds, all standard full metal jacket cartridges. Basic ammo, and of no value against these obnoxiously armored heretics. She sets it aside in case she needs to send herself to her Lord and Savior rather than become their slave.

The other magazine with three rounds in it—the one she used to ventilate her former mating partner and his companion—now, here is something. These rounds are in yellow-painted casings. Their projectile's tips grooved in such a manner as to not need the paint to stand out. She rolls one in her fingers, "Depleted uranium. High yield powder."

She looks back at the corpse of Spawngower. After he expired, she gathered her strength, spit venomously in an explosion of wrath and ran over to him. Kicked him repeatedly until she grew too tired and finally shuffled his body out from cover and into the storm.

His wound is extraordinary. How the single shot pierced him through his armor, admittedly much, much weaker than the plating the Knights are wrapped in, and how it went on to ruin Gruber as well. "Now, this is something."

Bee thinks back to the ship they took down here from Stake. It's difficult to tune out her new facial injury and focus on her memories. The entire time the Knights left her unmolested, as if she was some damsel in distress. Not a trained, calculating eye. Not a soldier observing them for weaknesses. The few marginally exposed points in their armor she noted.

The scope on the gun is a good one. Obviously more useful for destructive rounds like these yellow ones. A good shot—no. A *blessed* shot. That would put the brakes on these men. Maybe only one, but a man down becomes a force multiplier. One down, one to carry him. Possibly two to carry him. That's a devastating distraction, especially if they have to come back around and retrieve her.

"It might take their mind off me just long enough to get somewhere," she looks forward on the platform as spots of sunshine start to break through the storm. Infinitesimally quiet little pops occurring behind the clouds. The colorful swirls breaking through.

Crashing sounds. Bizarre notes puncturing the deafening drone of the storm. The barrage of the gems striking the shielded platform like some alien stampede. Gunfire.

It's all gunfire. "And it's coming this way. . ." Bee hunkers down in her elevated workstation, sets the rifle up and peers through the scope just as a Knight comes into view, moving aft.

†

"Fallen man is by his nature selfish, and though his God calls to him, he worries not about the end things until the end is upon him," Loognar shouts as he forces the 20de9 to reconfigure a shoulder into a light amplifying weapon. A hazy, thin beam sweeps across the platform where Commander Brigid and Brother Gonzaga are positioned, taking aim. The amplified light cuts through the metal and arcs upwards to cleave them in two. They dodge to either side and Gonzaga feels the searing heat lop off a corner to his armor.

"My own bishop, Bishop Chin Malichi Fritz taught that," Loognar says, stomping forward. "And the end is upon your man, there."

Brother Nonnatus races around with the archbishop's medpod in tow. Against the impressive clatter of the storm, he grabs a handhold on the platform and pulls up. The medpod strains to follow him as he clambers up and around. Out of the line of fire.

"You think your archbishop will die for you? When he has life at my hands? No! He will let you all die and carry on as an ambassador of the ZZH! What he preached as heresy yesterday, he will proclaim as gospel tomorrow!"

"Delusional," Brother Santa Cruz says as he ducks behind cover and then peeks out, taking aim. He fires, and his round ricochets off the 20de9's body. It rends the metal just a bit, and Santa Cruz sends a message over Visuals to his brothers.

As armor, this thing can't dodge our fire the way the others did. We can pound it down.

Cleopas responds, *It wants to. Loognar is using it as a shield. It's his victim.*

"Pound it, then," Brigid says and opens fire in a blast of rounds. "Make it choose between protecting him and protecting itself." The other Knights emerge and do likewise. Loognar cackles and sweeps his amplified light beam one way, fires sonic waves the other. The Knights dodge the best they can, keep their fire up.

A small node appears on the 20de9 armor's head and begins flashing intense light. The Knights' armor adjusts to filter it out. *Crowd control lights,* Brigid sends to the others. *Probably emitting a frequency noise to induce nausea and vomiting. Vertigo.*

"Aim at his weapons," Brother Pio says as he unloads into the light amplifying device on Loognar's shoulder. The device, like a shoulder mounted swiveling turret, tries to return fire but Pio can see the small blocks it's made from struggling to rearrange to avoid the gunfire. Fold and refold out of harm's way as whatever Loognar is doing to thwart it fights it internally.

Loognar himself bellows as the turret breaks his hold and wins, folds back down out of the bullets' way. He responds by forcing a new turret on the other shoulder only to have it hammered by fire. He unfolds machine guns and sweeps the deck.

Nonnatus comes down the far side of the platform, throws a packet of CQ4 at Loognar. The ZZH priest's armor stabs out with cubic project, impales the explosive. It explodes two meters away from his body. The concussion blast is enough to topple him off to the side. Loognar sweeps his laser towards Nonnatus.

Santa Cruz and Gonzaga move in, pummeling the 20de9 with gunfire. Loognar shoves up to his feet. Grabs Santa Cruz and aims his laser at him. As it fires Gonzaga shoves the muzzle of his gun into its barrel, unloading. Santa Cruz kicks up, striking the faceplate over Loognar's helmet. Loognar grabs him with his other arm and strikes Gonzaga with his freed hand.

Brigid and Cleopas move around, concentrate on Loognar's back. Loognar aims his machine guns that way, lighting up the platform all around the Knights. A tentacle-like protuberance sticks out from Loogar's armor, fires a wad towards Brigid and Cleopas. The wad bursts and expands into a spiderweb-like net that spreads wide enough to catch them even as they move. As they struggle against the strands, Loognar concentrates his fire into them.

Santa Cruz fires a volley of mortars high into the air. Several get hit by falling gems, but the rest arc hard back down and impact all along Loognar's shoulders and head. With Santa Cruz being so much closer to their explosions, he takes a beating as well. Loognar hurls him towards the edge of the platform and lunges at Gonzaga.

Pio gathers his CQ4 package and hurriedly mashes it into a concave shape, sets it and tosses at Loognar's feet. With the other Knights keeping fire on him, the ZZH priest's weapon systems are computing a kilometer a second. Gonzaga sees the CQ4 land and reacts. The 20de9's armored hand smashes into the floor grating between Gonzaga's legs. He pushes off it. Rolls backwards wildly. The explosion sends Loognar up into the air. He hits a cluster of piping overhead. Tears into them. They begin spewing gases out, occluding his silhouette. He comes crashing back down, his arm transformed into several stabbing weapons. He punches it into the floor grating beside Gonzaga. Instead of running, Gonzaga grabs them.

"Fools to the end," Loognar says as he lifts his arm. Gonzaga hanging on. The Knight lunges over the forearm, slaps a wad of CQ4 on Loognar's neck and shoves off. Loognar swings his stabbing arm at the Knight, striking him hard in the back. Gonzaga flies into the wall nearby. He rolls off to the side, groaning.

The CQ4 explodes, hurling Loognar out into the storm. He slides over by the edge and the 20de9 armor glitches. Fights against its leash held by Loognar to get out of the rain. He stands up, lasers swinging wildly at the body of the platform. Trying to incinerate any opponent.

Cleopas succeeds in cutting a strand of the web. "Here," he says and shows the commander the weak point he's created. Together they grab the section and yank. Brigid extends his TechHaft and ignites it. The exaggeratedly giant Merovingian axe blazes forth and he swings into it. Saws. Cleopas pulls free, turns and grabs Brigid. Heaves him out.

The other Knights see Loognar scrambling, and as he turns, they see Santa Cruz emerge on his back. He sprays a thick band of breaching foam all down Loognar's back. Loognar bends forward at the waist and extends several stabbing spikes out. Santa Cruz takes the hit and flails, falls off. But the breaching foam begins to smoke. Bubble.

Loognar screams. The Knights detect another sound—the drone itself screeching as it starts discharging damaged cubes. All at once the foam explodes. Loognar falls forward. Pio darts in and grabs Santa Cruz, who is still getting to his feet.

Loognar grabs them both, unloads his machine guns into them. Their armor blackens with the firepower. The other Knights lay their own gunfire into Loognar and his guns. Loognar smashes Pio and Santa Cruz together, then hits them both with his sonic pulses. The Knights fling off. At the same time, his guns still firing, one gives out. The other a moment later.

"Out of ammo," Brigid says. He grabs an explosive from his suit and throws it. It gets cut in half with a laser, exploding in the air between them. Then Loognar unfolds a long barrel from his suit and at the end, a small box on it starts sparking. A flame spews out, and he laughs wickedly as he belches flame all along the platform side.

†

"This is a test of faith," Bee says as she zeroes in with the sight. "If You are with me, Lord, if You are with the ZZH and Your truth, guide my hand," she prays. Following the melee through her scope, she is dazzled by the gout of flame.

She fires just as Loognar moves and the Knights react. The round strikes a thick undergirding and sharply ricochets. A fountain of sparks plumes up, then she hears it more than sees it somewhere else. Then above her head a meter, the round strikes.

She screams and ducks down, covering her head. Looks up and sees a blistered hole in the metal above. "How dare You, God?" she seethes. *"How dare You?"*

†

Gonzaga ducks off to the side, withdraws his TechHaft and ignites it. A tremendous bow and arrow come forth, and he shoots an energy arrow into Loognar's lower belly. The arrow has a trail line attached to it, glowing red with its semi-permanent energy particles. It's attached to his TechHaft, and he yanks it with all his might. Loognar falls off balance and out from under the overhang he is using as protection from the storm.

Gems rocket down like hail stones in tornado weather. The 20de9 suit reacts, pulling and trying with all its might to shed itself from him as gem after gem strikes it.

Loognar swipes at the trail line and severs it. The energy dissipates instantly, and he re-establishes his guns, opens fire again.

Brigid shouts, "Again!" and Gonzaga restrings another laser arrow. More pops occur in the atmosphere and more and more holes appear in the storm. Glorious swirls speckle the sky with their rainbow of beauty as the mechanized Knights and the darkness of the ZZH priest rage.

†

"Lord, I'm giving You one more chance. Be with me as I fire this weapon, guide this round into the devil-possessed person of our enemy, I pray to You," Bee says as she zeroes in on Brother Pio's neck. "I glorify You as I strike down these heretics who hate You and Your everlasting love. *Now, prove to me Your worth.*"

She takes a deep breath and holds it. Lets it slowly creep out as she eases back on the trigger. Wanting to be startled by the shot. Don't anticipate, just let it happen.

Tighter, tighter. Her breath is a third of the way out. Half now. Just a bit more and the rifle roars.

†

Brother Pio's head rings with an impressive concussion as he gets kicked to his knees by the impact. He rolls off to the side and Brother Santa Cruz stumbles to him. "Fire from behind us!" he calls out. Santa Cruz grabs Pio and drags him behind cover. Pops back up and launches a volley of mortars at Loognar.

The ZZH priest is still flailing wildly with his flame thrower, coating all around him as he's fighting against his unruly armor as well as with the attacking Knights.

Santa Cruz kneels beside Pio and rolls him over. Sees a sooty black dent in his helmet. "Right on the rim. Another few centimeters down and it would have skipped between it and your neck guard."

Pio coughs and groans hard. "That was. . . what was that?"

Santa Cruz looks back, sees where they left Rampart. "It came from that woman you rescued."

"No way."

"At least over there by her. More ZZH soldiers?"

Pio groans again. "Sure, they could have doubled back around or. . .or—"

"Or anything," Commander Brigid says over their comms. "Brother Cleopas, you and Santa Cruz take it wide back around there. If the woman is ZZH, stop her from helping Loognar. If not, see who's firing on us. Go."

"You good, buddy?" Santa Cruz asks as he makes eye contact with Cleopas rushing towards them.

"Yes. My guardian angel is pretty good about these close calls."

Santa Cruz pats him hard on the shoulder, then grabs and lifts him up. "Until Christ calls us home."

Cleopas makes it over to Santa Cruz and they jump a waist-high wall feature and dart through the storm to the next cover. Make their way aft down the centerline of the platform.

†

"Not a great way to build my faith in You, God," Bee says as she snarls and slams the gun down.

Somehow the humiliation of the fudged shot makes her head even worse. Seeing the two Knights dash off, she knows exactly what they're doing. "No way I'll even make progress taking them on," she whines. Pounds both her fists into the wall, then her knees.

Thoughts and fears boil up like sickness at the thought of being taken to some rape room or medical torture site. Who knows what the Knights 1513 really have. Maybe Loognar was right, and they don't take prisoners. They'd execute her right then, maybe? Or if Gruber was right, her fate is worse than that. The Knights are already doing something to clear up the storm. More and more pockmarks are appearing in the gray maelstrom overhead, allowing fresh sunlight through.

And they're overtaking Loognar.

She looks to the gun and thinks whether she can really turn it against herself. Her brain is muddled; stressed. *What was I trying to do? Fight until there's no more fighting left? What does that even look like? I am—*

She looks around, sees Spawngower's body nearby. A thought occurs to her like lightning out of the storm. So clear.

"'Til now, they've been treating me like a rescue. Some little damsel in distress, indeed. Those maintenance people were theirs in disguise. They must think—"

She grabs the rifle again. Rolls Spawngower over. Lays it in his arm and digs out his small frag gun. "You can make it up to me for being so worthless yet again, sweetie."

†

Brothers Santa Cruz and Cleopas are nearing the final corner to where they dropped off Bee minutes ago when they hear two more shots in rapid succession. Guns up, they clear the corner.

Santa Cruz sees the downed ZZH soldier and kicks him to the side to avoid tripping on him. Bee is huddled in the corner, bloody and hurt, knees drawn up to her chin and blood on her face. Her eyes wide, she sees them and screams.

"Stop him!" She shouts, pointing at the dead soldier. "Stop him from hurting me!"

Cleopas looks down, sees the gaping wound in his abdomen and another entrance wound in his head. He looks to Santa Cruz and gives the hand sign for *dead*.

Cleopas startles when he gets a good look at the woman. "Lord, be with us. What did he do to you?"

Bee just whimpers and cries. Touches her head, careful to cradle her hand protectively around her missing ear. The cut on her face bleeds freshly as she grimaces and weeps.

Santa Cruz turns to Bee says, "He's dead. Did you shoot him?"

Bee stutters manically, terrified. "He just— he just came around here and and and he had that gun—" she points to the rifle laying nearby, "—and he hurt me and then shot at you over. . . over there that way he shot at you. And then I just— I just I didn't want to be you know, *whatever* he was going to do and I just hit him or something and then I took this little gun I took the gun and I, I fired and fired and then you showed up."

The Knights both squat next to her. Cleopas takes the rifle in hand and examines it. Santa Cruz gently says, "Self-defense. He was trying to kill us and then you, whatever—"

"I'm a terrible person, oh Lord forgive me. . ." Bee puts her head in her hands. Her shoulders tremble. Santa Cruz lays a hand on her and she jumps. He pulls back. "I'm sorry we had to take you here. It's a battle. I'd rather have sent you to safety. We didn't have time or resources and—"

"Is he dead?" Bee interjects, extremely fearful.

"Yes."

"Then get me to safety."

"Working on it. We'll get you to medical. I vow it."

Cleopas looks up from the body and says, "Brother, look at these." He holds up the magazine of yellow-painted rounds.

Santa Cruz takes it, looks at the tips, the markings and puts it together. "Those are extra high-power depleted uranium. These bad boys are the rifle version of bunker busters."

"He must have hit Brother Pio with that."

Santa Cruz snorts. "Terrible shot, though." He does not notice Bee sour at the comment. "Might turn the tide, though."

†

Commander Brigid sees the 20de9 try to peel off Loognar like tearing glue from a surface. Stretchy but solid at the same time, peeling back leaving strings of material, only to have it snap back into place around him.

"How is he controlling that?" He demands out loud, still moving to provide fire while dodging attacks.

"He must have one of those devices like what Gonzaga had," Brother Nonnatus says.

"Those only identify friendlies," Brother Pio says as he fires a pin-sized rocket into Loognar's back. "They don't take control of the drone."

"Well, his does."

Brother Gonzaga gets the alert just as his brother Knights do. Brigid shouts, "I3 inbound!" Gonzaga moves to get behind Loognar and shoot another arrow when he sees the 20de9 fight against its master, unfolding and trying to stretch away. It reveals some kind of canister-looking device on Loognar's person. As the drone struggles and shifts, remolds around the ZZH priest, the canister positions up above his head. When the armor fully envelops him again, the top of the canister is like a rim sticking out of the back of where the head would be.

"That's it," he says. So confident that the Lord has revealed this to him, he ducks and rewinds his Visuals' feed, takes a still shot of the canister. Sends it out with the message, *There it is. That's the control.*

Santa Cruz responds, *I can hit that from here.*

Brigid sends, *Get it done, then.*

Gonzaga knocks an energy arrow and shoots it into Loognar.

†

"Go, go!" Brother Santa Cruz shouts as Brother Cleopas takes off from their position, running at full speed towards Loognar. Santa Cruz takes the rifle with the uranium rounds in it and posts up on the workstation. He maneuvers the controls to lift it up high, right into the falling gems from the storm. Bee screams as the gems strike all around her. She curls up into the fetal position under what little overhang she has. The Knight is unaffected by the onslaught. His concentration too great.

High up enough, he gets the shot lined up.

Loognar sees a spot on the platform in front of him where the cloud seeding has created a hole. Fresh sunshine and respite from the blistering downpour. He steps into it, praising God for giving his disobedient suit a moment to concentrate on what he's commanding it to do rather than trying to betray him and avoid the jewel storm.

"My plan is complete, and now you will die," he says. "Your archbishop will witness to our truth, and I will disappear and be remembered only as a glorious martyr for this cause. My cause."

"Not God's cause?" Brigid says as they continue to lay down fire.

"One in the same, heretic. I have prayed fervently to receive the revelation that this is what He wants."

Cleopas emerges from the side, barreling towards Loognar. Gonzaga heaves on the arrow. Santa Cruz takes a deep breath and holds it. Lets it slowly creep out as he eases back on the trigger. Wanting to be startled by the shot. Don't anticipate, just let it happen.

Tighter, tighter. His breath is a third of the way out. Half now. Just a bit more and the rifle roars.

The top of the 20de9's armor rocks forward as sparks explode from the destroyed canister. Cleopas takes a flying leap and hammers into Loognar, knocking him back. Combined with Gonzaga puling on the trail line from the arrow, Loognar stumbles out of the patch of sunshine and right into an overshadowed spot of downpour.

Cleopas falls off to the side and the Knights watch as the freed 20de9 begins to dodge the incoming gems by opening small holes in itself. Reaction fast, opened and closed, opened and closed.

And underneath them, Loongar.

The ZZH priest dances in complete agony as his suit of armor picks its own survival over his. Instantly opening holes to allow the raining gems to fall through, nailing him over and over again. He screams, bellows. Flings his arms around like a man swatting away a swarming mass of stinging insects.

He falls over, pelted a hundred times and then a thousand more. Rolling from one side to the next until the combat drone heaves itself fully off him. A blanket with a mind of its own, unwrapping itself from someone cuddled inside.

The severely damaged 20de9 reforms into a hovering train-like formation and rushes off toward a patch of sunlight in the storm. The patch moves with the winds high up in the sky as they blow the swirling gases around. The 20de9 follows, even as the patch leaves the edge of the platform and carries off further into the world. The drone cruises right off the lip of the platform's starboard edge, and without a solid surface underneath it to repel against and therefore float, it falls downwards the gulf of distance to the next surface.

A new patch of sunlight shines over Loognar like a spotlight. The man is absolutely broken. Already glowing purple from internal bruising, bleeding everywhere. He jitters and coughs a throaty, wet sound.

"Santa Cruz, you and the girl, get down here on the double," Brigid says. He walks over to Loognar, who is trapped in a forever moan of suffering. His respirator still on, cracked and foggy. One eye rolls up to Brigid, and in it, the commander sees true hate.

"We'll try and help you," Brigid says. "I'll call rescue."

Loognar does what he can with his broken mouth to smile. Gurgles a sarcastic laugh. "You... have... no... love... for— for me."

"I do." Brigid says. A message scrolls across his Visuals just then, *Ieiunium Rota inbound.* He looks up. "Get ready for the Fast Wheel. It's time."

"Sir?" Pio asks. He looks to Loognar. "What's the call?"

Cleopas is getting the archbishop ready, and he leans over the medpod. "Excuse me, Your Grace?"

The Knights turn to look at Cleopas, who has his helmet near the viewing glass. He listens intently, says, "Yes, Archbishop." He leans up and turns to his brothers. "Archbishop Hrutt... he says to put Loognar in the medpod. With that life support gear we took."

"That'll kill the archbishop," Gonzaga says. "You said earlier if we unhook him—"

"Correct," Cleopas says. "The archbishop wants to lay down his life for his friend in Christ. John 15:13."

The Knights regard one another for a precious moment they don't have. Brigid clears his throat, says, "You heard the archbishop." He looks down at Loognar, who's one eye is frozen with incomprehension at the change of plans. "We do have love for you. As Christ commanded, we have love."

Loognar's lips quake. Trying to say something, but he cannot. A tear falls from his eye, and he looks away.

Favorite Way to Fly

Brother Cleopas opens the medpod and gently removes Archbishop Hrutt. Brother Santa Cruz brought a respirator off the dead ZZH soldier by the platform, and they get it on Hrutt.

The archbishop tries to stand and does well enough to lean on Brothers Pio and Nonnatus. He slumps between them, an arm strung around both their necks. All his strength dedicated to holding his head up high, lips moving in silent prayer. Eyes focused on a hole in the storm where God's brilliant array of color beams through. He smiles.

Santa Cruz maintains their perimeter while the other Knights work. Cleopas and Gonzaga gather up Loognar's broken form and lay him out in the pod. Cleopas cuts away his tattered clothing and shuts the lid, allowing the machine's program to take over. A scanner array on an arch over the pod's bed runs up and down, examining him. Tiny surgical arms unfold from the sides, start an IV. Insert a port into his side. Run a clear tube up one nostril.

Cleopas can see that though only half conscious, Loognar's relief is immediate. Cleopas prays for him. Turns around toward his brothers.

"Get your gear ready, it's show time," Commander Brigid says. He reaches behind himself, grabs a thin rectangular box the length of his back. Detached, he unpacks from it a large spool connected by a metal cable to a yellow rubber bladder with a gas charged cylinder at its base. The spool clips onto the center point of his back between his shoulder blades. He stands ready with the yellow bladder in hand.

The other Knights do the same. Cleopas reaches under the medpod and retrieves a rectangular box that is sized for the pod. Blows off a layer of dust on it. Prepares Loognar.

Pio connects the archbishop to himself, and Gonzaga gets Bee. Says, "We're not far away from getting you fixed up, okay?"

Bee won't make eye contact. Nods slightly and nothing more.

Brigid snaps his fingers to get their attention. "There, inbound," he says as he points to the coordinates in the sky he's just received.

The distinctive operating sound of the *Ieiunium Rota* penetrates the air before it. Still immersed inside the cloud coverage, the Knights hear it before they see it. A gravelly low bass tone rumbling in its motor chugging combined with a high-pitched scree that would be at home with gears shearing and flailing about.

Santa Cruz claps. "Home free, now, boys." He turns to Bee, who is disconcerted by the cacophony. He gives her a thumbs up, says, "This is my favorite way to fly."

"What's it going to do?" she asks.

"Watch your balloon, keep your body loose, and make sure you exhale before it snatches you up."

"What?"

Santa Cruz waves off the question, looks at Gonzaga. "Got your grappling hook?"

Gonzaga smiles. "Yeah, and my personal transponder."

"Then you're ready to be one of us." At that, the sound of the Wheel Ship suddenly becomes much clearer. He turns back to the sky.

True to its name, the *Ieiunium Rota* appears as a giant spinning wheel. Bursting through the storm clouds, it's a spherical center with a tremendous rotary portion spinning upright along its center axis. Diving down to them, its motor sound becomes deafening.

"Put them up!" Brigid shouts and heaves his rubber bladder up into the air. His suit's strength enhancements hurl the thing high up, the spool unfurls the trail line and the small gas-charged cylinder punctures with a staccato shot. The bladder instantly inflates into a huge yellow balloon. It's joined by all the others.

The Knights run into a line, straight and evenly spaced as they can get it. The storm whips at the balloons. On the spool is a small battery that sends an electrical charge up the trail line where it's filled with electro-reactive particles. The particles, when charged, form stiff chains and help to hold the trail line rigid. Cleopas maneuvers the medpod to the end and stands between it and the others. The wheel ship adjusts its trajectory and swoops down.

"I love these!" Santa Cruz hollers with joy as the Wheel Ship's rotating portion extends a V-shaped hook that snatches directly under the balloon. The contacts kill the electrical charge and with an explosive heave he's yanked from the surface and into the air a hundred meters. He ecstatically hoots the entire way.

Bee watches as each Knight propels upwards in a split second. The Wheel Ship zooms overhead, the earsplitting noise of the storm overcome by the earsplitting noise of the rescue vehicle. Time slows down to a microsecond as the extraction reaches her and Gonzaga. She screams in terror as their balloon is caught. The tremendous rotation of the recovery wheel cranes them upward in a colossal pull. Like being shot out of a cannon.

The moment of contact with the V-hook, the racing speed of rotation, the absolute fury of it all. Steals her breath away. Punches it out of her. The storm races down and past her as if there was a planet-sized vacuum beneath her feet, drawing it all that way. They swing aft at what feels like a million kilometers per hour. In the blink of an eye they are being towed by the wheel ship as it ascends, something inside its guts winching them as fast as they flew up. She sees the menacing gray and black of the storm, the gorgeous colors of the atmosphere, all of it while leaving the brutalized platform beneath them.

Bee drops onto the metallic floor of whatever compartment they're in, draws air into her burning lungs, and starts to scream again. In the corner, Santa Cruz is clapping and hollering with joy.

Declaration of Resplendence

With the I3 oriented like a rolling wheel, the receiving bay is located on the bottom with both the flight drive and pilot cockpit above. The entire bay is forged from one piece of an exceptionally thick impact-resistant and space-capable poly-glass. Fully transparent. The view it offers is second to none.

The Knights crowd into it and drop in their flight chairs with a collective heavy sigh. Finally helmetless, they breathe out and wipe the sweat drenching them. Archbishop Hrutt is gently placed into a chair as well, between Commander Brigid and Brother Cleopas. Cleopas detaches his suit's first aid kit and does what he can to assess him.

As they rise above the remnants of the storm, into the full glory of the swirling colors of Zaffre Asperity, the archbishop smiles.

"What a. . . tremendous gift. . . this— this is," he wheezes out. "To be. . . welcomed out of this life. . . and into God's hands by— by this, His beauty."

The gases roll around on and off the glass like gentle tides of radiant splendor. Beneath them, falling ever further downward toward the planet's surface as they ascend into the upper atmosphere, the giant storm crawls like a darkened bottomfeeder through an ocean of pure rainbow. Bolts of lightning illuminate it like veins. Holes punched through it with the cloud seeding. The pinpoints below them, each gorgeous.

Bee Rampart sits in her chair, studying the Knights. Each rugged and handsome in his own way. Full beards on many, which she fells jealous over. Many of the ZZH have a hard time developing Anything more than patchwork.

Dumbfounded just enough by this, she asks before she even realizes she is speaking, "You're all monks, are you not?"

Brother Gonzaga, still so fresh to that adopted state, is surprised to hear himself included in it. "We are. Final vows, every man."

"I see." She recalls graduating from her primary education on Xewl. Top of her class. Her parental mating pair were so proud of her. None of her other siblings distinguished themselves like she did. They went on to do menial tasks. But not her. God had smiled on her.

On Xewl, as in any city or planet they occupy, the ZZH requires laying on of hands for any religious situation. Even their nuns, who simply transition into monks when their rotation is triggered. Bee supposes it is one way the ZZH differentiated themselves from the Catholic heresy when they developed their doctrines.

Her educators asked her to assume a priestly role, the headmaster nearly begging. *Someone of your capabilities, image the souls you can bring to Christ. . . look at your accomplishments thus far, can you image your future?* So much praise for a child still in primary school. Accomplishments? How she doggedly memorized her catechism? How she argued all the other children down if they strayed from their beliefs? She was an athlete, though she would be hard-pressed to ever do that rotary rescue nonsense again. No thrill. Only sheer suicidal terror.

Of her parental mating pair, the one who produced the sperm for her conception was named Kurlos. He spent three days trying to convince her to enter seminary. She was so resistant that he accused her of an inflated ego. And by the end he told her she was listening to temptation. Demonic temptation for her dreams when there should be none other than helping evangelize.

Bee hated Kurlos then, as she still does today.

Those that do not receive the laying on of hands are free to transition and attempt mating. She declined any holy orders. She desired to propagate and spread their truth in that manner.

Bee Rampart has never conceived, as either male or female, and it burns with bitterness inside her. She is too good to merely be a priest. Loognar is a priest and look at him. Denied her right to be a parent when God would not cooperate with her and her mating partner. Kurlos was a parent and look at him. If she cannot be successful with heretics through convincing, then it shall be through coercion.

But these imbeciles she aligned herself with, Loognar's ragtag collection of half-baked soldiers who were mostly lifted from security details and military misfits, though they shared her militant views . . . look at them.

"The only priest here is the dying man, then," She glances at the archbishop. Turns to Loognar, inside the medpod. They placed him near the entrance to the receiving bay; the only spot inside where there was room enough. "And *him*."

Brother Pio says, "I assume so. We're with the Order of Those Washed in the Water and Blood from His Side. That man is with another religion. I believe he said he was a priest in their religion. I can't recall how to properly pronounce the name, but I guess it's commonly enough called—"

"ZZH." She finishes for him.

"You know them, eh?"

"Well enough," she stares directly at Loognar. He cannot see her from how he is laying down, but she focuses her glare enough to where she hopes he can feel it dialed in. Like a magnifying glass over a worthless insect. She hopes Loognar can suffer from its heat. "I do not associate with them."

Brother Nonnatus says, "I think most mean well. The ones you encountered were . . . a sect, I guess. A splinter group. Extremists."

Extremists. Pfft. "Obviously they were failures," Bee says, seeing the tip of Loognar's nose through the medpod glass. Cocked off to the side after being struck in the gem storm, she is impressed at how his entire life can be represented by a single facial feature. Broken and useless. Offtrack and ugly. "They deserved death."

"We didn't want them to die," Brigid says. His tone is quiet, but stern. "Our goal was to sneak into Stake and retrieve the archbishop. But we knew—"

"You knew they wanted to be martyred for their cause," Bee says. "You knew you would spill blood."

"Pray for . . . their souls, brothers . . . and sister," the archbishop says. He groans and lays a hand on his chest. Stripped of his cassock and crucifix, he is an old and wiry man in little more than a dirty undershirt and shorts. Barefooted. His skin is changing colors, his veins so dark they look like tattoos of river fingers spreading through the marsh of his flesh. As a medical doctor as well as his religious education, Archbishop Hrutt must have some thorough knowledge of what is happening to him. The ZZH process interrupted. He has preached against this treatment. "They belong to. . . to. . . God as well."

"We will, your Excellency." Brigid says.

"Rest, Archbishop. " Cleopas says as he examines the readouts on his first aid monitor. "There's still some time."

Archbishop Hrutt lets a knowing smile cross his lips.

"I'm just glad you were able to get away," Pio says to Bee. A change of subject after seeing how the archbishop's demeanor has eased. Flattened. It communicates the end is near. Better to focus on life for a moment. A reprieve. "It was divine providence that we ran into one another."

Bee looks at him and immediately looks away. She knows the look on her face will betray how stupid she thinks he is. "I'm glad as well. I was worried you'd think I was with— *them*. I didn't want to die."

"No, no."

She can't help but snicker and let loose a sorrowful laugh. "You killed them all. Why not me?"

"We didn't want to kill anyone, and we take great pains to adhere to the Just War Theory."

"I don't think there really is one," Bee says and huffs. "We either fall in line or are made to. Simple." She watches as the atmosphere falls away and is replaced with the blackness of space. Below her feet is a scattering of millions of stars, each a hair's breadth in size at this distance. She knows how titanic each one actually is. She feels like that is the same magnitude of the lie Loognar fed her. The ZZH fed her. Her entire life fed her.

Brother Santa Cruz clears his throat. "Just War Theory and the force you're alluding to are very different. One aligns with God's principles, the other aligns with fallen nature's principles. We've chosen God's side in all this, despite our fallen nature."

"Do you struggle with it?" Bee examines the Knight, the one she thinks is the most at peace with the ugly things his God's principles ask of him.

Resolute, he says, "Always. I'm a fallen creature, in need of God. But I choose God over force."

Bee shrugs and starts playing with a frayed piece of her exposure suit. "I don't struggle with it. He's made known how He feels about a thing like me."

The archbishop suddenly groans loudly. He trembles violently, and Cleopas shares a look with the Knights. In his hand is the health monitor he's hooked up to Hrutt. Cleopas places one hand on his shoulder, squeezes gently to support him.

The archbishop struggles for just a moment. A runner of blood spills down his chin from the corner of his mouth. Then he stops shuddering as quickly as he began, opens his eyes widely. Smiles radiantly. "Glory to God in the highest, brothers."

The Knights lean forward in their chair straps. Brigid undoes his and kneels at the archbishop's side. Takes his hand.

The archbishop says, "Resplendent! His beauty is resplendent," and he stares off into the distance as his body relaxes. His breathing eases and diminishes with every movement of his chest. No more labor. No more agony. Resplendent peace.

Cleopas turns his monitor off and reaches up, gingerly pulls the archbishop's eyelids closed. Makes the Sign of the Cross over himself.

Pio clears his throat and says, "Lord, in Your infinite mercy, we commend the soul of our brother here to You. We praise You for his time with us, his dedication to Your Church, Your people. His steadfast resolve to evangelize the souls of all Your creation who would listen. We praise You for his enduring strength in these final trials and ask that You judge his soul worthy of Your promises. We love You.

"For the soul of Archbishop Hrutt, we pray: Eternal rest grant unto him, O Lord, and let perpetual light shine upon him. May his soul and all the souls of the faithful departed, through the mercy of God, rest in peace. Amen."

"Amen," the word echoes inside the receiving bay by one voice composed of several men. Bee does not join in but finds her lips silently moving with the word. She despises herself for the thoughtless reaction to say it.

The Knights relax back into their chairs. Death is no stranger to this team, but when someone is called home from them, they still know the moment is solemn and to be observed.

Cleopas removes his Rosary from a compartment in his armor and begins praying. Pio pats him on the shoulder and asks him to lead the team in it. They offer it for Hrutt, and it is beautiful.

†

Later, as the wheel ship comes alongside HQ's carrier and begins to dock, the Knights prepare themselves. Brother Gonzaga opens a compartment in his armor and removes the stuffed pink doll from the morale strip theater. Sits it on his lap. Rotates it so the blue button eyes look at Brother Cleopas. He wiggles it, makes a silly look. Cleopas laughs, not sure what to make of it.

Brother Santa Cruz points, says, "They issue those in the academy now."

Cleopas exhales and brightly looks at his brothers. "Man, wait until I tell Mom I was back on Stake. She won't believe me."

Brother Nonnatus snickers, says, "Wait until you tell your mom your buddy over there rigged the GravCore to destroy it."

Brother Pio shrugs, keeps tending to his business. Cleopas shakes his head, "I might leave that out for now. But it was good to be home."

Bee Rampart ignores them, remains lost in her ill-colored thoughts.

Left with Either Devotion or a Rodent Warren

Spec Ops Unit #7-1a is transferred to the mobile HQ ship where they part ways with both Bee Rampart and Loognar. They and the Archbishop's body are transported back to Nicaea Neo, the adopted home world of the Knights of Those Washed in the Water and Blood from His Side. Named after the ancient Greek city of Nicaea, sieged and reclaimed by the original crusader Knights in Earth Year 1097 from opposing forces known as the Seljuk Turks. The Seljuk Turks had captured it from Christians nearly two decades prior, and its reclamation by the Christian military during what became known as the First Crusade was a great source of inspiration.

It seemed fitting to the surveyors and settlers here on Nicaea Neo to memorialize the first galvanizing effort of their crusader forefathers to name it this way. An homage.

The Knights 1513 presence on the planet is extraordinary, and their membership constitutes the sole occupation of the surface. Under the planet's four vast oceans, there is a sentient race of aquatic crustacean-like beings with whom the Knights have developed a lasting peace. And brotherly love. In testimony to the message of Christ the Knights brought with them, the race, known to themselves as Broxari and "Crusties" to the Knights, received Our Lord and converted as a species to His teachings. They cannot breathe an open atmosphere but have formed their own religious societies under the water, receive Holy Orders, celebrate Mass and continue Christ's mission.

Under the oceans they have built vast churches from coral and volcanic rock, spackled them with a type of phosphorescent algae that perpetually lights the way to their hallowed sanctuaries. Many are built next to underwater vent tubes that heat the surrounding water well enough to allow tall seaweed grasses to grow. Colorful fish nest in these veritable forests, darting in and out of the swaying blades. Jewels on fins, forever animated.

In orbit, the Knights have constructed an artificial ring around the entire equator. The ring houses several parts of their economy, such as shipyards, significant importing and exporting, communications and planetary defense measures. By keeping these industries off-planet, they nullify any untoward effects on the environment, and especially their oceans. Nicaea Neo is the Knights' primary construction site for their non-atmospheric capable ships. Building them in space alleviates them of any concern for constructing them on the surface and then launching them off-world.

On the surface, among the impressive stretches of rocky crescents that form the dramatic shoreline, the Knights' main fortress resides. A string of waterfalls is constantly fed by inland rivers, pouring over their lips and down into the ocean. Stridently clean, breathtakingly beautiful. One more panoramic view of God's glory forever more.

And there in the center of all of it is the Basilica of Our Most Precious Sacrament. The tallest structure in all of their fortress, or anything the Knights have built on Nicaea Neo. A tribute to God, reaching high to the heavens and showing the greatest achievement of the universe is to strive to its Creator.

All other Basilicas are patterned after it. The stained-glass stories high, sunlight passing through and illuminating like rubies, emeralds, topazes, diamonds and a thousand more. The rose window is a glorious tribute telling its holy message in picture to anyone with eyes to see. Its choir tells its holy message to anyone with ears to hear. Its incense telling its holy message to anyone with a nose to smell. Its stone, metal, ceramic and glass walls, different slabs here and features there, telling its holy message to anyone with touch to feel.

But today, its symphony of church bells ring fifteen times and pause for a breathless moment. Then ring thirteen more times. Everyone gathers there to pay honor and give thanks to God and celebrate the lives of their own.

†

Archbishop Theodore Joseph Hrutt from the archdiocese of Polycarp on Xewl is laid to rest at the Basilica, with Cardinal Wysman Ruv himself presiding over the funeral Mass. Archbishop Hrutt receives full honors as a member of Knights of Those Washed in the Water and Blood from His Side, clerical division. His body is laid to rest there in Grove of Our Lord's Last Supper, the dedicated graveyard for ordained ministers in the embracing shadow of the Basilica.

It is beautiful, celebrating the archbishop's life and sustained evangelical efforts to bring all souls he came into contact with to God through the Catholic Church. His ultimate sacrifice for his captor, Amit Hiram Loognar, is hailed as a prime example of Christ's command to love thy neighbor. Greater love hath no man than this, that a man lay down his life for his friends.

†

Loognar is taken before a FedNet court to answer for his actions. As expected, his own ZZH Tiberian Council disavows him before the secular authority and washes their hands of it. They vehemently refuse to assume any financial responsibility, to say nothing of the blood on Loognar's hands. The Church of Jesus Christ of Latter-Day Saints accuse the ZZH of murder and forced expulsion from Xewl. No different than when Joseph Smith first founded them, and they had to endure coerced migration on Earth. The Carhovian authorities demand reparations for all they've lost. The maintenance crew's company make the same claim, as well as the water reclamation company who bought Stake to reopen it for its untapped resources. The ZZH refuse to entertain any of their motions, and FedNet becomes so bogged down in litigation it closes out everything else associated with Loognar as quickly as possible. Things become lost in the shuffle.

The names of Loognar's soldiers—all listed as deceased—are given as part of a general accounting process and the ZZH notifies their families. One name, Benedict/Bee Rampart, is among them, and neither the ZZH nor FedNet bother to give the Knights the list. Someone may have noticed the overlap in their own reports with a Bee Rampart, the only survivor of the maintenance crew. Nor do the Knights receive a notification from the maintenance crew's company that they have no listed survivors.

The FedNet court finds Loognar guilty on all counts and sentences him to death. Loognar does not fight it. His own church does not contest it either. Even though the Knights rally against it, citing Archbishop Hrutt's personal sacrifice as one reason to let him live, FedNet ignores them. Loognar is summarily executed one month after his criminal trial closes. He refused all clergy to be present, not that the ZZH offered to send one anyway. His body fed to the composting mechanisms of a space station to be recycled into life-sustaining elements there.

The rest becomes a confused, bureaucratic pile. As organized and clean as a rodent warren.

†

Bee Rampart disembarks from her civilian transport into a way station outside the orbit of a small, rocky planet called IREF-7.

The travelers with her, a motley hodgepodge of various races arriving here for the same reason she is—anonymity, ignore her, and wisely so. Her face burns terribly. Swollen.

She allowed the Knights medical unit to stitch up her gash and clean up the wound left by her missing ear, but no more than that. They offered to take a DNA sample and regrow her an ear in a "morally acceptable process," as they called it. She declined it; a sample would reveal her ZZH-copyrighted DNA. Through her youth, as are all children born into them, she was chemically and hormonally adjusted to their way of life. Corrected to God's intended design. Realigned to sequential hermaphroditism.

Their religion. It is an eighth sacrament to the ZZH, occurring after infant baptism but before Reconciliation. As is those two, Reconfiguration as it is known, is a prerequisite to Confirmation. But their indelible mark is left on the children down to the level of their genetic building blocks.

Adult converts have it harder. Look at that ridiculous archbishop.

But by the Knights growing a new ear for her, she would be discovered. And now that the ZZH has written her off, they won't help her either. She needs a black-market organ.

She looks around for a moment at the old and dingy spaceport. Metal corridors on one side where years prior they had a hull integrity blowout, killing everyone inside as it sucked them into the void of space. Now repaired with crude metal sheeting, daring space to try it again. The other side is a dull white plastic. It is textured over with small dots like the skin of a reptile. Along that wall are innumerable marquees, flashing the same advertisements on digital screens in no fewer than a hundred languages. The pictures are big, the writing is minimal. On each in their bottom right is a touchpad that will analyze the digit placed there to take a best guess at what language they can most likely read, then display it.

Bee sees several of those touchpads are greasy, cracked or both. She grimaces and does her best to not look at the near seizure-inducing ads. They do, however, produce better light than the overheads. That effect is nauseating to those conditioned to having light come down from above rather than from their side. The overhead lights are inconsistent as she guardedly strolls the corridor. One is too bright, the next too dim. The one after that nearly dead, so watery and weak her eyes try and refocus. A buzzing quality to the next one, the one after that is completely dead. And every variation of that pattern is everywhere.

The smells of a mishmash of planetary cultures stain the air. Whether it's food or actual beings, she does not know. Probably both.

"Well, I asked to come here," she says in a tired, put upon voice. "Whatever."

The space station has a quiet reputation for anyone seeking anonymity. Vessels are in and out at all hours of each day's cycle. One can enter a teeming crowd here and be lost to civilization if they desire. For a supposedly dead suspect in a vicious terrorist incident, Bee desires that very much.

She meanders down the corridor, bumping into other travelers. Packed in like cattle in this segment. Shoulder to shoulder with shoppers. Past the sizzling meat of some nearly transparent flesh on a grill. Fluid tanks occupied by still-living fish, waiting to be picked and butchered for meals. Ice chests full of whatever is already dead. Dangling strings hanging from a display, skewered through odd vegetables in front of another storefront. Various beings vying for her attention, wiggling fruits and wraps in front of her. Packaged sandwiches her system probably can't digest anyway. She ignores them. Not interested. Not hungry.

She wants the comms bank.

After passing through the throng of merchants, she sees it. Two rows of interplanetary communications setups. Galactic phones. The Knights gave her traveling money; a card loaded with enough credits to travel and eat much better than she has. Got to conserve her funds. Where she told them she'd like to go is not where she went. It's further, and she took a circuitous route. That in and of itself cost her more of her resources.

She's on her own, and the traveler's card is all she has. The ZZH doesn't care about her. If she reveals herself back to them, she knows for certain they'll arrest her and offer her up as some goodwill sacrifice for what Loognar did. That will end in execution.

The comms set-up is mercifully less populated. She finds a quiet comms setup between two that are marked out of order. One has a chunky red sauce smeared over the touchscreen. Scattered remnants of food thrown at it, settled in a heap at its base. Apparently, the being who tried to use it couldn't read the languages the out of order sign is written in. Lost money to it only to discover it's not working. A harsh way to discover that.

Bee pays her fee and dials in the contact code she has. It rings twice and is promptly answered.

A lovely female voice, cheeriness in every syllable. A perfect tenor, impeccable speaking pace. "Gosnell PTE corporation, this is Destiny speaking. How may I help you?"

"I need to speak with Dawood Thorstad."

"Whom should I tell him is calling, please?" a practiced song. So rehearsed. So fake.

"Tell him B.R. He'll know."

"Thank you. Please hold," and the voice switches over to a pleasant holding tone. It shifts up and down in a major register, AI-generated on the spot to give the caller a custom form of music while they wait. Gosnell PTE's customer surveys show this form of hold music is more appealing than others. Bee Rampart doesn't like it.

Bee waits, watching the connection timer on the comms setup. Every second it counts up equals more money. She grits her teeth as it crosses higher than she wanted to spend in the get-go, starts to groan loudly. Considers hanging up. Finally, after a fury has boiled inside her, the line clicks over to a ringing. From there, the percussive sound of someone un-cradling a handheld device.

"Thorstad," he lisps in a deep voice. It's just like this man to use a handheld rather than video.

"It's Bee Rampart." She says, eyeballing the counter. "Hurry up. My money is running low."

"Rampart. . . I, uh. . . last I heard the whole Loognar thing was—"

"A blood-soaked screw job." She says, pointedly enough to drive it home. "I made it out. They think I'm dead. Leave it alone."

"Okay. . ."

"Thorstad, does your offer still stand?"

"Well, Rampart, I guess." Confusion borne on surprise. "But you— you said it, the offer, I mean, goes against your beliefs. I, uh. . ."

"Not anymore," Bee Rampart says with more conviction than she ever had when she professed the doctrines of the UnZerre FulZzhea WarHeight. That was a lifetime ago. "I'll transmit my location. Come get me. We've got work to do."

Afterward

Thank you, Dear Reader, for following us on this adventure. This is actually the second Knights book to be written, coming on the heels of *Stigmata Invicta*, though it serves a prequel. One of *SI*'s beta readers, a buddy of Ryan's named Matt James, asked for more information on the Knights and on Brother Cleopas in particular.

We already had *Vindicare Hope* written in first draft form, and we thought it'd be cool to write another prequel story about the same size as *VH*. Since *VH* was about equal to half a novel in length, we'd package them together so you, the reader, would get a single prequel novel.

The second story would need to be something that focused on Cleopas. Thus, *Rescued ex Inferna* was conceived. (Fun fact: the title *Rescued ex Inferna* was originally what we were going to call both novellas packaged together, since both stories involved rescues. It transferred over to Cleopas's story when we split them up.)

But, *REI* blew up to novel size. (Another fun Fact: if you're counting the total words, it's bigger than *SI*). So, instead of releasing a prequel book composed of two novellas, you get what you got. One novel, one novella, and hopefully two cool stories. If you liked it, please thank Matt James for making a fairly innocuous statement about wanting to know more about Cleopas. If you didn't, please blame us for taking Matt seriously. But you should like it. All good people do.

If other prequel stories pop up, we'll write them. But as for now, we're pushing forward to new adventures about Commander Brigid's team with Brother Becket, who featured in *VH*.

Mining asteroids is something that interests both Joe and Ryan, and it seemed like a cool setting. The idea of a decommissioned anything is fascinating—Ryan enjoys seeing photographs of old, abandoned factories and all the rusting hulks of machinery left behind. Same for mines. There's something unpredictable and dangerous about them no matter what. These sites are dangerous, and worth posting KEEP OUT signs, but not worth actually dealing with whatever dangers people are supposed to keep from. It's romantic in an apocalyptic way.

We read about some gas giants who have such particular mixtures in their atmospheres that they literally rain jewels of one kind or another. Diamond storms, et cetera. How cool is that? What a great setting for a climax.

Since the Knights are Catholic, we thought we should start integrating other faiths that run counter to Catholic beliefs. We made up the ZZH, though there are Christian denominations that express their same basic tenets. They're just a thousand years or more behind in technology.

The 20de9 drones popped up in a spur of the moment writing, something to give the Knights a bigger threat while on Stake. 20de9 is just the rearranged letters of the Enforcement Droid Series 209, or ED 209 from Robocop. A fun little wink and nod to our generation's pop culture. (Final fun fact: in the climax of *SI* we had Brother Gonzaga get into a loader suit and fight the big bad guy, something inspired from *Aliens*).

Bee/Benedict Rampart was a late addition. She didn't feature in any outline; she too just popped up and seemed like a cool future villain to drop in there. One fun thing about writing a series—and this one has no foreseeable end; we're not writing a simple trilogy or even set of trilogies or whatever else—is we can plant a seed in one book only to show how big it's grown in a future novel. You saw Bee this time, and you might see Benedict the next time. Or we could all die from a meteor tomorrow and you'll never see either form of Rampart again. So, uh . . . anyway . . .

We'd like to thank the usual suspects for helping us on this book: Patrick Sayles, who generated the cover art, Paula Hays at Floralies

Creative, who did the cover and back cover lettering and layouts, and Catherine Lueckenotte for her editorial pass. As per our usual, Catherine did not edit this afterward, so if there's a goof, it rests on us.

God bless you all and thank you again for reading. Stay tuned. The next book is already being put down on paper.

CMC

CARL MICHAEL CURTIS

Carl Michael Curtis is the pen name of Catholic authors Joe Ralston and Ryan Sayles. *Stigmata Invicta* was their first work together, and the beginning of the *Knights 1513* series. *Rescued ex Inferna* serves as a prequel to *Stigmata Invicta*, alongside the prequel side story, *Vindicare Hope.*

Joe Ralston has spent his life collecting memories, stories, and experiences. From his days as a ranch cowboy, riding bulls, working as a bouncer, soldier, police officer, doing executive protection, and as a construction scuba diver to being an adventurer and explorer, he has dedicated himself to the pursuit of adventuring.

Ryan Sayles married his high school sweetheart. Through his wife's selfless generosity, his quiver has been filled with seven arrows. He drove boats for the military and policed in bad neighborhoods. Now he is a tradesman. He's published several secular novels in the crime genre.

www.ingramcontent.com/pod-product-compliance
Lightning Source LLC
Chambersburg PA
CBHW020913200626
46814CB00001BA/318